Right now, right here, I know that Mireya Sawyer is mine.

"I love you," I tell her simply, wanting to say it again and again and again, as many times as I can before this is over. She keeps her eyes closed, groans as I bite at her neck, leaving red marks as I go, sucking gently on her soft, bronzed skin. Exotic, wild, beautiful. That's how I see her. A streak of angry perfection with her legs wrapped around my body and her hands touching my chest, feeling up my tattoos, tracing down my muscles.

I can still smell and taste her pussy on my face, and it's making me crazy, churning my lust into a frenzy. We grind against the wall, grunting and whimpering like animals, drawn halfway out of this world and into the next.

BOOKS BY C.M. STUNICH

The Seven Wicked Series

First
Second
Third
Fourth
Fifth
Sixth
Seventh

Houses Novels

The House of Gray and Graves
The House of Hands and Hearts and Hair
The House of Sticks and Bones

The Huntswomen Trilogy

The Feed
The Hunt
The Throne

Indigo Lewis Novels

Indigo & Iris
Indigo & The Colonel
Indigo & Lynx

Never Say Never Trilogy & Never Too Late Series

Tasting Never
Finding Never
Keeping Never
Never Can Tell

Triple M Series

Losing Me, Finding You
Loving Me, Trusting You
Needing Me, Wanting You

A Duet

Paint Me Beautiful
Color Me Pretty

Hard Rock Roots

Real Ugly
Get Bent
Tough Luck

Stand Alone Novels

She Lies Twisted
Hell Inc.
A Werewolf Christmas (A Short Story)
Fuck Valentine's Day (A Short Story)
Clan of the Griffin Riders: Chryer's Crest
DeadBorn
Broken Pasts
Crushing Summer

C.M. Stunich

Sarian Royal

Loving Me, Trusting You

For information address Sarian Royal Indie Publishing, 1863 Pioneer Pkwy. E Ste. 203, Springfield, OR 97477-3907.
www.sarianroyal.com

ISBN-10: 1938623622 (pbk.)
ISBN-13: 978-1-938623-62-2 (pbk.)

this book is dedicated to the following people, in no particular order, simply for being awesome:

Susan Lynn, Lola Stark, The Triple M Book Club, Amanda Heath, Sali Benbow-Powers, Melissa Stewart-Allum, Rhea French, Brandy Little, Lance MacCarty, Amanda Carroll and the numerous other amazing people who have and continue to believe in and support my work.

but most of all, this book is dedicated to those who have or will be told that they can't or shouldn't do something because of their gender: I believe in you.

Gaine

CHAPTER 1

"What in the holy hell is wrong with that woman?" Austin asks, shading his eyes against the harsh burn of the sun. My helmet's still on, and I'm peering out the visor at the remnants of Mireya Sawyer's soul. They're scattered across the yellow desert for all of Triple M to see, laid bare and sizzling hot. Even if I didn't know her as well as I do, I could see that she's bleeding inside, hurtin' so hard she can't breathe. My first instinct is to cross the dry ground that separates us and take her into my arms, whisper into her hair and tell her that everything's going to be okay, that I'll take care of her forever.

She'd probably kick me in the fucking nuts.

A smile teases the edge of my lips as I rub at the broken heart tattoo on my shoulder. Austin isn't happy about the sudden stop, but I don't mind. I'd do anything for Mireya Sawyer. Even wait around for seven plus friggin' years while she pined for my best friend.

"Should I go talk to her?" Amy Cross asks, sneaking up between Austin and me, and curling her delicate fingers around his arm. Brunette hair whips around her face, hiding the expression of concern that's there, genuine and sympathetic. She's a miracle that, girl. The one person on this earth that I think is capable of handling Austin. She's calm, collected, and she don't hold no fucking grudge against Mireya. I feel good knowing she's Austin's soul mate. I just hope he's aware of how lucky he is.

"Nah," I say, watching through the visor, waiting with my breath caught in my chest for that day that might never come, for the day that Mireya Sawyer looks me in the eyes and tells me she loves me right back. I've told her before. Just once. It didn't go over so well. I plan on doing it again, but I don't know when. If I have to, I'll wait another seven years. I'd rather not, thank you very much, but I will. I'd wait forever if I had to.

I glance over at Beck who's busy checking out Amy's ass. When Austin sees, he growls low in his throat and our friend backs off, running his hand through his red hair and chuckling. Dumb as a Goddamn doornail, but ten times tougher. I really believe that Beck could take out twenty men by himself. Wouldn't surprise me a bit.

"She's just … dealing with some old shit," I say as Austin sighs and glances back at the group behind us. Triple M. Our family. Our friends. The people we'd do anything for, that would do anything for us. It's a confusing time right now, but they're all still here and they're not asking questions. I think it's because we all knew deep down that Kent Diamond was a Goddamn lunatic. Well, okay, for me it wasn't even deep down, but thing is, he did a lot of good for us all, rescued us when nobody else was there, gave us a home and a family. He might've been an asshole, and a backstabber, but he was still the one that gathered us all together, whatever his reasons.

But now he's dead.

Austin didn't bother to check before we left, but I did. I felt for a pulse, and I got nothin'. I don't think Sparks cared either way. All that mattered to him was Amy, and that was that. He took Kent out without a second thought. Guess love will make you do shit like that without thinking. It's a violently gentle emotion, ain't it? A contradiction in and of itself. I know it's been screwing with me forever. Especially when I saw that stupid bitch, Tray Walker.

Fuck. I wanted to kill that son of a bitch with my bare hands, feel the life drain out of him while I gazed into his eyes and showed him exactly how I felt about what he did to Mireya. Stupid motherfucker. But it wasn't my decision. It was hers. Beck gave her the knife, and we walked out. She had blood on her hands when she came out, but not a lot. I don't know what happened, and she doesn't want to talk about it with anyone. Not a single soul.

"We can't sit on the side of the highway all day," Austin warns, but I'm not sure who he's talking to exactly. He's in charge now, so he better get used to it.

"Okay, Pres," I say, lifting up my visor and feeling the burn of the sun on my skin. "So what do you want to do about it?" Austin gives me a look, blowing out a rush of air like he isn't quite sure he's ready for all this. I don't tell him, but to me and Beck, he's always been in charge. He's the only one we've ever really listened to.

"Give her five minutes," Amy says, so quiet that I almost don't catch her words. Austin does though. And he hangs all over them like a kid on the monkey bars. *Jesus. This boy is so head over heels, it's hard to look at him. I hope he realizes it.* "I think she needs this. If you rush her, she'll hang onto the pain. Let her go for a minute, please?" Amy asks, pressing a kiss to the leather sleeve of Austin's jacket. His arm curls around her waist protectively, and his eyes soften a bit. Jesus.

I turn away. I can't look at that. Not right now. I'm jealous, and I don't want to be. I just want to be happy. I just want to be with Mireya Sawyer.

I turn around to give her some privacy and focus my gaze on Melissa Diamond. She's slumped over Kent's bike, holding onto the handlebars like they'll be able to save her from the downward spiral she's started on. The flirty, wicked blonde bombshell she was a few days ago is gone. Disappeared without a trace. Despite all the things she's done to me, all the flirting and the teasing and the bullshit, I feel sorry for her. Really, I do. Poor thing's going to have to reinvent herself, figure out what it was she wanted in the first place. I do not envy her that fucking task.

I pull my helmet off with a sigh and walk over to my bike, tossing it onto the back and pulling out a cigarette. As I light up, I take a deep breath and try my best not to look over my shoulder at Mireya. She needs her space, I know that. But I can't resist. Like that douche, Orpheus, I turn and look at her, even though I shouldn't.

Her head is back and her dark hair is billowing in the breeze.

Ash falls from the tip of my cigarette and hits the toe of my boot as I gaze, completely raptured by this wild woman. My cock gets rock solid at the thought of her brushing her lips down my stomach, dragging that gorgeous hair across my skin. Mireya is a hot fuck, don't get me wrong, but that's not why I'm interested.

I pull my cigarette out with two fingers and exhale into the hot, dry air.

Mireya is the one.

I don't just believe in all of that fairytale shit, I eat it for breakfast. I *live* that fucking shit. Because without it, the world is a bleak, bleak place. Don't even want to imagine how anybody gets along without it. Even people like Austin who deny it eventually fall for it. We all do. Or we die real pissed off. Now, I don't know if there's heaven or hell or anything like that, but I do know that if I go without a chance to have Mireya, my soul is going to be seriously fucked up. This wanting can only go on so long before it bleeds you dry. Right now, I'm ready for a transfusion. Seven years is a long time, sweetheart. A long, long time.

Mireya drops her chin to her chest, shakes out her hands and spins around. She pounds the earth with her knee-high boots and licks her dry lips. Her dark eyes are faraway, but still beautiful. Deadly. She's been pissed off ever since that night. I can't figure out why, and she won't discuss it, so what am I supposed to do? I feel like a kicked puppy for Christ's sake, and I'm a grown ass man.

"Don't do it," Beck whispers as he saunters by and flips me the finger. "You're acting a damn fool, Kelley." I ignore him and put my cigarette back in my mouth.

"You alright there, lover?"

"Screw you, Gaine," Mireya says as she storms past and mounts her fucking motorcycle like I wish she'd mount me, muscular thighs clenching tight, fingers wrapping the bars. She squeezes them so hard, her knuckles pop. "I don't want to hear any of your dime store romance bull. Just leave me alone right now, okay?"

I should be offended, but I'm not. Kind of used to this shit by now. Used to it but ready for it to stop. Soon. I watch as Mireya closes her eyes and tries to get a grip on her emotions. If she'd let me, I could help her. As of right now, I'm in the dark. I don't know what happened with Walker or why she's feeling the way she's feeling. Did she kill him? Is this guilt? Or is he still alive? Is this fear? I have no clue. Mireya Sawyer is not the kind of woman that's easy to read. Over time, I've gotten better, but I'm no expert.

I drop my cigarette to the ground and crush it out with the sole of my boot, watching as Mireya's eyes open and trail over to Austin and Amy, happy in their little couple cocoon. She gazes at them with pain, but no envy. Not anymore. I think she's moved on. Or at least, I fucking hope so.

"And Gaine, I can see your Goddamn hard-on. It's pointing straight at my fucking face. A little respect here? I'm hurting and you want to dive into my vagina. Piss off." I roll my eyes and try not to get mad. If I do, it'll just start this fire between us that I'd rather not have burning. Mireya can turn any fight into a brawl, any brawl into an all out war. I keep telling myself that it's a defense mechanism, but my tongue's got a life of its own sometimes.

"You know what I want, Mireya, and it ain't just your pussy." Beck whistles, and some catcalls pass down the line, but I ignore 'em, watching Sawyer's beautiful bronze face squinch up in distaste.

"Really, Gaine? You want a happily ever after? Is that it?" Mireya smiles wicked nasty, grabbing her helmet and jamming it onto her skull like she's trying to punish herself for something. She lifts her visor up to glare at me. "Well, keep searching cowboy, because you're not going to find it here."

Mireya starts up her bike with a roar, drops her visor, and disappears down the highway without another word, leaving the rest of us to catch up behind her.

Mireya
CHAPTER 2

Gaine Kelley is such an asshole. He doesn't know that he is, but he is. The biggest fucking asshole to ever walk this earth. I don't want to look at him. I don't want to see his face. And most especially, I don't want to hear him say it again. *I love you.* I don't love him. That's for sure. We've fucked a couple of times, so what? If he expects me to give him the key to my heart, he's going to be sorely disappointed. That crusty, old organ was chained up and locked away a long time ago. And I threw away the key when I saw Austin look at Amy for the first time. I knew it then, just knew it. Winning him back was never an option. I knew, but I still tried, and I failed. And now ...

Now, I have blood on my hands.

I swallow hard and pull myself together. When you're flying down the highway at seventy miles an hour, the wind in your face, nothing between your body and the road but a bit of denim and leather, you've got to pay attention or you'll end up as roadkill. I've seen it happen before, and I'm not willing to end it that way. If I'm going to go, it's going to be spectacular. I deserve that at least, don't I?

I leave the intercom off in my helmet. I don't want to hear what any of them have to say, and I sure as shit don't want to listen to Nickelback. If Austin tries to play that crap again, I will kill him. *Like you did Walker.* I try to convince myself that I should feel bad, but I don't. I don't feel a lick of guilt for putting that fucker down. When I slid that blade across his throat, I cried tears of relief. Call me sadistic or mental, I don't care. He hurt me in ways that may never heal. I have to learn to live with the scars, or I won't survive. So I killed a man and I don't feel the way I should about it. This is my cross to bear. This is my trial to overcome, to accept that I am a monster because they made me that way.

My next step is to figure out where I go from here, how to find something out there worth living for. Austin was ... I guess he never really was that thing for me, but he was something, someone to hold onto at night, someone to run to during the day. But he wasn't that perfect, special something we're all searching for, that thing that Gaine believes he's found in me. *Too much responsibility*, I think as I hit the corner and take it hard, tilting my bike so low I could brush the ground with my fingers, taste the concrete and watch it wear away at me. For a split second, I almost let it, almost drop through that last bit of space and watch myself spin away into nothingness. But then I pull my bike back up and rocket down the empty, flat stretch of road towards the sunset. If anything, there are a few people left in this world that owe me a pound of flesh. I don't want to go to the grave with a debt hanging over my head.

Another motorcycle whips up beside me, and I don't even have to look to know that it's Austin's. I can tell by the sound of the engine, that's how familiar it is to me, how much it used to mean. I know he wants me to switch to the intercom, but why? So he can bitch at me? Tell me to fall back in line?

Fuck this.

I will never again allow a man to control me, whether directly or indirectly. This friggin' community is full of misogynistic bull from both sides. I've got girls from other gangs telling me I'm not worth anything but the heat between my legs, that I should be a good old lady and hop on the bike of a person with a penis. My response? You ain't never seen this bitch ride.

I give Austin and Amy a one fingered salute and gun it, kicking up dust in my wake and scarring the road with rubber. The good thing about being in a fake ass MC is that nobody really cares what kind of bike you ride so long as you ride one like a God and have respect for the machinery. Me, I can outrun Austin's custom clunker any day. I've got a Triumph Bonneville. This baby could run circles around him.

I speed up and hit a small crest in the road, launching myself high, silhouetted against the sky for the rest of Triple

M to see, a dark shadow bathed in light. When I crash to the pavement again, the air kisses my skin and steals away my pain, hiding it in the rush of wind and the sizzling heat for a few, brief beautiful moments.

See, some people, like that stupid bitch, Amy Cross, they like to bury their noses in books to escape. Me? I like to straddle my bike and find a new place, somewhere I've never been so I can see something I've never seen. That's what I live for, that's my escape. I hide in experiences and lose myself in air and mileage and the scent of gas, shiny alloy wheels, stainless steel headers, chromed upswept silencers.

So when that beauty is threatened, I get upset. Really upset. Livid even.

I swing around the corner, past a genuine freaking cactus, and spot a smattering of people in the distance, dark against the sunlight. They've got bikes aplenty and they're using them to block the roadway.

Ay, Dios mio. What the fuck is this shit? Malditos estúpidos.

I know I'm getting pissed because I'm starting to pull out the Spanish. I only do that when things get rough. And things are going to get *really* rough. I mean, I knew that. We all knew that. We've been lucky to get as many days without being accosted as we've had. *Might have to move back to Spain with my broke ass mother.* Ugh. Even the thought makes me shiver.

I hit the brakes and slow down, so Austin can catch up to me. I can *feel* his glare through the helmet, but I ignore it, sliding back into the ranks with Beck and Kimmi. I can't look at Gaine right now, but I do flick on my intercom.

"You disobeying the new Pres on purpose, Sawyer?" Beck asks, chuckling.

"Shut your fucking mouth, Evans," Austin snaps back at him. "Deal with outer turmoil then inner, you know that."

"Aye, aye, Captain!" Beck chortles, not at all worried about the cluster of shadowy figures. Why should he be? The man is absolutely insane. He's the perfect soldier, capable of downing a dozen men by himself. I've seen it many times. *Brawn over brains* should be Beck's motto.

We start to slow, filling the road with shining helmets and beautiful bikes, works of art in metal and chrome, curious faces and nervous twitching. You don't mess with another gang and walk away, no matter what they did to you. I don't even have to see their colors to know who we're up against.

Bested by Crows.

Great.

Suddenly, I feel my chest tighten and my mind start to spin. With my thoughts rocketing into space, drawing me away, clouding me in blurry stars of distant memories, I almost miss the sound of a loud pop. Seconds later, I lose control of my bike and hit a dusty patch on the road with my wheels spinning every which way. The bike starts to roll and my mind goes blank.

I remember leading the women out on a pride parade, flaunting that inner beauty and that hard wiring that all women have inside themselves somewhere. Tray never let on to me that he was going to take our bikes away, never even hinted at it. And then he caved to peer pressure and everything just went to shit. I remember pulling into the garage with the other girls, how my cheeks felt flushed, the smile on my face.

And then I remember the pain. The violation. The horror.

My bike slides out from under me and goes spinning, rolling down the road like a boulder in an avalanche. *Whoosh, whoosh, whoosh.* It turns and scrapes along the pavement, smashing and sliding and grinding until it hits the row of motorcycles in front of us, slamming into a sexy little custom deal with a crunch and a violent screech.

I expect to go down after it, get trampled by the roaring rush of tires behind me, torn to pieces by my friends and family.

That doesn't happen. Instead, I end up in front of Gaine, smashed against his chest with my mind running in slow motion, imagining faces I knew and trusted leering over me. My mind goes blank again, totally white, and I slump against the handlebars while we roll to a stop.

I hear people shouting over the intercom, but I can't be bothered to listen to them. Vaguely, I recognize the voices, but I'm still lost in time, drowning in emotion. Each and every spot on my skin where Walker's blood touched me burns like fire, sinks into my flesh and poisons my bloodstream.

"Bastard took a fucking shot at her!" *Kimmi.*

"Which one?" *Austin.*

"Guy in the front with the beard. Shot out the front fuckin' tire. Austin?!" *Gaine.*

"I got him. Keep Amy safe." *Austin.*

"No worries, Pres. Watch your woman, I'll blow his friggin' head off." *Beck.*

"Keep it tame for now, Beck." *Austin.*

Gaine is shaking me, flipping up his visor with one hand and cradling my waist with the other. I have no idea how he grabbed me mid-fall like that, but it's impressive. Maybe later, I'll remember to thank him for it. But that's pretty doubtful.

"*You gonna be my Old Lady or not, Sawyer? I ain't got time for uppity bitches.*"

Walker is dead, but I can still hear his voice. A decade later and I can hear it in my ear, unwanted, burrowing into my brain and scarring me in irreparable ways. *Why, why, why?* I'm tired of being the victim though. Thoroughly fucking *exhausted* by it.

"Mireya! Wake the hell up!" Gaine grabs my helmet and tosses it to the pavement where it bounces and skids to a stop just inches from the boots of the man who fired a gun at my fucking bike.

"I've always said it, but nobody listens," the man in the front says. Will Walker. My mind goes white again, tries to cover up the pain and the hate and the anger. "Bitches can't ride. It's just a biological fact."

There's something inside every one of us that will make us snap, that will turn us from people into animals. For me, it was this. My rapist, the brother of the man that betrayed me, is standing up in front of my MC telling me I can't ride? Without a second thought, I'm pushing away from Gaine and spinning off his bike. I see Austin and Kimmi, guns raised, faces stoic. Beck stands perfectly still, a smile on his sweaty face, no weapons in his hands. He doesn't need 'em.

Surreptitiously, I slip my fingers into Gaine's saddlebag and lift out the tire iron he keeps in there for emergencies. And this, this for sure qualifies as an emergency.

"State your business or get the fuck out of our way," Austin says, standing tall and sandy haired, so beautiful I could cry. He was *mine* for awhile. Maybe not as often as I wanted or as deeply, but he used to belong to me. And now … My eyes shift back to Amy. Her eyes are wide, but to her credit, she doesn't look afraid. A religious Southern girl yanked out of the bible belt and bent over a freaking pool table now looks perfectly at home standing in the center of a ring of bikes, the people looking on all covered in tattoos and piercings, leather and hard lives. I hate her so damn much, but I respect her, too. The guy in front of me, Will, I just loathe the bastard.

Will just laughs and shakes his head like he can't even believe he's having to stoop to answer our Pres's question. This sort of disrespect has to be taken care of now, before word spreads and we end up the hunted rather than the hunters. I move a step forward and Will's greasy eyes swing to my face, glistening like old oil on pavement. I want to kill him, too. I won't lie. Taking this tire iron and bashing in the front of his skull would make my life damn near complete.

"Business? Austin Sparks, the brand spankin' new president of Triple M, has the audacity to ask me that stupid fucking question?"

"I think what he's trying to say, rather politely, I might add, is that you better get up and fuck off before we blow your Goddamn brains out. How's that sound?" Kimmi asks, not caring that her breasts are holding center stage, bulging out the top of her leather corset and bouncing when she takes another step forward. I love that woman. Bravest damn bitch I know. She thinks I hate her, but that isn't true. I just want her to think I do. Don't ask me why. I don't give out my secrets.

Kimmi flips some red-orange hair over her shoulder and adjusts the sunglasses on her face, pushing them up and flicking her tongue across her lips.

"One of you boys better answer me real quick or I'm going to get angry here, and you don't want to see me angry." She laughs and her earrings sway in the breeze.

"What are you doing with that?" Gaine whispers from behind me, but I ignore him, crossing my arms over my chest and hiding the tire iron in the folds of me leather jacket. From above, the sun beats down on the black fabric and heats me up from within, boiling my rage into a frothing fury. *It's one thing to disrespect me, but to disrespect my bike*? There aren't even words to describe how I'm feeling right now. Blank, white hot, empty, pissed. My hands are shaking, but I don't let anyone see.

"Where the fuck is Tray?" Will asks, but I'm sure he already knows. He keeps looking at me with this little flicker in the back of his dark eyes. He knows what happened to his brother.

"How the hell should I know?" Austin begins, arm poised and steady, holding the gun perfectly still. He never wavers, but his eyes slide along the group of men in front of us, taking in their stances, the weapons that he can see, the ones he can't. There isn't a single woman among them. Pity. I'd have liked some of my old friends to see me now, see what they're missing out on.

"He's six feet under if he's lucky. Rotting forgotten in a morgue while the police pretend to give a shit, if he's not."

Will's nostrils flare, but he doesn't look at me. A few faces turn my way, but they don't stay, hovering there, remembering when I was Mrs. Walker, when I rode with Bested and smiled the whole way, before things changed, before my world was destroyed and my life shattered into fragments that I'm still working on picking up, piece by piece. Behind me, bodies shift and clicks sound loud as jets in the quiet air.

Let's just hope nobody accidentally stumbles upon us. MC business should stay MC business. Period.

"We don't want any trouble now," Austin says, and I can't help but see the way Amy's lips part when she's looking at him. Even though I shouldn't be able to, I swear I can hear her sigh from here. *Ugh.* I look at my bike lying fucked and forgotten on the concrete, glad that I sold off my custom piece last year. Better she found a home between someone else's thighs than get trashed like this. "Tray and Kent had something going on that I don't know nothin' about. We've moved on, and I suggest you do, too. Let sleeping dogs lie if you catch my drift."

Will takes a step forward and the men behind him shift, muscles tensing, terrible prison tattoos winking at me from empty eyed skulls and the faces of big breasted women. Austin does the same and violence sifts through the air like flour, coating each and every one one of us. Even little Amy looks like she could throw a punch or two. But it's not going to go that far, not yet. This is all a formality here, a chance to strut and throw muscular chests around, grunt like friggin' animals.

"I killed him," I say, moving just another few inches forward, towards my damaged bike. "I slit that pig's throat and laughed while the blood flowed from him like rain. If I could, I'd have carved him into bacon and sizzled a bite for you to savor." I grin, and I don't hold back. I don't care how crazy I look or sound, it's nothing compared to the inner turmoil inside of me. I think again of the other girls, the ones that stayed with Bested by Crows. What ever happened to them? Did they suffer the way I suffered? *Do* they suffer?

I make sure all these stupid fucks can see in my eyes how

much I despise them, how little worth I see in them. If I could, I'll kill each and every one one of them right now, strike them down with lightning and watch their corpses sizzle. The world would be better off that way. Besides, Mireya Sawyer knows how to carry a grudge and she firmly believes in the whole *an eye for an eye* and *a tooth for a tooth* thing. I will extract my vengeance, one way or another.

Finally, I get Will's attention and he swings his 9mm over to me, focusing the sight on the center of my chest. He wants to shoot me just as much as I want to smash this tire iron into his face, but he knows that the second either of us moves, the rest of our people move and neither will benefit. We'll all go down in a hail of gunfire and find ourselves on the way to hell, bodies still and bathed in blood, bikes abandoned.

"You miss my dick, bitch?" he asks me, but I don't respond. I reach out and grab the handlebar of my poor Bonneville, yanking her up with a scream of metal and the cry of an abused engine. She's trashed, absolutely friggin' trashed. I let go and the spirit in the metal dies, flitting away in the heat soaked afternoon to whatever heaven there is for machinery. When she hits the pavement again, she's just a hunk of parts and discarded faith.

"You owe me a fucking bike," I say as I turn to face Will fully. He looks out at me from under his dark, shaggy eyebrows and the thin lips under his beard twitch imperceptibly.

"And you owe me a fucking brother. What are you gonna do about that, Mrs. Walker? Can't exactly head down to the dealership and pick up another." I smile because I can tell he doesn't believe me. He doesn't really think his brother's dead.

"It's Sawyer," I say, lifting my chin and squeezing my fingers tight around the metal under my coat, not so much to make sure I don't drop it but rather to keep myself in check, to make sure I don't *use* it. "Tray and I got a divorce after he raped me. Don't tell me you've forgotten?"

"You might've been divorced on paper, but it was never made official in the group, Mrs. Walker. By all right and reason, you belong to Bested by Crows. Now, why don't I make you an offer you can't refuse? You tell me where Tray is and you come ride along with us and forget your busted bike. We'll call it all even and the rest of y'all can go on your way. I don't give a fuck what you did to Kent Diamond or anybody else."

I laugh then, eyes focused on Will, waiting for that perfect moment when he realizes that I'm not kidding around, that I really did take that blade that Beck gave me, that I slid it along Tray's stubbled throat.

"Will, you're living in a world of your own creation, a disillusion so strong it's got its hands wrapped around your throat. One day, you'll wake up and you'll realize what it is that you've been missing, but by then, it'll be too late."

I pull the tire iron out of my jacket and get rewarded with a chorus of hammers clicking back, ready to pump me full of holes. I lay it on my shoulder and turn around, watching the toes of my boots as I move forward towards the row of gleaming metallic beauties before me. In the past, I might've climbed onto the back of Austin's bike, but today, that's no longer an option for me.

I raise my chin and spot Gaine staring at me, dark hair almost red-brown in the sunlight, eyes hard and unyielding. Nobody moves and nobody speaks as I drop my weapon back into his saddlebag and climb up behind him, sliding my arms around the hard body of the nicest man I've ever met.

The one I refuse to fall in love with.

Gaine

CHAPTER 3

The intercom stays quiet for awhile. Nobody's willing to weigh in on what just went down between the two MCs. There's a lot of bad blood between us, and now, it's startin' to spoil like roadkill in the hot Southern sun. This can only end bad, we all know that. Our only goal from this point forward is going to make sure that it ends worse for them than it does for us. *My* only goal is to keep Mireya safe, mentally and physically. Right now, with her wrapped tight around me, fingers twitching gently on my belly, I can almost pretend she's gonna let me, that she's going to smile up at me and touch her hands to my cheeks.

"First stop in the next town, I'm getting myself a new ride," she growls through the crackling microphone, shattering my illusion with a single sentence. Mireya Sawyer is tough, I get it. And she doesn't *need* anybody to watch over her. Doesn't mean I don't want to though.

"I don't think so," Austin replies, taking the lead, playing Road Captain just the way he's always done. I think he's going to have to learn to delegate, but I haven't had the chance to bring that up yet. Right now, Beck and I are just trying to make sure he stays afloat as President. It's not easy to fall in love, kill an old friend, and take over a motorcycle gang in a single week. "Mireya, you need to learn that there are boundaries for a reason. You damn near got yourself shot back there. You're riding with Gaine until I decide otherwise."

"The fuck, Austin?" Mireya screams, and I swear, I see a few bikes swerve at the outburst. "I'm not taking any Goddamn orders from you."

"Then you're out, Sawyer. This isn't a game. You'll listen to what I have to say or you'll leave. That's the way it is. And don't even say what I think you're gonna say. This has nothing to do with Amy and everything to do with you." Austin pauses. "And this isn't a man/woman thing neither, so don't even start on that."

"You cock sucking son of a – "

"Ain't that a little harsh, Austin? I mean, it isn't Mireya's fault she got her bike trashed." Maybe I shouldn't speak up, but I can't help myself. Austin might be my best friend, but when it comes to Mireya, he never knows what to do, never has. He's been stringing her along forever without even realizing it. Man's as dense as a week old loaf of bread, but just as tough. I know I should cut him some slack, but I just want to see Mireya happy. That fear I felt when I got that phone call from Amy really lit my ass on fire. I can't rest until I convince her to take me - mind, body, and soul. I'd like to call her mine, too, but I'm not holding out for that. Mireya isn't a woman that wants to be owned or tamed.

"Fuck off, Gaine," she snarls, squeezing me tight. Wish it was out of affection and not anger, but hey, I'll take what I can get. I can feel her full breasts smashing against my back, can practically *taste* the heat between her thighs. She's crushed so tight against my spine that I can't miss the warmth contained there in that blessed domain. Like a needle to my veins, Mireya gets into me and swirls around my bloodstream, poisons me with need and desire. I'm so wrapped up in her that I barely hear the rest of the voices coming through the intercom.

"I think I'm going to be sick," Amy whispers softly, and Beck starts laughing like he's trying to cough up a damn hairball, making highly inappropriate pregnancy jokes while he's at it. Austin tells him to shut the fuck up, but it's Mireya who finally puts a stop to the nonsense.

"Beck, you insensitive sack of shit, this is Amy's hometown. Show some respect."

The group goes silent as we approach the faintly lit sign on the side of the road. It's just about dark out now, so it's hard to make out the words *Welcome to Wilkes, Friendliest Little Town There Ever Was*, but there isn't really a need to. Amy breathes them against the mic like a curse, and I swear, I can hear her heart pounding from back here. Or maybe that's Mireya's. Maybe she's remembering the moment she laid eyes on the little brunette and lost her chance at Austin forever. I clamp my hands tight on the handlebars and resist the urge to reach down and curl my fingers around hers.

"We'll stay at the same place as last time. Finances are all screwed up right now, so let's make it two a room, just for now." There aren't many complaints at that. Most folks end up shackin' up together anyhow. "Don't talk to anybody else, don't fuck anything up, got it?" A chorus of shouts and cheers ring through the mic, weak at first, but getting better. Losing Kent was like cutting off a diseased limb. It ain't so pretty at first, but in the long run, it'll make everything better. With Austin at the helm, we can't go wrong. "Beck, Gaine, Kimmi, Mireya, meet me in the bar after everything's settled and we'll talk."

"You got it, boss," Beck says, laughing maniacally, like there's something actually funny about that.

We roll into the little town like a dark curse, idling up next to silver SUVs and mud covered trucks. We don't fit in here, that much is obvious. And now that the festival's over, we might not be welcome. I don't tell any of this to Austin though as we park best we can in the remaining spaces in the garage. There's no cordoned off section for us this time, no welcome mat. I can only imagine the look on the faces of the folks behind the counter when we march inside, chains rattling, tattoos bright under the fluorescent lights, and ask for twenty-five odd rooms.

Mireya slides off the bike like I'm offensive to her somehow and tosses her borrowed helmet to me, swinging her ebony hair over her shoulder and combing it out with her long, bronze fingers. I watch her through my visor and try to wait her out. Wouldn't help if I waltzed inside with a massive hard-on cloggin' up my jeans. If she notices, she doesn't let on and turns away, watching Amy with narrowed eyes as Austin takes her face between his hands and kisses her hard and fierce, like he'll never get enough. And I know he won't. She's his soul mate, that girl. I hope he gets the balls and realizes it soon. I can't tell my girl how I feel, so he better damn well take advantage of the fact that he *can*.

As soon as Mireya's attention is diverted, I take my helmet off and climb off my bike, giving the girl a gentle pat to tell her how proud I am. I swear, my little baby has a soul. Ain't nobody gonna tell me otherwise.

With a smile, I turn to Beck and watch him ruffling up his red hair, grinning like the asshole I know he is. Fucker's got a pair on him, too. Bravest dumb ass this side of the Mason-Dixon.

"Room with me?" I ask him as he brushes dust off his pants and winks at Kimmi's girlfriend, drawing a smile from the girl even as Kimmi flips him off.

"Nah, brother. Tonight, I'm performing a public service and making sure the ex Mrs. Diamond doesn't get herself into no trouble." Beck stands up straight and leans in close to me. "We're hittin' the bar tonight and then after, well, if she needs some comforting, I'll be right there at her bedside with my entire body at her service." I roll my eyes and curse under my breath.

"You're such a dumb shit. You'll never learn your lesson, will you? That woman is trouble." Beck grins, big and wide and sloppy. The tanned skin on his face pulls back tight and his lower lip cracks.

"Yeah, but she's *my* trouble now. With Kent gone, you never know what might happen." Without waiting for another insult from me, Beck whistles and swings his key ring around his finger, moving off towards the glass doors that frame a set of stairs up to the main lobby. By the time he rolls out of there, I'm all alone. With a sigh and a string of unspoken curse words, I move after him, arriving just in time to see Austin passing out room keys.

Mireya gives me a look when I walk in.

"Awfully warm welcome, don't you think?" I ask as I pause next to her and tuck my hands in the front pockets of my jeans. She lets her eyes slide off of me to trail around the weary-eyed group in front of us, our brothers and sisters in leather and ink. These are the folks that society cast out, but who weren't right to drift down to the underbelly neither. These are the people that don't fit in, but can't be left out. Good people, for the most part. If Kent had picked a different crowd, maybe things would've gone his way, but you can only push people like us so far before we fight back.

"Kid behind the counter scored some weed off Diamond when we first got here. He had to be gently reminded of that fact." Mireya sounds bored, but her eyes are anything but. They're full and whirling, spinning a million miles an hour to nowhere. "Stupid shit actually thinks we're gonna call the cops on him if he doesn't comply." Mireya gives me a wan smile which I don't return.

"Who are you rooming with?" I ask tentatively, and she shrugs.

"You, I guess, since there's nobody else," she says, taking a plastic key from Amy's outstretched hand, turning towards the bank of elevators on the right that are already filled to capacity with a bunch of Triple M'ers and a pair of old folks in Hawaiian shirts who, admittedly, look a little terrified.

"And what if I don't want to room with you?" I call after her, feeling a little stir in my belly. *Want* isn't strong enough of a word when it comes to Mireya. I don't just *want* to room with her, I'm practically desperate for it. Already, I can feel my dick rising to the challenge, chasing after her tight ass as she sashays over to the metal doors, pauses, and then turns left towards the stairs. I start to move after her when she pauses again, fingers clutching the handle.

I know that everyone's starin' at me, thinking I'm a damn a fool, a stupid ass who can't seem to get the fact that his love ain't mutual. But I can't help myself. I am head over heels and way too far gone to see straight anymore.

"Oh, please, Kelley," she says, making sure her voice echoes across the mostly empty lobby. Only Triple M's here to witness my mockery. I try not to look at Austin and Amy standing by my left shoulder or at Beck who's feelin' up the widowed Diamond. "We both know there's not a lick of truth in that question. Stop being an asshole and get us some extra towels." Mireya yanks open the door and moves inside without waiting for an answer. That's her problem, and mine, too, maybe. She knows she doesn't have to wait for me because I'm always waiting around for her. Maybe I should show her that I'm not just going to sit here and rot, be her backup plan?

But I know without even asking myself that I won't do that. She's the only thing I see in full color anymore. Everything else is just black and white.

With a sigh, I move after her, finding her waiting at the next landing by the time I get there.

"I figured you might have trouble finding the room," is all she says before she takes off again. Her face looks ashen in the harsh, white lighting, drawn and tired, but with no hint of anything in particular. More like she's just tired of plain ol' living.

"You alright there, babe?" I ask her, glad I'm behind her, so I can't see her scrunch up her face at the nickname. I know Sawyer doesn't like to be called anything but what the ink on her birth certificate says. She especially hates bein' called after food. Austin's *sugar* this and *sugar* that really pissed her off. I wonder if she misses it now or how she feels when she hears Austin calling Amy that?

"Why wouldn't I be alright?" she snaps, kicking open the door to the third floor with a whole lot more force than necessary. "I mean, I lost my bike, faced down a group of people who used to be family and relived the pain they've scarred me with. I have to say, I'm feeling just plucky." I hear her mutter something under her breath as I move to catch up and grab the room door before it swings closed behind her. I have a feeling she might not let me in if it does.

"What I meant was, do you want to talk about it?" I ask her, trying not to get flustered. Getting pissed at Mireya doesn't help anything. All it does is reaffirm whatever it is she's thinking about you. Trust me, I know that from personal experience.

"No."

Just that, a single word. It's all I'm worth nowadays. She used to talk to me, tell me everything, but that was before I uttered those three stupid words. *I love you.* The girl won't even look at me straight anymore. I royally fucked it, spilt the blood of my heart before she was ready to see it and now I'm drownin' in it.

Mireya slings the bag she's got over her shoulder onto the floor and drops to her knees, unzipping it with long, red nails. She tries to pretend that her hands aren't shaking, but I can see it, even from across the room. After her omission to Walker, I know the truth now: she took a man's life. I get it. Even if he deserved it, even if he hurt her so bad she couldn't sleep for months after. No matter what she shows on the outside, on the in, Mireya Sawyer's a good person and this isn't gonna be easy for her.

"You comin' down to meet with Austin in the bar?" I ask when she starts gettin' out some lacy naughty nothings. *Damn. I sure as shit hope she isn't planning on wearing those tonight.*

"No."

Again, just a single word. I narrow my eyes and move over to her, crouching down beside her and trying to play friend instead of interested lover. She likes me better that way.

"Don't make me tell you the badger story again because I will. Austin wants us all down there, and if you disobey him again, you're gonna get yourself into trouble." Mireya slams her fist into the bag and turns to glare at me. Our faces are inches apart. I don't miss that. Neither does she.

"No man can own me, Gaine," she growls. I can feel her hot breath against my dry lips. I want so desperately to reach out and take her in my arms, hold her and brush her hair back. I want to kiss her and show her the world's not all bad, that there are men out there who'd rather cut off their own dicks than abuse a lady in the ways she's been abused. I want to hold her and protect her, press my lips to her eyelids while she's falling asleep naked in my arms at night.

Instead, I get to crouch there with loins burning and my fists clenched tight at my sides.

"Austin isn't tryin' to own anybody. He's our Pres, Mireya, and he needs us behind him. We're his best damn fuckin' friends. The group needs to know that we support him, that we're with him one hundred percent." A piece of ebony hair falls across her forehead and it takes every ounce of self-control inside of me not to reach out and brush it back behind her ear. Her red, red lips are moist and shiny with fresh lipstick, beckoning me, calling out to me in a language that's older than time. *Shit, damn and God Bless America, I want to kiss this girl so bad it* hurts.

Mireya stays stone still, staring at me, taking me in. I don't know what she sees. A guy with a stubbly chin and a sunburned nose? A man who's only been with three other women in the past five years because he's been waiting on her ass? Who felt guilty after each and every one of them, like he betrayed her? I don't know. But whatever it is, it's not enough. She rises to her feet and starts towards the bathroom.

I move after her, but I keep my distance. I don't want her to feel pressured by me, just supported. It's not an easy line to toe.

"I'll tell you what," I say as she steps onto the white tiled floor with a click of her boots. "You come downstairs with me, and I will beg, kiss and plead until Austin promises to get you a new bike. How about that?"

Mireya pauses for a moment with her hand on the light switch and her dark brows bunched. In the mirror, I catch a glimpse of her profile, her sculpted jaw, her ripe lips, her full breasts.

"You already tired of sharing yours?" she asks, throwing her lacy panties on the counter. She turns around to face me and puts her hands on her hips. "What if he says no? Then what? You gonna let me drive? I need a guarantee here, Kelley." I give her a look, raising a single eyebrow.

"Life isn't about guarantees, Sawyer. It's all chance and circumstance, but I can promise you I'll do my best."

"Not good enough," she says, and we stand there staring at each other for a long, slow moment. I know not much time is passing, but it feels like a lot with the heavy weight of her gaze on me, measuring me, testing me with a single look.

"Okay," I say finally. I might cringe while I'm doing it, but I say it and I mean it. "If you want to sit in front, I'll be your ol' lady." Mireya smiles and this time, it's genuine.

"Fine then, cowboy. You're on. I'll meet you downstairs in ten."

And then she slams the door in my face.

Mireya
CHAPTER 4

When I get down to the bar, the boys are already there nursing beers and pissing off the man behind the counter who looks like he hasn't slept in weeks. Kimmi, the most masculine one of them all, raises her glass to the ceiling and salutes me.

"We thought you weren't going to show," she says with a smile. I keep a frown on my face. I want her to think I hate her. I don't know why, I just do. It makes things easier, I guess. The less people I have to worry about, that I have to consider when making decisions, the better things will be. And I don't *ever* want to end up in a situation where I believe in everyone and have no one, better I ration out my approval. Right now, I can't think of a single person who has it. Austin used to.

I look at him looking straight back at me, dark eyes soft and sandy, blonde hair gleaming in the light. He's so *fucking* beautiful and now he's gone. Forever. I will never have those strong arms around me again, never taste those warm lips.

With a sigh, I approach the bar and order up whatever it is that they're having.

"Glad you could make it, sugar," Austin says, but I ignore him, sliding my beer close and squeezing it between my hands. I have no desire to drink tonight. I'd rather just slide into bed and forget the world for awhile, but here I am and I'm going to make the most of it. I lift the bottle up to my lips and drink deep. "And I'm sorry about calling you out earlier, but I had to make an example." I laugh so hard that I almost spit out my drink.

"Right. You did real good there, boss. Thanks for chewing me out over the com." I slam the last of my beer and order another. I overheard Beck say he was taking Mel out tonight. If that's the case, then I'm riding shotgun. What else am I supposed to do? Sit in a room alone with Gaine and watch him make puppy dog eyes at me? If he thinks it makes me feel better, he's wrong. I can't even look at his face anymore without drowning in *need*. I don't want him to need me. I don't want anyone to need me. I want to simply exist and be a part of the road and the wind. I need oil and chrome and burnt rubber, not kisses and sweet nothings. As shitty as it is, I can always buy a new bike, always fix one up, always start over with a new piece of metal, breathe life into it and run away. With love, you don't get a do over. It just happens the way it happens, and if it fucks you, so what? There's nothing you can do about it. Walker shoved that principle deep into my heart and the thorns have been cutting me ever since. And then there's little Amy Cross, Southern Bell Bitch Virgin from the middle of nowhere. I never expected her, thought I'd have at least a slice of Austin's life for the rest of mine.

I down my next beer and pretend I don't feel Gaine watching me.

"You know it wasn't personal, Mireya," he says, and in his voice, I can tell he feels bad for me. That just pisses me off even more. I squeeze my fists tight and say nothing.

"Can we move on, please? You invited us down here for a reason, right?"

Austin sighs and shakes his head.

"I did. Frankly, I'm a little overwhelmed. Everything just happened so damn fast, I don't know what to do with myself. We ain't got a lot left to be honest with y'all. The last few … ventures Kimmi and I undertook didn't exactly go over successfully."

"Well, what the shit does that mean?" Beck asks, slamming his drink on the counter and making the bartender jump. The man glowers at us, but with a green eyed glare from Beck, he finally moves away and focuses his attention on an old man that stumbles in and flops down on the seat farthest from us.

"It means that after we finish doing what we need to do here, we go straight to Fort Walton, recharge with some fresh supplies and lay low on the coast, somewhere that doesn't belong to anybody else. I don't think we need a turf war layered on top of all this shit," Kimmi says with a sigh, brushing some of her bright red curls back from her face. "But before we go, I think we should check with Broken Dallas, the MC that owns Fort Walton. I don't want to step on any toes. Let's just let 'em know that we'll be in and out, no questions asked. That way, if Bested wants to stop by and pay us a visit, they'll have to go through them first."

"Sounds good to me," Beck says.

"Of course it does," I growl at him from across the counter. "You're a blundering idiot that doesn't think things through. You want to *rob a bank*?" I hiss. "You think that's a good idea right now? The cops are going to be looking for somebody to pin those murders on. You don't think we should be worried about that?"

"I think," Austin says, interrupting me before I can really get going. He doesn't want to hear what I have to say, that's for sure. Once I get started, I won't be able to stop. I think I'll just keep talking until the words turn to screams and then sobs. I've got a lot going on inside right now, most of which I don't understand. I feel conflicted and lost. I don't like it. I don't like it at all. "That the cops don't give a shit about some broken ass bikers. They'll call it a gang war and write it off like they always do. Nobody but us cares whether we live or die, and that's," Austin says, rising to his feet as little Miss Perfect appears from the elevator and casts a shy smile his way. "Why I think avoiding Bested by Crows is more important than avoiding the cops. Let's just get to Fort

Walton, get this money and have a little sand and surf."

"You asked us down here for our opinions, right?" I ask him, spinning around on the chair as he steps back and wets his lips. He wanted a 'meeting', so he's going to get one. I don't care that Miss Amy walked into the room all saccharine sweet, the white fabric of the dress she's just changed into swirling about her delicate ankles as she pauses by the elevator banks and tosses Austin a smile. To his credit, the man pauses and turns to look at me, tall and sweaty, dirty from a hard day's ride. I want to feel something for him, *anything* for him, but I don't. I feel nothing but emptiness. I stare Austin's dark eyes down. "Well, I think coming back here is a fucking mistake. We're, what, rescuing another poor, Southern belle from her daddy's hard hand? That's not what we're about, Austin. Triple M is counting on you to take care of them, not get them hauled into a police station for questioning. We need to ride fast and lay low. I say we get the hell out of here and don't look back."

Austin stares at me for a long moment and sighs, putting out a hand and squeezing my shoulder.

"You've got good points, Sawyer, but I have to do this."

"For who?"

He looks me straight in the eye when he answers.

"For Amy."

I grit my teeth solid, but don't try to stop him as he walks away.

"Why did he even call us down here, if he wasn't willing

to listen?" I ask, grabbing my beer and draining it with one last eye roll towards the ceiling. *Hombres.* They think with their nuts first, their hearts second, and their brains never.

"Well," Kimmi says, ever the Austin advocate. He could advise us to ride to hell and back and that girl would stand by his side and toot his horn for all the world to hear. "We need to choose a new Road Captain, somebody to scout out the road ahead of us, decide where we're going to refuel, where we're going to sleep." Kimmi nurses her beer for a moment and brushes some hair behind her ear, sending her bright, ruby red earring swinging like a pendulum. Her green eyes are vibrant, like fresh cut grass, and I can smell her perfume from here. Such a doll, but a badass, too. I really do like her, even if she pisses me off. "I was going to wait for Austin to come back because this sounds fucking pompous as shit, but … what do you think about me being the Vice President?" She looks up and casts her eyes down the counter, focusing her pinprick pupils on me.

"What do I give a shit? You're the one that has to tell the group that you got cherry picked by their new leader." Gaine coughs and opens his mouth to interject, but Kimmi's already pursed her pink lips and started in on me.

"Who says we need a popular vote? He's the Pres. His word his law, and he wants me to be Vice. You have a problem with that, princess?" I order yet another beer, desperate for the alcohol to hit my system and do *something* to it. I've become immune to booze over the years. After all, we're bikers, we drink. That's what we do. Right now, I doubt anything less than a gallon of moonshine could knock me off this stool onto my ass.

"We going to pretend to be a real MC now? Maybe we should vote in a Treasurer and a Sergeant-at-arms? Have 1% stitched onto our jackets? No, no, I know. Let's all sit around and watch *Sons of Anarchy* and then bitch about how we're not following all the rules set down by a fucking TV program?" The beer comes up and I close my lips around it, sucking down the bitter hops in a few controlled contractions of my throat. When it comes, I keep going. "Or maybe we should chase down Bested by Crows and ask what we're doing wrong?" I look Kimmi right in the face, letting the anger swirl around me like a dark cloud. I don't mean to be this way. Somewhere inside of myself, I get that I'm difficult, but I can't stop the outbursts. I feel like a little girl trapped inside a woman's body. I have the idea of how I should act, but feel like I have no control. My fists clench at my sides tight and my nails dig into my palms, drawing the slightest sting of blood. It drips down to my knuckle and rolls to the floor with a silent splash I swear everybody around me can hear. "Don't try to mimic them, Kimmi. Don't let Austin try to mimic them. We are what we are, and we're better than everybody else. In a 'real' MC, you wouldn't be Vice. You wouldn't even be a member. Remember that next time you guys decide to make plans. We should be fighting everything they are and showing people that it goes beyond the bullshit, beyond the jackets and the emblems." I touch a hand to my chest, and I have no idea where all of this is coming from. Maybe it's just been bottled up inside for so long, I don't know what to do with it anymore? "It's about the wind and the road and the sound of a purring engine. It's about being free and owning yourself, doing what's right for you and nobody else. That's it."

And then before anybody can say a thing, before they can see the bit of wetness that's streaming down my face, I turn around and walk away, hips swaying, hair flowing behind me. I feel powerful and weak at the same time, like I'm a perfect conundrum, something to be feared and worshipped both.

I hit the glass doors of the lobby with both hands and emerge into liquid heat that washes over me like a wave, drenching my body in sweat, plastering my hair to my forehead.

"Fucking Southern summer shit," I murmur. I hate the heat. I'll be honest. Growing up in Seville, in Spain, the weather was one of the things that I hated the most. Three hundred days a year it was sunny, bright and hot. At least fifty of those days were akin to living on the sun with soaring temperatures that made the city look like a ghost town. I don't miss it there, and I *hate* this. I like places that have a definition between the seasons, where you can see fall change to winter, winter to spring, spring to summer. There's a magic to that. Not like this long, oppressive blanket of stifling heat.

I growl under my breath and dig around in the pockets

of my jacket for a smoke, pulling one out and placing it between my lips with trembling hands. The leather comes off next, peeled away from sticky skin and slung over my shoulder as I cross the street without checking either way. This is a one horse town, so to speak, one of those places where everything closes down after five o'clock.

"Sawyer, wait up."

I don't wait. I keep going, ignoring Gaine's voice as I step up on the sidewalk and under the pale blue-white glow of the bar's single sign.

"Back off, Gaine. I used to think your obsession with me was cute. Now, it's just plain fucking creepy." I kick open the heavy wooden door with my foot. Probably a little overdramatic, but it feels damn good. Inside, a couple of lazy drunks and a group of young kids stare at me with interest. This place must just worship the antique bike show every year because instead of the hopping joint it was a few weeks back, now it looks like a dive.

I move over to the bar with Gaine on my heels and toss my coat over a stool before sitting down and ordering yet another beer. I could get to my drunk with something else, but it wouldn't feel right. A good beer buzz is the only thing that sounds good to me right about now.

I run my fingers over the mangled top of the bar, tracing scratches with my nails and pretending that Gaine didn't slide onto the stool next to mine.

"You feel any better after that outburst?" he asks, and I glance up at him, lips pursed and eyes narrowed. Here's the thing about Gaine Kelley: no matter how hard I try, how loud I yell, how fierce I get, he never goes away. For years, I've been trying to swat the asshole off like a fly in the hot summer sun and still, he persists. To tell you the truth, I can better understand why Austin *doesn't* want me than I can understand why Gaine *does.* I don't know what man would want to take on a woman with the emotional scars I have, to deal with someone who has a temper even *she* doesn't fully understand. Something is seriously wrong with me, and yet, Gaine acts like I'm a fucking goddess. At first, I thought it was youth and inexperience. Now, I just think he's nuts. *Loco hijo de puta.*

"Sure, Gaine. I've had a revelation and am going to become a saint!" I hold my hands in the air and shake them around. "Praise the Blessed Virgin. *Gloria a Dios!*" I drop my fists back to the bar and wrap my fingers around the pale yellow label. When I glance at it, I don't recognize the brand. Probably something local, homegrown, and tasteless. The night I danced on this bar, that I filmed Austin and Amy together, I had no idea how much my life was going to change in such a short time. I'd gotten used to the way things were. I *liked* them that way, and now? I feel more alone than ever.

Kelley drums his fingers on the counter and watches me with eyes that glitter like the night sky. They're so dark that in the right light, his pupils melt into his irises and make him look otherworldly. I won't deny that it's sexy. Gaine is as attractive as they come, but I'm not in the mood to be swept off my feet by a man, especially not one that's five years my junior.

"Are you done yet?" he asks me and his voice slips out of that Southern sultry drawl and into a bit of New York. Oh yeah. He thinks I don't know where he comes from, but I do. We can hide from our pasts, but eventually, they'll catch up with us. It's best to keep a net waiting just in case. "Because I'd like to have an actual conversation with you."

"This is the mood I'm in tonight, Gaine. If you don't like it, leave. You don't owe me anything." I finish my drink and start in on the next. The bartender here is good. I don't like having to ask.

I stare at the dirty mirror above the rows of bottles and try to imagine that there's another world in there, one that doesn't fuck you at every turn, where people care and shit smells like roses. *Hah. Fat chance.*

"No, but I owe you everything, Mireya," Gaine whispers, bending close. The bartender sets a beer down next to his wrist, the one with the koi fish tattoos. I hate the damn things, but I guess I can't complain. I've got a tramp stamp on my back, right above my ass crack. It's a winged pig. You know that phrase, *when pigs fly*? Sounded like a good idea after a night of tequila shots. I do my best to keep it hidden at all times.

"How's that, Gaine?" I ask, turning my head slightly as the doors to the bar swing open and in walk Beck and Melissa. God. What a train wreck that girl is. If I thought I was messed up, Mel has completely lost it. She doesn't even look like the same woman. She's not wearing any makeup and her clothes are as plain as can be, just a white tee and a pair of dirty jeans. Her hair is loose and stringy and her lips are stuck in a permanent frown. I mean, I never thought she actually liked Kent, but maybe I was wrong. Maybe she did love the asshole?

Beck waves at us and grins, but I turn away without acknowledging him. Gaine gives him a nod of his chin and spins back to face me.

"Because I like you, Sawyer." He tries to smile, but I don't return the favor. Instead, I focus on his pinched nose, his rough lips, the speckle of stubble across his jaw and throat. Usually, Gaine keeps himself nice and clean and smooth. It's one of the things I like about him. I wish I could tell him, ask him to shave it all off, so I can run my fingers down his throat, but we don't have that kind of relationship, he and I. He'd like that, sure he would, and that's what this is all about. I don't know why he's chosen now to pursue me at full speed, but he has and it's already getting old.

"And I like you, too, Gaine. As a *friend*. Don't be as clueless about me as I was about Austin. We're friends, and we have fun together. That's that." I notice I've knocked out another beer. *When did that happen*? The soft, yellow lighting in the room is starting to blur at the edges and the dirty wood floors don't seem so trashed. I smile and push aside my empty bottle to make room for another.

"Then as a friend, I'm worried about you." Gaine pauses

and licks his lips, looking around the room like he's trying to sort out rival spies from the local clientele. "How did you … take care of Walker?" I laugh and the sound isn't pretty. I wish I could laugh like my *mamá*, toss my head back and not care that I'm broke and single and alone, just let my hair hang and smile while the sound of bells peals from my throat.

"I'm not talking about that with you or anybody else. Now leave me the fuck alone." I close my eyes and let my lashes rest on my cheek, sipping my drink and swirling the liquid around on my tongue. I swallow it quick and try not to choke as my mind conjures up images of Walker lying unconscious in a pool of red. I can't decide if it's a dream or a nightmare.

"You sure you don't want to party it up with us?" Beck asks, appearing out of nowhere behind my left shoulder. I ignore him completely, but the man can't take a hint worth crap. "Couple of the college kids are home for the summer and want to live it up with some real, live bikers." He winks at us and flicks his tongue over his lower lip. "Couple of good lookin' fellas over there and a few girls that'd make their mamas cry if they saw the skirts they were wearin'." I turn to glare at him and spot the group surrounding the table next to Mel. She's flipped a nice, little 180, grinning and pulling at the silver hoop earrings she's been wearing for days. The bitch is as shallow as a puddle and half as deep. *Figures. If anybody could get over the death of their husband and the surprise of his betrayal in less than a week, it'd be her*. Not that I think Mel is over hurting. Pain doesn't disappear that fast, no matter how far you go or how fast you run. I should know better. I'm the one that got raped by my own husband.

My hand clamps around my beer and I spin away from Gaine, snatching my coat and sashaying over to the group. There are a couple guys with big shoulders and easy grins, a girl in a trench coat that hits her mid-thigh and does little to hide the tattoo on her left leg, and a set of skinny bitches in slinky red and black dresses that don't exactly look like they belong here in Wilkes, Small Town, USA.

"You guys looking to have some fun?" I ask them, liking the way their gazes turn towards me and sweep me up and down and back again, absorbing, glorifying what and who I am with a single glance. I smile.

"We want to take a ride on your bike," one of the guys says unashamedly. He has nice eyes and bright blonde hair, but he's stupid as shit. I can already tell. I nurse my drink and bite my lip, noticing the way his gaze holds on the line of cleavage peeking up above the neckline of my gray wife beater. I like this old thing, even if it's riddled with holes and twice as old as I am.

"I don't do joyrides, kid," I tell him, pushing Melissa over with my hip. She gives me a strange look but moves anyway, propping her hand on her chin. Gaine and Beck follow us over and only one of them is smiling. I'll give you a single guess.

"Mireya, I ain't done talking to you yet," Gaine says, not

caring that he's being eye fucked by all six of the college girls. I keep drinking my beer and ignore him.

"You have such a sexy voice," says the chick in the trench coat, touching his arm with her fingers. Gaine ignores her, keeping his eyes on me. "You're not from around here, are you?"

"This stupid fucker is from New York City," Beck shouts with an ugly belly laugh. "Thinks if he pitches his voice to match mine, he'll be hotter than two rabbits screwin' in a wool sack." The girls start tittering and reaching out to poke at Beck's massive biceps. He, of course, laps up the attention like a dog in heat.

"You going to give us a ride or what?" says Trench Coat Girl. I rest my chin on my folded fingers and examine the rose tattoo she's got climbing up her leg like a trellis.

"We'll give you a ride, sweetheart, but it's not going to be on a bike." The boys whistle and a couple of the girls snort with laughter, but this girl, the redhead with the twisted smile doesn't seem to mind. I look over at Gaine and push myself to my feet, enjoying the sway of a body slowly succumbing to bitter, brown poison.

I lean in close to Gaine's ear and brush my lips against his lobe. There's a small scar here that slices through his flesh and leaves a jagged, red mark. I have no idea where it came from, but that doesn't stop me from running my tongue across it, tasting the sweaty salt of his skin with a gentle flick.

"If you want to talk to me, you'll play with me first."

"Like hell I will," he growls back at me, but as soon as his hand comes up and his fingers brush the bare skin of my shoulder, he pauses and leans into me. He doesn't mean to do it; it just happens. "What do you want from me, Sawyer?" I suck in a cloud of cigarette smoke and the heady scent of booze, breathing out against Gaine's neck and watching as the hair on the back of his hand stands on end. And I'm sure it's not the only part of his body that's standing at attention.

"A night of fun, a frozen slice of reality where pain doesn't exist and pleasure reigns king. Can you do that for me?" A part of me realizes I'm not playing fair, that I'm stretching Gaine to his limit. He's not Austin or Beck; Gaine doesn't pick up random fucks. I *love* that about him. I admire him even though I don't understand him, yet I just keep doing what I'm doing and I don't know why. Do I want him to hurt as much as I do? No. I just don't know how to stop. "Play with me tonight and I'll talk to you tomorrow."

"And you'll listen?" he asks, voice gruff and kind of breathy, like he doesn't know what to do with the air in his lungs if he isn't kissing me. I pull back and look him in the face, lean forward and breathe in the scent of oil and dirt and masculine spice. I press a kiss to the spot below his lip where he used to wear a piercing. He hardly wears it anymore, but I think it's hot. I wonder if I can convince him to put it in again?

"I'll hear you out," I promise as Gaine pulls back a bit

and then tangles his fingers in my hair, kissing my mouth so hard it hurts. I can taste his desire and his need on his lips, hot and spicy, so bright it burns my tongue and brings a drip of sweat rolling down my chest and between my breasts. There's a flash of jealousy inside of me and for an instant, I think maybe that I don't want to share. *Ridiculous, Mireya. You know booze makes you sentimental.* I ignore that blip of thought and pull back, turning around and touching my fingers to the side of Trench Girl's face.

"What's your name, butterfly?" I ask her, watching as her friends stare in open fascination, drinking me in like I'm an exotic spice, something flavorful and forbidden.

"Crystal," she says, her lips parting like a flower, half in surprise and half in desire. I can see the way she's staring at Gaine, eyes catching on his rounded biceps, his flat chest, the square lines of his pecs beneath the tight cotton of his T-shirt. The fabric's stretched over his body like a second skin, leaving little to the imagination. I can even make out his belly button from here. I follow Crystal's gaze and then touch her mouth with a single finger, bringing her eyes back to mine. They're pale and colorless, like glass, with tiny flecks of green, a nice match to that headful of red hair.

"Do you like Gaine, Crystal?" I ask her as I move my hands down and unbutton the clasps on her jacket. She reaches up her fingers to stop me, but then pauses when she sees him start backing away towards the door.

"He's cute," she says which nearly pulls a scowl from my mouth. I almost want to shove her back and pick somebody else. Cute? Gaine isn't cute. He's young and cut and muscular, one of those guys that's got that nice, gritty edge on the outside, but who cleans up real nice and always smells good. Cute doesn't really work for me. But then I open Crystal's jacket and find out what she's hiding underneath. It's a black lace dress stretched tight over her tanned body, almost tasteless but classy enough that it works. I can see why she kept the coat on. She looks like she's ready for a night out in the city, not a boring slump at a dive bar with tearful soft rock and cheap drinks.

I look over my shoulder and watch as Gaine tosses a wad of bills on the counter and gives me a look that's part hunger and part melancholy. I ignore it and turn my attention back to Crystal, listening to the sound of the doors swinging open and shuttering closed.

While her friends laugh and heckle her behind us, goaded on by Beck's ridiculous one-liners, I lean in and whisper in her ear.

“Do you want to fuck him?” I ask. I'm not shy about it. Tonight isn't about being shy. I don't need to bring a shy girl up to my room and walk her through the delicacies of sex. I need somebody that's going to give and take equally, who I think will leave that room tonight or tomorrow without any fantasies about what might or could be.

“Yes,” she whispers, completely enraptured. She doesn't seem drunk though, just wild, a bit of untamed spirit back home for the summer, a small town girl with big town dreams. They're a dime a dozen, but at least I know how to handle them. Austin and I used to … play around sometimes. But Gaine's not like that. And I'm forcing him to be. I keep the *why* off the tip of my tongue and smile at Crystal.

"Then come with me."

I turn away and start towards the door with catcalls and whistles abounding behind me. Either the girl will follow or she won't. This is the perfect way to test her, see if she's really up to it. My feeling here is that little Miss Crystal wants Gaine, that I'm inconsequential. Sometimes, they come for me. Mostly they come for the guys, but that's alright. That's what we're both there for anyway. I just like to watch.

I make it halfway across the street before I hear her heels behind me, clacking across the cement in hurried steps. When she finally catches up to me, her arms are crossed over her chest, keeping the jacket closed.

"Where are we going?" she asks, looking up and down the quiet street with wide, fearful eyes. I'm about to take her inside the hotel when I see Gaine leaning against the street entrance to the parking garage with a cigarette between his lips and his arms crossed over his broad chest. When he turns away and moves down the steps, I change my direction and follow. "You're not going to, like, rape and murder me, are you?" Crystal asks, steps slowing as I start down the cement stairs without waiting to see if she's going to follow.

"Sweetie, if you have to ask that question, maybe you should go? After all, this world is one sick and fucked up dirty place. I've been hurt bad by it before, and I can promise you that it'll show no mercy." I hit the oily pavement and move across the brightly lit lot like a jaguar hunting prey. Gaine's already waiting for me, cigarette dangling from his lips while he stares with glittering eyes. I like the power I have over him. I admit it. I like that he wants me, *craves* me.

Without a single word passing between us, Gaine grabs his cig between two fingers and flings it to the cement, wrapping his arms around my waist and pulling me to him, kissing me hard and possessing me with his lips. We've been here, done this before. He's said things to me before, things that I can never forgive. *I love you.*

But he can't. Nobody can. At this point in my life, there is nothing here to love but a sharp edged bitch who doesn't remember how to feel. Numb. That's all I am anymore. Just numb.

I feel Gaine's body, hard and angular, the perfect opposite to my soft curves, my breasts. He crushes me against him as I tangle my fingers in his dark hair and pull, drawing a groan from his lips and a pleasant grinding against my hips when his cock responds to my call.

"Don't be selfish now," I whisper against his mouth, drawing back and glancing over my shoulder. Against all the odds, Crystal is standing behind me with her coat gaping open, staring at us both with a heated expression. She made a stupid mistake coming down here. There's a very, very good chance and a high likelihood that had we been a part of any other MC, that bad things might've happened. I should be warning her off, telling her how lucky she is to have that boring life she hates, but I can't do it. The animal inside of me is raging out of control, a lioness unleashed on the hunt. I can't control myself anymore. I've never *really* been able to control myself. On the outside, it seems like I am, but inside, I'm screaming. "Come here," I tell the girl, beckoning with my fingers for her to approach. She's steady on her high heels, running her tongue across her lower lip.

"How old are you, babe?" Gaine asks, narrowing his dark eyes suspiciously. When he looks at me, they shine like jewels forged from the deepest recesses of the earth, something old and condensed and burning with molten heat. When he looks at her, they may as well be flint. They're cold, unfeeling. I wonder how far I can push him?

"Twenty-two," she says, and I can almost see Gaine's face fall. He wanted a way out, some way to say no to me without bearing the brunt of my anger. He's trapped now. I laugh and press a kiss to his ear, teasing the little wisps of hair that tickle his neck. I twirl them around my finger and absorb the liquid heat from his fingertips. If I focus too hard on that feeling, that intensity, I'll get swept in and sucked away. *Estoy ardiendo.*

"Twenty-fucking-two," I whisper into Gaine's ear. Just six years younger than me and a whole world away. I step back and put my hand against his broad chest, splaying my fingers against his rapidly beating heart. With a simple push, I get him right where I want him, sitting on the edge of his bike. Without any prompting from me, Crystal moves forward and wraps her hands around Gaine's neck, dropping the shy girl routine completely. Her teeth nibble his lip and he kisses her back, mildly, like he's kissin' his damn grandma or something.

"Oh come on, Gaine Kelley," I tell him, sliding Crystal's trench from her shoulders and tossing it over the back of Gaine's bike along with my jacket. "Don't tell me you've never been in a ménage à trois before. Show me some of that New York City slick, baby." I run my hands over Crystal's hips and reach down to the hard bulge of denim between Gaine's legs. His belt buckle comes undone next and then his zipper.

He starts to kiss her for real then, reaching up and taking hold of her hips, right above my hands, squeezing with calloused fingers and gripping tight. My lips touch Crystal's neck, taste the tangy bite of perfume while my nostrils fill with the sweet scent of shampoo. She smells like a dozen other girls I've shared with Austin over the years, like some I've had all to myself. I prefer men, but I haven't been very discriminate. I should've been, maybe, should've tried to find something in myself to value, to ration out rather than give away, but I never could follow the healing process to that natural conclusion. After ... what happened to me with Walker and everything, I think I wanted to make sex not such a big deal. So I've had a lot of it. Too much maybe.

But that doesn't matter right now. Right now, there's just three hot bodies and a whole sea of hormones, teasing us, bringing us to life, filling the air with pheromones that are nearly irresistible.

Gaine grunts as I free him from his boxers, stroking the smoothness of his shaft, the hot, sweaty heat of his skin. His moans fill her mouth as my breasts press against the thin bones in her shoulders. Crystal's not like me. In all the places I'm round, she's flat and trim. Her hips are small, her breasts smaller. She's delicate, like a doll. If we'd have been born in different places, I don't think she would've survived, not my life anyway.

My hands move away from Gaine's cock, and Crystal's take my place, stroking and teasing, drawing his male essence up like a magician casting a spell. I tickle my fingers down her body until I find the hem of her dress, drawing it up and exposing her bronzed ass, perfect from lazing around in the summer sun.

"Ride him for me," I whisper in her ear, watching over her shoulder as Gaine's eyes open and find mine. He's hot and flustered, three shades of red in his cheeks and forehead. I have to admit, Gaine's is the only face besides Austin's that I can remember the expression on after sex. Hot, flushed, sweaty, wide-eyed and openmouthed. "Ride him hard, Crystal." I grab the sides of her thong with my fingers and drag it down to her ankles as she leans forward and nips at Gaine's ears with a chuckle.

The fucker doesn't look like a red-blooded man with a passion. Instead, he sits there with his eyes on mine and his lips downturned.

"We're not here to do your friggin' taxes, Gaine," I whisper up at him as Crystal strokes him with a light, fluttery touch of nails and kisses at his throat. "Show some respect, and fuck the girl while I watch."

It all happens in a split second. One minute, there I am crouched behind Crystal, pulling her panties over her heels, and the next, she's stumbling back and landing on her ass on the oil soaked pavement while Gaine zips up his jeans with a growl.

"No."

That's it. A single word. And I'm supposed to get what he means from that and that alone. I fucking hate men. Talking doesn't disintegrate dicks, you know? It's okay to actually say what's going on inside those thick skulls of yours.

"No, *what*?" I snarl back at him, rising to my feet and tossing Crystal's thong to the cement near my boots. "I don't know what that means, Gaine." I flip hair over my shoulder and shiver as it brushes along my neck. I'm so hot it hurts inside. But broken, too. I feel like a volcano ready to explode with all of this molten heat filling the hole inside me. I think I'm trembling as Gaine takes a step closer to me, but I'm not sure.

"Kiss me," he says, and I don't like the tone in his voice. I look into his dark eyes, shimmering like metal under the hot sun, reflecting back all of that faraway energy, that untouchable power that only grazes us gently, hinting at its presence but never overpowering. I swallow and cross my arms over my chest. When his hands come down and his fingers touch my waist, diving in through the rips of my T-shirt and making love to my skin with each soft stroke, I shove him back.

"What the fuck?" asks Crystal, who's struggling to get to her feet, swaying like she's drunk even though I know she's not. I could see how Gaine might have that effect on someone. I take in the square set of his jaw, the way the skin on his cheeks tightens like he's bitin' his tongue or something. "What's going on?"

"I want to kiss you, Mireya Sawyer, and nobody else."

"Oh, Jesus fucking Christ!" I scream, letting my head fall back and my eyes flicker shut. I can't take the strain. Gaine might not know he's putting any on me, but he is. He's loading me to the breaking point and I can't take it anymore. He wants me. Fine. But I don't want him, not like that. I'm not ready to bind myself to somebody else's soul. I don't know if I'll ever be. Sometimes I even consider hopping on the back of my bike and just heading off into the world alone. I think things could be better that way.

I drop my chin to my chest and narrow my eyes. This is how I defend myself, how I've always defended myself – with anger.

I take a step back.

"You're twenty-three years old for fuck's sake, Gaine. You don't know shit about shit. Act your age and have a good time. Stop brooding around waiting for me because you're going to waiting a hell of a long time." I poke his chest for emphasis, feeling cruel, like a wicked stepmother pointing her finger at the young hero. My fingertip brushes his chest, shocking me with a burst of static electricity that lifts the hairs on the back of my neck.

"What in the hell is going on here? I came down here for a good time. I don't want to deal with any fucking drama." Crystal's mumbling under her breath, snatching her panties from the ground and stuffing them in the pocket of her trench as she tosses it over her shoulders. Neither Gaine nor I pay her any attention.

"Mireya," he says, taking a step forward, making me feel like I'm the young, immature one, like he's got the wisdom of fucking ages shoved up his tight, firm ass. His fingers encircle my wrist, strong but not forceful, burning me with the pain he carries around for me. I don't know why he does it, why he cares so much, but ever since he joined Triple M, he's had his eyes on me. Everybody knows it, and maybe I'm the only one who doesn't know why. "I don't want to fuck that girl or any other girl for that matter. You're the only one I'm interested in. You're the only woman I'd let on the back of my bike, the only girl I want wrapped around me in the bed or out of it." He pauses as Crystal chucks a box of matches at the side of his head. They hit him in the temple, but he doesn't flinch, just stands there as they bounce off and clatter to the pavement. I flip the bitch off.

"Have fun with your old lady, asshole," she says as she storms off in a flurry of flowers and a swish of hair.

"Don't feed me lines, Gaine. You know that shit doesn't

work on me." I pull my wrist away, even as my body begs me to step closer, to let him hold me, to trust him the way I've never trusted anyone else. I don't need a man to take care of me. I can take care of myself.

I spin away and start towards the doors to the hotel, listening as his footsteps sound behind me, following close enough to make me sweat but far enough away that when I turn around, he's out of range. I clench my fists at my sides and stare him down, focus on those gray-brown eyes and that desperate frown, the single piercing in his eyebrow and the broken heart tattoo on his shoulder. Neither of us needs to talk about that either. I know why he got it and when. It's me. I broke his heart and I continue to hold a piece, whether I want it or not.

"I'm going to say this one time and one time only, Gaine Kelley. The day I surrender my heart to you is the day the earth crumbles into the sea. That organ is blackened and long dead. The woman you think you're in love with died the day the girl she used to be was betrayed one too many times. Back off and let me wither away in peace."

This time, when I turn to go, he doesn't follow, and I make it all the way up to the hotel room before the tears hit like a flood, sliding down my cheeks the same moment my knees hit the carpet and my hair hangs down around my face. My stomach clenches in painful spasms as I sob, letting salty pain hit the floor in miniature puddles of agony and despair. My fingers clench tight, scraping across the rough fibers until they're red and painful.

Tray Walker.

I loved a man once, gave him my heart and he stole everything from me. And now … now …

"He's dead," I whisper the words aloud, just to make them real, just so I can remember pulling the blade across his throat. And then my elbows collapse and my forehead hits the ground as I cry so hard I can't breathe, hurt so much I can't think, regret so much I can't believe that things will ever get better. And I cry because I'm upset for all the wrong reasons. I'm upset that Tray didn't get what was coming to him, that he didn't suffer half as much as I have.

I hold myself there for awhile, both terrified and hopeful that Gaine will come up and find me in the most compromising position I've ever been in, feeling both vulnerable and tender in all the wrong places.

But he doesn't come, and after God only knows how long, I force myself up, little by little. It's almost painful to rise to my knees, to sniffle back the tears, to wipe my hand across my face and force my lips down into their near permanent frown.

For too long, I've been subsisting on anger and hate and frustration, coasting through life on fumes. I want to change, but can I? I touch my fingers to my cheeks, feel the wetness and the heat. I want revenge, not just for me, but for anybody that's suffered like I suffered.

I want revenge, but the question is: will it bring me peace?

Guess there's only one way to find out.

Gaine
CHAPTER 5

When Mireya walks away and leaves me alone in the parking lot, I just about flip shit and end up cracking my helmet when I kick it against a cement pillar. I run my hand through my hair and sit on the edge of my bike with my forehead against my palm, elbow resting on my knee.

"You alright there, cowboy?" Beck asks, voice echoing from across the room. I don't look up at him and simply shake my head. He won't get it. Beck doesn't operate the same way I do. He's not a one woman kind of man. I can't even *imagine* him getting his panties into a wad over a girl, not even Melissa Diamond who I see is nowhere in sight.

"Fine," I growl. "Just sittin' here with a heart split in two and a pair of the bluest balls you ever did see." Beck laughs at me which doesn't help. I raise my face to glare at him, and all it does is make him piss his damn pants.

"You poor kid, you," he guffaws, slappin' his damn knee.

"You've got it worse than Austin Sparks." I stand up and grab my damaged helmet, tossing it onto the back of my bike as I start to move away. Beck doesn't let me get far, jogging to catch up with me and putting a hand on my shoulder.

"Listen, Kelley," he says, and something in his voice makes me stop. When I turn to glance at him, I don't see that mischievous bullshit rolling around in his face. He actually looks, for a single heartbeat in time, *serious.* "Mireya has to heal on her own. You can't just come in and sweep her off her damn feet. You didn't fall in love with a princess, so you can't play prince. Mireya Sawyer's a fuckin' knight, armor, spear and all. Let her fight her own battles. All you need to do is show her what path to ride down."

"Ain't no damn fairytale, Beck," I say, although I wish it was. I wouldn't mind a good old fashioned happy ending for Mireya and me. Beck scratches at his goatee with chipped fingernails and knuckles emblazoned with the worst word there is. *Hopeless.* I like it best when I can only see the right one. Hope's an important part of life, you know?

"I know, asshole. It's just a saying for Christ's sake. What I'm trying to say is, that woman could start a fight in an empty house. Just let her be, and try not to smother her for God's sake. Give her a little lovin' and a lot of space."

"I've been giving her space for *years*, Beck." I try to bring up a timeline in my head and find that my stomach's in knots. Seven years I've been with Triple M. From the second I saw her face, I was head over heels. Took me three years to get her to even look at me, and when she did, she didn't see in me what I always saw in her.

"You're pussy whipped without the damn pussy, ain't ya?" Beck asks, and when he starts laughing again, I leave him behind, heading into the lobby and up the stairs. I think about what Beck said, but it doesn't feel like a revelation. I've been leaving Mireya to her own devices for a long while now. I thought maybe with Austin out of the picture, things might be different, but I have a bad feeling that they're not going to be, that things will stay the same until I make them different.

So I march down the hallway to the door, unlock it and find that she's thrown the chain.

"Mireya!" I yell into the crack. I can see the ends of the beds, but not much else. "Let me in." I wait patiently for a moment, but don't get any response. I listen for the sound of the shower, but don't hear much of anything. "Mireya!" I slam my fist on the door and nearly sock a punch to Austin's jaw when he materializes behind me.

"You're goin' to wake the whole damn floor," he says to me as I spin around and find him and Amy standing behind me. They're both smiling, both wrapped up in each other. I hope to high hell that the man has got his shit together and told the girl how he feels. Seems obvious enough, but sometimes it's just nice to hear that stuff said.

"I can't get into my own room," I tell him, crossing my arms over my chest and examining the dress Amy's got on. It's a swishy, silky floral thing, not something you'd see any of the Triple M women wearing on a regular basis. I smile. "Think I've just been kicked to the curb for the night."

"Oh, please, would you get over yourself?" Mireya growls out from behind me, shutting the door and unhooking the chain. When she flings it open, the three of us are treated to quite a show.

Mireya Sawyer's half friggin' naked.

"Oh my," Amy says with a bit of a giggle. She clamps her hand over her mouth quick but not quick enough. Mireya narrows her slanted eyes at the girl and plants a hand on her outthrust hip. Long, bronze legs peek out at us from inside a silken robe and my body reacts instantly, muscles clenching tight, pants gettin' tighter. My dick responds to Mireya like its been commanded by those full breasts, that taught belly, those rounded hips. The only fucking thing she's wearing is a pair of black and purple lacy panties and some sort of top that's got see through bits on the side and not a whole lot of fabric anywhere else.

I lean forward and put my hand against the door frame, trying to stay calm and push back the overwhelming wave of heat I feel between us. Or maybe it's just me. Maybe she doesn't feel anything at all?

I notice that Mireya's eyes take in Austin, watching to see if he's looking at her the same way he used to. I don't know what she sees, but all I can tell is that he feels sorry for her. *God, I sure as shit hope she doesn't pick up on that.*

"Mireya," he says, clearing his throat and looking down at the floor. His sandy hair falls over his forehead and obscures his eyes. Good move. If Mireya gets even the smallest inkling that he's pitying her, she's going to flip the fuck out and kick some ass. That is for fucking sure. "Tomorrow, Amy's friend is going to be joining us." He pauses again, like he isn't sure he wants to ask what he's about to ask.

"And?" she asks, ignoring me purposely and watching Amy take in her wild femininity with furtive glances. I doubt she's had much exposure to strong women like Mireya Sawyer. Poor Amy could use a good role model, and God, Mireya, whether she knows it or not, is the perfect example of overcoming hardship. She's got a spirit made of steel and a take-no-crap attitude that makes me want to stand by her side forever, fight whatever battles she sends me into. I'd defend this woman to the end of the earth.

I watch her, standing there unashamedly with her body on display, proud of who and what she is and know that she's not simply a woman in a man's world. Mireya is much more than that. She's a woman who takes the norm and flips it on its head, even though she doesn't realize that she's doing it.

I smile, and she glares at me.

"What're you smirking at, asshole?" she growls as I push past her, purposely rubbing my erection against her thigh as I squeeze by. She notices. I know she does.

"Well, the girl's going to need a sponsor," he begins and already, Mireya's shaking her head.

"Nuh uh. Not happening, Sparks. Go fuck yourself."

Mireya steps back and starts to slam the door when I put my hand out and stop it, the muscles in my biceps bunching above Sawyer's head. She looks up at me, and then turns so that she's glaring at me over her shoulder.

"I need a woman I can trust to take the girl in," Austin pleads, moving forward and reaching out a hand. I give him a look before he can make contact with Mireya's arm. Touching her right now would probably be a bad idea. Can't imagine that she'd take it well. She rolls her eyes and looks back around, past Austin and straight at Amy. "I've already got a prospect, and Amy's still learning the ropes herself." He tries to smile. "Please? I'd owe ya one."

"Why should I bother with this chick?" She pauses and clenches her jaw tight. "I don't even have a fucking bike." Austin's brows pinch together and he opens his mouth to speak when I drop my hand to Mireya's shoulder and slide the other up the back of her robe. Goose bumps rise across her skin, but surprisingly, she doesn't stop me. Instead, I feel a flare of warmth from her, almost like she was waiting for this. *Hot damn.* Neither Austin nor Amy sees.

"Ain't any good spots in town to buy a bike here, but what if we stopped on the way to Fort Walton and hooked her up with something good. I mean, if she's going to have a prospect, the woman needs a bike, right?" Austin pauses and glances back at Amy who's no longer smiling. She nods her chin once and he sighs, running a hand through his blonde hair.

"It's not exactly in the budget," he says. "But if you'll

agree to take Christy on, then I suppose we could make it work. I need somebody to really make her feel welcome. It's not gonna be easy."

"Fine. But I want something nice. If you try to saddle me with a Suzuki Savage, I'll kick you in the balls and throw the girl off the back. Got it?" Before Austin can answer, Mireya's slamming the door and spinning around. My fingers glide along her hip as she turns, and I clamp down hard, pulling her against me, reigniting the passion I felt in the garage. "What the fuck do you think you're doing?" she asks, but she doesn't throw me off. Good sign. "You had your chance tonight and you blew it."

I frown at her, but I manage to catch her gaze. Something ain't right. She looks like she's been crying maybe? *What the fuck*? I almost ask if she's alright, but manage to catch my tongue in time. Mireya isn't about to spill her heart out to little old me.

"I didn't want to share you with another woman," I tell her instead. "I don't want to share you with anyone. How about I save all the fuckin' for you?" She rolls her eyes and pushes away from me, untangling herself from my arms in a cloud of perfume, trailing flowers and sweet soap behind her as she moves away, dark hair wet, trailing down her back and begging me to bury my face in the crook of her neck.

"Gaine, you've obviously got some issues. Your mama abandon you as a child or something? If you need somebody to help you through your mommy issues, find another old lady to do it with."

"Oh come on now, Mireya. You know my attraction for you has got nothin' to do with that. Fuck, if I had mommy issues, don't you think I'd have played 'em out with Old Barbie." I see her lip twitch, I know I do. Old Barbie's the oldest person, man or woman, that's in Triple M. She's so old, her wrinkles have got wrinkles. Woman's got deeper lines than the Grand Canyon and hair that's gone white but still in dreads. Bitch is tough as leather. "And much as I fancy her, I want more than sex in my life."

"I'm telling Barb you're talkin' nasty about her," Mireya says, dropping her robe off her shoulders and tossing it onto the chair near the window. "Is that why you always look so far away when you're fucking? Thinking about that old bat, hmm?" I watch Mireya's body, curvy and muscular, feminine but strong, as she moves over to her bag and starts to dig through the fabric, either unaware of the effect on me or not caring that she's got me all hot and fucking bothered. My hands are trembling and my throat's gone dry.

I'm standing here watching a round, firm ass move around the room draped in lace. Any red-blooded man would go nuts in my position. Doesn't help that I'm head over the heels for the girl.

"You know it," I say, but my voice doesn't hold any laughter. Instead, it comes out in a croak, like if I let forth all that I was feeling inside, that I'd explode. I don't want to go back to joking around and pretending that I just want to be friends with benefits like she and Austin were.

I watch as Mireya pulls out a pair of faded jeans and sets

them aside. It's just busy work, what she's doing, pretending to set out her outfit. I've never seen her plan out her clothes even an hour in advance. She's avoiding me. I think about whether I should talk about what happened downstairs and decide against it. No. No. Maybe Beck, asshole that he is, is right? Maybe I've been going about dealing with Mireya in all the wrong ways? She's a woman, sure, but that doesn't mean she necessarily wants to talk everything out.

Instead, I step forward and come up behind her, pressing my erection against the silken crease in her panties, smelling her floral perfume and letting it sit on my tongue when I open my mouth to whisper in her ear.

"Somehow though," I begin as she stiffens in my arms. "The only woman I can imagine that's prettier than Old Barb is standing right in front of me." Mireya shakes her head and her wet hair slides along my face.

"I'm going to tell her you said that," she says, grabbing the zipper on her duffel and sliding it closed. All she's managed to dig out are a pair of jeans and a black thong. I smile when she spins and turns to face me, our mouths so close we could kiss if either of us took a single breath. "She's a jealous bitch, too. I once saw her shoot a man in the foot for even looking at another woman." Mireya shrugs, but I can tell from the look in her eyes that even she knows we're past the jokes and the silly sayings and the gossip. I don't want that anymore and she knows it. "I don't want to belong to anybody, Gaine," she says and her voice starts off more tender than I've ever heard it, fading just a bit when she says my name so that her callous attitude is plastered across her face when she's finished.

"Babe," I tell her, leaning towards her and pressing my forehead to hers. "You don't need to be." I lift my face up and press a kiss to her hairline. She's frowning and the skin around her nose is wrinkled, but she isn't pulling away. Or punching me in the balls, so I think we're doin' good. "Because no matter what you say, no matter what you do, I'm yours."

My hands rise up and slide around her waist, pulling her tight as my lips find hers, hot and bothered and sticky with moisture. The air conditioner doesn't seem to be working right in this room, so it's a bit hotter than it should be, making Mireya's skin slick where my fingers find it underneath the edge of her lacy nothing. I kiss her the way a woman should be kissed, like there's nowhere else I'd rather be, like I'm worshipping her with my mouth. She's always wearing these fruit flavored lipsticks and whatnot, so I'm used to that taste. Only problem is, it isn't her. The lipstick isn't what I want to savor when my mouth is up tight to hers. Tonight, for what may very well be the first time, she's au naturel, no makeup, just soft skin and lips that hold no lies, only secrets. Wonder if I can kiss them all out of her?

I hold her gentle at first, like she's made of glass. I can't help it. I'm a man, and I love a woman. I want to protect her, to treat her nice, keep her safe. But then I think about how strong she is, how independent. Maybe I don't need to be so careful? Maybe my slow approach, my caution, that's what's fuckin' me hard?

So I squeeze tighter, flexing my muscles so that Mireya's pressed so hard into me that her breasts bulge out above the wire in her corset, rising full and golden against my chest. I can't hold back any longer, so I dig my fingers into her back, pressing against her skin through the ribbons that lace up her top, and hold onto the edges. It doesn't take much. Just a quick surge of strength and the two sides pull apart, bows unraveling until the purple ribbon is sliding to the floor in a pool of satin.

The whole time, I don't take my mouth off of hers. If I do, she'll start to protest, I know she will. I can't let her find a reason to quit because out of principle, she will. That's Mireya Sawyer for ya.

I use my body to maneuver us to the side, pushing her back until her knees hit the bed and she collapses with me on top. Her legs spread with a groan and her fingers easily find my belt buckle, unhooking it with expertise and letting it hang, metal clanking as she undoes my zipper.

My tongue hooks around hers, teasing and tangling, fighting against the rage that always seems to build up inside of her during sex. Sometimes, I can tell she wants to quit, to walk away and never look back. Sex hasn't always been good to Mireya Sawyer. My hands clench painfully around the comforter as I struggle to control my own anger at Bested by Crows. Just the simple *thought* of anyone fucking with this woman makes me want to destroy the damn world. To know it actually happened? Agony. *I'm going to find every last fuck that made her suffer, and I'm going to rip their damn heads off.* Beating their bikes up before felt good, but it wasn't enough. I don't know if it'll ever be enough, not until they've suffered even half as much as she has.

I push down my urges and try to help her through hers, moving my hands up her sides and grabbing the corset, pulling it out from between us just as Mireya frees my cock, letting it spring forward into her hand where she grips it tight and unyielding, holding hard enough that her grip straddles that line between pleasure and pain. Her nails dig into my skin enough to bite but not bleed. She knows me so fucking well, it's scary. Wonder if she knows how easily she reads me.

The corset goes flying and suddenly my hands are on her breasts, kneading and massaging the soft flesh, teasing her dark nipples into points as I groan into her mouth and taste sweet surrender. It's not complete, but it's there, just enough that she can let go of her anger and enjoy herself. In the morning, she'll be back to normal, pretending like nothing at all ever happened between us, but I can feel it. One day, I'd like to see how far I can get her to go, how deep she'll let me dig. Right now, this is enough, just holding her is enough.

We come up for air, and she releases my dick, drawing a disappointed groan from my lips. My shirt comes up and off, and soon, our sweaty flesh is pressed together, sliding wet and moist across one another as the air conditioner sputters to life behind us for a brief moment before dying away again.

I tangle my hand in her wet hair and wrap it around my knuckles, pulling gently, bringing her mouth up to mine for another kiss. Down below, she pushes aside her panties and guides me into her warmth, letting my cock slide slippery and slick into that silken wetness. I can feel the muscles in my back and ass clenching tight, holding me back from going bat shit friggin' nuts and fucking her so hard she screams. For a split second, I don't think I'm going to be able to control myself, that all of my emotions and my want and my need are going to come out right here and now and make themselves known. But at the last moment, I hold it back and dive into her with controlled thrusts, sliding my dick along her ridges, teasing her thrashing body into bucking twitches and drawing guttural groans from her smooth throat.

My hands move down and cup her ass, drawing her closer to the edge of the bed, so I can find my feet and use the power of my entire body to pleasure her. I stand up tall and let my head fall back, eyes drifting to the ceiling as Mireya hooks her ankles behind my back and holds on for dear life, letting me slam her into the bed over and over again, shaking the whole damn thing enough that I'm pretty fucking sure our downstairs neighbors are gettin' an earful.

"Fuck, Mireya," I say because that's all I really can say. There are a whole host of other things that want to come out, but I keep 'em back because I have to. The last time I let loose, I told her I loved her and she pulled away from me like I was nuts. Now, I have a stupid ass heart tattoo on my shoulder and every damn day I get to look in the mirror and get reminded that she doesn't love me back.

"Fuck you, Gaine," she growls as her back arches and her body spasms tight around me. She says that all the time because, well, she is Mireya friggin' Sawyer. "Fuck you to hell and back!" she screams as she claws at the bedding with her long, red nails, tears the comforter to shit and comes all over me, drenching me with her warm heat. *I seriously love this woman so fucking hard.* I pause for a moment, body pulsing, muscles flexing involuntarily. I want to spill my seed inside of her, but I hold back. We should be using a condom, and even though I know the damn pull out method is shit halfway out a bull's ass, it's better than nothing.

When Mireya releases me, I move back and she pushes herself up on shaky arms. I notice she won't meet my eyes this time, staring at any and everything else in the room as she stands up on quivering legs and flicks the switch on the lamp, plunging us into darkness punctuated only by breath and the beating of heavy hearts.

When she falls to her knees before me and takes my cock into her mouth, I wonder if things will ever change, if they'll ever be different, if Mireya will ever love me the way I love her.

As she slides that perfect mouth along my cock, teases my balls with her fingers and whispers curse words against my skin, I know that I don't rightly give a fuck. If I have to chase after her forever, then I'll do it. After all, what's the fun in catching something that's easy? It's all about the challenge, ain't it?

I come inside Mireya's mouth and I whisper the words in my head that I don't dare to say aloud.

I love you, Mireya fucking Sawyer.

Mireya
CHAPTER 6

I slept with Gaine even though I knew it was a bad idea. Something was different about last night. Something is different about *me*, and I don't fucking like it. *Damn you, Tray. Cock sucker. Fuck wad. Pendejo.* I run my hands down my face and stare at myself in the mirror. I wish the asshole had a grave, so I could go and dance on it, maybe spit at the dirt and swear a lot. Instead, his body's probably been swept up by the police, quickly cremated and forgotten about. Nobody pushes hard to find out who murdered a loser fucking criminal. Still, I know that it's his death that's doing this to me, making me act so strange, so ... *vulnerable.* I shiver. Vulnerable is not a good place to be, not for anyone, especially not for a woman in a world of bikers.

I slide my red lipstick across my mouth and promise myself that the heavy makeup isn't a mask, that I don't use it to hide how I'm feeling inside. Might be a lie, but it makes me feel better. I pucker my lips and slide my finger into my mouth to remove any excess before grabbing my jacket and heading out the door.

With my fingers clamped around the handle I pause and glance back at Gaine.

He's still sleeping, lying out naked on his back with a damn hard-on. Staring at his sleeping face, his stubbled jaw, his fall of dark hair, I almost, *almost* feel a smile twitch my lips. At the last second I manage to push it back, muttering under my breath about the young, useless piece of ass that was crowding my bed last night.

When I get into the hallway, I see that Amy Cross is already waiting for me.

"I was just about to knock," she says with a smile. I stare at her, and I don't bother to hide my distaste. She might think I hate her because Austin likes her better than me. While I'm not going to lie and say that I don't feel any animosity towards her for that, it isn't why I feel so angry when I look at her. Amy might not have had a perfect life, but she had an okay one, and she threw it away to come live this life. While I can't deny that the open road has its appeal, that wind in your face and metal between your thighs is its own sort of heaven, I can tell you that I wouldn't have given up a cushy existence to come out here completely unprepared and vulnerable. Amy Cross is like a sitting duck, waiting to be manipulated. If she were to be kidnapped by another gang, I don't even want to *think* about what would happen to her. So I'm pissed off. I'm pissed at her, at Austin, at the world. I'm just mad about freaking everything, so I take it out on everyone. It might not be right, but that's where I'm at for the time being.

"Where's Austin?" I snap at her, taking in her obviously new jeans, her crisp T-shirt. Somebody went clothing shopping this morning. I frown and try not to let my face go into an all out scowl. Once it gets there, it's hard to pull it back. Little Amy with the heart shaped face might not be able to handle my full wrath. She looks over her shoulder at the cracked door across the hall. Inside, I can hear Kimmi and Austin arguing about something in low voices.

Fucking bank robbers.

Jesus, who would have known?

"So what, I'm supposed to take you to this bar?" I quip, wrinkling my nose and checking the tire iron I shoved into the back of my jeans. I've got a knife in the front pocket and a hand covered in rings, just in case. I'm prepared for anything at anytime. Bested by Crows *will* be back, and they *will* be looking for me. If they catch me off guard, I *will* suffer, no ifs, ands, or buts about it.

Amy nods and tucks some hair behind her ear. I hate the way she always looks at the floor before meeting my gaze. I want to tell myself it's because she's so submissive, that she's afraid to look at me, but I don't think that's it at all. I think she's gathering herself, pulling her thoughts into an organized procession, so that she knows how to look, how to react. It's a good skill, one that I'm pretty fucking certain I don't have or will ever have.

"Just me and you?" I ask and she opens her mouth to respond.

"Nah, sugar pie, you got me!"

I roll my eyes to the ceiling and glance over at Beck. He's strutting down the hallway like the piece of shit ginger fuck that he is, grinning from ear to ear and looking like the cat that got the cream.

"And Gaine if he's up for it." I look over my shoulder and make sure the door is closed firmly behind me. I'd like to stay away from Gaine Kelley for the day if at all possible. I look back at Beck. His goatee is gone, shaved clean away for the first time in probably three years. His shirt is soaked in sweat and I'm pretty sure it's the same one he was wearing last night.

"He's asleep. Leave him the fuck alone." Beck laughs at me and even elbows Amy who gets real wide-eyed and doe like. I glare at Austin's friend and it isn't difficult for me to remember why, despite his physical perfection, we've never slept together. *Ay, qué idiota*! "And why the hell are you hairless all of a sudden?" I gesture at my chin while Beck's grin grows to grotesque proportions, stretching across his sunburnt face like a disease.

"Ain't the only place I'm hairless now," he says with another laugh.

"Oh." That's all that comes out of Amy's mouth before I'm turning on my heel and marching down the hallway towards the elevators. The ache between my brows has grown into a massive migraine already, and it's not even eight o'clock yet. This day is not looking good.

"Hey, hold up, I gotta thank you for turning down that girl last night. What was her name? Cassie?"

"Crystal." I spit the word out like a curse as I jam my thumb on the button for the elevator.

"Yeah, yeah, that was it. Anyhow, I gotta thank you for turning her down. Woo wee, that girl was crazy. Shaved every damn inch of my body from head to toe. Got off on it crazy hard, too." Beck tries to show me the gleaming tats on his forearms, the reapers, skulls and tombstones shining like they were freshly inked. "Let's just say, I never had such a weird ass lay in all my life."

The elevator doors slide open and I step inside, slumping against the railing with a sigh as I watch Amy covering her mouth and trying not to laugh. Beck notices and thumps her on the back hard enough that she stumbles.

"You like war stories there, sugar pie?" he asks, laughing his annoying ass off while the doors begin to slide closed. But not nearly fast enough. My stomach drops when I see Gaine come flying out of the hotel room, pants unzipped, boots in his hand. His hair is stuck up every which way and his eyes are sticky with sleep.

"Yo, wait up!" he calls, and I'm tempted to hit Beck in the nuts, so he'll drop his arm and let the doors slide closed. No such luck. Instead, Gaine comes sliding into the elevator in his socks, looking like a much more attractive version of Tom Cruise in *Risky Business*. "Shit, fuck," he says, dropping his adopted Southern accent. "Why the hell did you sneak out like that?" he asks me as I do my best to keep our arms from touching. I don't know what's up with me, but when I look into Gaine's face, I feel something untwisting inside, falling away from my heart, leaving it bare and nervous. It's beating reminds me of the hooves of a herd of wild horses, pounding the earth and making my fingers quiver. I squeeze them tight around my arms, curling my nails into the leather of my jacket. *What's with the nerves all of a sudden? I'm too old for this love shit.*

I get out a cigarette and put it between my lips, watching Gaine as he leans back and slips his boots on.

"I didn't sneak anywhere. I got up to take care of my shit. Who invited you anyway?" Gaine gives me a look while Beck chuckles in the background. The fucker thinks everything under the sun is funny. I wish he wasn't such a badass or I'd have beaten the crap out of him already.

"I did," Amy chirps up like a stupid songbird or something. My hands clench tight as I wonder when the two of them had the chance to chat. "Well, not directly, but when we were having drinks the other day, I said he should come help me rescue Christy." She smiles and puts her hand on Gaine's arm. Inside of me, something snaps and the cigarette drops out of my mouth, hitting my boot and bouncing across the elevator. I want to hit her, I won't lie. Instead, I clench my hands at my sides and glare so hard, I'm sure she can feel my gaze pummeling her perfect skin, incinerating her.

Amy's hand falls to her side as Gaine bends down and picks up the cigarette, handing it to me with a weird look on his face. His lips twitch a bit as he watches me, saying things with his eyes that he dare not speak aloud, especially not with company. I fold my arms across my chest and fall back with a grunt.

When the doors on the first floor open up, I'm the first one out, stomping across the lobby in knee-high leather boots and a scowl that could melt metal. People part when they see me coming and nobody complains. Behind me, Beck, Gaine and Amy struggle to keep up, following me out into the muggy afternoon and the silent roar of summer. There aren't many people, hardly any cars, but the sounds ambush me, crushing me with the buzz of insects and the whirring of air conditioning units.

"Oh, thank goodness," Amy says from behind me. "There's Christy's car. She should be inside. I tried to get her to come to the hotel directly, but her uncle owns it so … " I tune her out and don't respond, just roll my eyes and wonder who thought it was a good idea to meet at the twenty-four dive in the middle of this shitty town. It's not exactly inconspicuous. There isn't a single other car parked outside the crappy little building.

Gaine catches up to me and walks shoulder to shoulder with me as we make our way to the front doors and push them open together. Inside the bar, sitting alone on the cracked black leather of an old stool isn't Christy, the unassuming Southern belle. Instead, it's Will fucking

Walker. swear on the very depths of my soul that it will be the last.

Mireya
CHAPTER 7

He doesn't turn to look at us when we enter, just sits there nursing a beer like he doesn't have a care in the world. This early in the morning, he's the only patron. Even the bartender is missing. Not a good sign.

I pause and pull the tire iron out of my jeans, pausing only when I hear the click of a hammer being pulled back.

"Drop the gun, sweetheart," says a voice from behind and to my left. I don't even look, letting Beck work his magic behind me. As long as there's less than four armed men, we'll probably be alright.

"What the fuck is this shit?" I ask Will, feeling my heart clenching with rage, begging me to charge forward and unleash the pain I'm nursing onto the world. If I could, if I let it go, would that make things different? If I did that, would the weird emotions I'm feeling towards Gaine be able to become something else? Only one way to find out.

I move forward and pause only when Will turns and levels his 9mm on my chest, pursing my lips and barely blinking when Gaine steps up beside me, a gun held out in front of him. Didn't even know he had it to be honest with you. I'm not used to scuffles like this. Triple M pretty much stays on the sidelines. We have minor brawls, fist fights, maybe a swinging baseball bat here and there, but nothing that requires firepower. Can't say that I like it much.

I examine Kelley's metal, a sleek piece of silver that doesn't mean much to me. I'm a bike girl, not a gun girl. You'd think the two interests would go hand in hand, but trust me, there's a difference.

"Now, I'm not here to start shit with y'all. I simply want an answer to my question." I spit at the floor and bark out a laugh, letting my eyes slide surreptitiously around the room. I want to know how many of his people are here and where they're at and what they're up to. I doubt Austin expected anything to happen to us during a two minute walk across the street. I didn't hear any bikes pull into town last night, so I'm guessing the whole MC isn't here, probably just a few guys. That puts things in our favor. If we're not back in ten, I'm sure half of Triple M will be down here at Austin's behest. I know he wouldn't let anything happen to his precious little Amy Cross. Speaking of which, I glance over my shoulder and find her with a can of pepper spray in hand, eyes narrowed, nostrils flared. She looks *pissed.*

"Where's Christy?" she asks, bringing my mind back around to her friend. *Oh, fuck. This could be bad, really bad.* I swing my gaze back around to Will Walker as he rises from the stool with a grunt, leather creaking as he stretches his arms above his head and gives us a crooked toothed smile. *Hillbilly fuck with ugly ass teeth. God, I sure would like to see those yellow monstrosities lying chipped and ruined on the splintery wood floor.* I clench my fingers around the metal and lick my lips.

"Your friend is fine," Will says with a wink, and I notice that Gaine stiffens, finger tightening like it's having a muscle spasm, going stiff as a board. I know he knows about my past. In a night of blind idiocy, I spilled everything to him. Maybe not the best choice I ever made, but what's done is done. Gaine knows more than anyone else about what I went through back then and vengeance is burning in his blood. Thing is, this vengeance is *mine* for the taking. "She's just hangin' in the back with some of my boys." My body goes cold then, straight from molten to ice. The transition is so quick that it makes me dizzy, and I almost sway on my feet. Only Gaine's solidness beside me keeps me still. *Why the fuck is that, I wonder*?

"You touch her and you can forget shit, Walker. I will cut off your nuts and feed 'em to you, one misshapen, sterile, inbred bite at a time. And then I'll move onto your dick. You don't even want to know what sort of creative ideas I have for that useless piece of hypocrisy." Will just laughs and shakes his head, secure in his fallacies and his stupidity, his ignorance and all the horrible misogynistic bull that's floating around this community. Biker bitches don't mean shit, not to him, not to a lot of people.

I start to wonder if I was put on this earth to prove them wrong.

"Beck, you okay back there?" I ask, voice neutral, calm. I won't give anything away. Don't have to. Sometimes, when other people think less of you, it's best to let 'em. Then, when it's time to come in and kick their ass, they won't see it coming. *El día que se muere, la tierra va a llorar lágrimas de alegría.*

Will doesn't think women are worth a damn, so he doesn't think they're a threat to be reckoned with.

"All good back here, lady cakes," he says, and I smile.

Two steps forward, elbow cocked back, and then I slam the tire iron against the side of Will's face. He doesn't scream, doesn't cry out, just drops to the floor like a sack of fucking potatoes. Shouts ring out from behind the door to the back room where I stumbled upon Austin fucking Amy for the first time. What a momentous occasion that was. I didn't think anything of it then. I just thought she was another random fuck, a girl that would disappear into a history of blurry faces. I wonder sometimes if the most important events in life are cloaked in obscurity on purpose, just to screw with us.

Gaine doesn't hesitate in firing back, one handed mind you which is pretty damn impressive. His other arm comes out and snakes around my waist, pulling me tight against his hot body, the pulsing thrum of energy he carries around with him always. I was immune to it, or at least I thought I was. Until now. Now, even in a hail of gunfire, I feel like I'm bent over the fire, heating back up and rising like steam. That coldness fades away in a split second, retreating back to whence it came, and then I'm just hot and angry again. And compared to that strange coldness, it's a fucking blessing.

"What the fuck were you thinking, Mireya Sawyer?" he says and he sounds like a New Yorker again. He's been surrounded by viscous, Southern drawls since he was sixteen, so it's rubbed off on him pretty heavily, but like me, when he gets stressed, it's back to resting on his laurels. I've got Castilian, and he's got Upstate New York. What a pair we make.

"Screw you, Kelley," I say, even as we drop to the floor in a flurry of activity. Vaguely, I remember Amy and feel a surge of panic in my chest. I try to check for her, but Gaine's yanking me behind a table and holding me tight against him while the room quiets down and an eerie silence descends. I don't see Beck or Amy, but I pray to God that she's alright. If I were to get her killed, Austin would never forgive me. *I* would never forgive me. I might not like the girl, but I feel responsible towards her somehow. Maybe it's some latent mothering bullshit or something? I don't know. I just don't want her to get killed by a bunch of rapists with guns.

"The fuck is wrong with you? Do you have a death wish or somethin'?" Gaine whispers in my ear while we wait in tense anticipation for somebody to make the next move. Things have got to happen fast from this point on, before the cops get here. Nobody wants to deal with cops.

"Don't talk to me like I'm stupid, Gaine," I growl at him, pausing my rant early to listen to the sound of a door swinging open. A couple pairs of boots move into my vision and a blonde girl with red eyes and wet cheeks falls to her knees not six feet from where we're crouching.

"Where the fuck is Tray? We want honest answers this time." My hands clench involuntarily, curling into fists so tight, I feel like the bones might burst from my skin and cut me open. *Mack.* Tray's *other* brother. Unfortunate isn't it that the world seems to breed idiots in excess.

I untangle myself from Gaine's arms, despite his protests and rise to my feet. They won't shoot me. Yet. They want to hear what I have to say. I need to keep it that way until I get the girl back. I may not know her personally, but I know what they'll do to her if they take her out of here. She will be doomed to a short, painful life of hell, and it'll be at least partially my fault. I hope that she's escaped my fate thus far.

I look down at the girl before I bother acknowledging Mack. She seems alright, a little roughed up maybe, but she doesn't have that vacant look in her eye like she's been betrayed. *Got here just in time, I reckon.*

My eyes move up a pair of dusty boots, past faded jeans, a red tee and onto a baby face that will never cross over into handsome. I imagine that Mack will always look like a kid, probably right up until the day he gets wrinkled up like a fucking prune. Tray stole all the good genes in this family, the physical ones anyway. There wasn't much else worth having to be found in this lineup. I stare at Mack and try to reconcile what I use to think about him with what he did to me, and what he's doing now.

He looks over at his brother's crumpled form and wrinkles his nose. The three men behind him keep their eyes on Gaine when he stands up behind me. They just saw me smash Will's face in with a tire iron and they're not taking me seriously. Oh, well. Their ignorance is my bliss.

"If he's dead, you're done, Mireya." I try not to laugh. Nobody else might've noticed, but I can hear the soft clink of chains behind the bar. Once Beck gets to the other side, these guys are all done for. They may as well kiss the world goodbye. I smile instead.

"I can only hope," I say, and Mack's blue eyes flick up to mine and hold there with grim determination. Inside, he's a fucking pussy. On the outside, he's playing a good game. I always thought he could be an actor if he wanted, would probably enjoy it, too. And I'm not a hundred percent certain, but I think he's gay as well. Not that it matters to me, but I wonder what his ignorant asshole buddies would say if they found out. "You want Tray back? You're going to have to do an awful lot of traveling to find his ass."

Mack holds up his gun, points it straight at my face. I hold my hand out to keep Gaine from reacting in my defense. He's always been good in a fight before, always stood by my side, but I don't know if I've ever seen him so protective. I can't tell if I hate it or ... No. No. I hate it. I can take care of my damn self.

"And what the fuck is that supposed to mean?" Mack asks, stepping forward aggressively, his shaking shoulders the only indication that he's actually terrified by the situation.

"You don't owe them anything, Mireya," Gaine whispers, voice so low that I'm probably the only one that can hear it. "Just keep quiet and wait 'em out. I think I hear sirens anyhow."

I ignore him.

"I mean, if his pathetic, miserable, useless soul is still floating around somewhere, it's buried in the depths of hell. It's going to take an awful lot of good riding to find him down there."

Beck explodes from behind the bar like a machine, muscles hard as rocks, joints like pistons. He pounds the space between the man closest to him in seconds, slamming his elbow into the blonde's temple and dropping him before any of the others can even turn to look.

I move forward, taking advantage of Beck's movements to cloak the iron in my hand until it's too late, swinging it hard and drawing blood from Mack's forehead as he crumples. Deep down, a monster stirs and kicks, begging me to keep swinging, to destroy this man and all the rest with a pounding beat of rage and violence. *Take that vengeance and destroy them.* There's a good chance that I'll get arrested then, or that I won't be able to stop. My arm draws back and all of a sudden, my hand's missing my weapon. I spin to find Gaine behind me and nearly kick him in the balls when he reaches out and grabs me around the waist, tossing me over his shoulder like a helpless heroine in a romance novel.

"Put me the fuck down!" I scream, but he's already spinning us around, flashing me a quick look at Amy Cross, who's still alive, thankfully, and a panoramic view of the dazed Crows as we sprint towards the front door and burst out into the heat, trailing Beck behind us. He's got Amy's friend scooped up in his arms and is booking it with Amy at his heels.

I hear Austin's voice before I see him, and fortunately for him, Gaine chooses that moment to set me down. He's lucky. I was about three seconds away from tearing out a clump of his hair and then castrating him.

"What in the holy hell of fuck is goin' on in there?"

"Questions later, Pres. We have got to get the hell out of here. Now."

Gaine tries to take my hand, but I shove him back and throw him the hardest glare I have.

"You pick me up like that again, and I will kill you," I snarl. He looks at me for a second and then turns away, moving towards the doors of the hotel with a blank expression on his sweaty face.

I watch his strong back, and I try not to think the thought that's swirling around in the back of my mind.

Gaine just damn near saved me from making one of the biggest fucking mistakes of my life. I want revenge, but I'm not an animal. Somehow, he seems to know me better than

I do.

That scares the shit out of me.

Gaine
CHAPTER 8

I must've been out of my fucking mind to pick up Mireya Sawyer and toss her over my shoulder like that. No shit. I should be dead right now. But I'm not. That's a good thing, right? Is this progress? I want to ask someone about it, but there's nobody to talk to right now, not when I've got Mireya wrapped around me on the open road, making my dick so hard it hurts. I think I'm driving a little crooked, but nobody mentions anything on the intercom.

"We are so fucking screwed," Kimmi says, sighing so hard it echoes around the mic and makes my ears bleed. "They are going to chase us to the edge of the earth and back. I'm starting to wonder how desperate our future measures are going to have to be. I can't pull a job with Bested on my back." We're on a private channel, Mireya, Beck, Austin, Amy, Kimmi, and me. Mostly, it's just been Kimmi and Austin chatting back and forth. Things don't sound promising.

"We should still hit Fort Walton," Austin says, but he doesn't sound convinced. These types of dirty deeds used to be taken care of by Kent and who the hell knows who else. Not us, that's for fuck's sure. "Let's make contact with Broken Dallas, let 'em know our intentions and see how they like bein' swarmed with unwanted guests. Bested by Crows hasn't exactly gotten famous for their manners." Mireya sighs behind me, shifting just a bit, so that her breasts press hard against my back, warming me up from deep down and making me crazy for it. Last night was nice, but it wasn't enough. Unfortunately, with all of this shit going down, I don't know how to make her pay attention to me.

"We're going to have to make tough choices, Austin," she says, sliding her hands down my belly and tucking her fingers into the waistband of my jeans. *Jesus Mother Mary of fucking fuck*. I try not to let a groan slip. *Why the hell is she sitting so close though*? *She could lean back if she wanted. God knows there's enough room back there.* "We're going to have to decide how far we're willing to go to keep this group safe, to uphold our dignity, and to make sure that the open road stays open." Her hands dip lower, rubbing over the stiff bulge in my pants, making me clench the handlebars so hard I'm afraid they're going to snap. "We don't want to get backed into a position where choices are made for us, not in a situation like this. I need to know how bloody this is going to get." Mireya unzips me and for the life of me, I can't figure out what the hell she's doin'.

"I don't want anyone to get hurt," Austin says, and I can feel Mireya sucking in a big breath behind me. "Anyone that means anythin' to me, that is." The zipper comes down and Mireya's hand slides in, taking advantage of the fact that I didn't have time to wear shit all under my jeans. Her fingers wrap my cock, giving me a shock of white hot pleasure and a confusing slew of emotions. *She ain't pissed at me*? I wonder as I switch off my mic and let out a groan that gets lost in the rush of wind around us. I could flat-out shout and nobody would hear me.

"So we have the go ahead to make things right?" Kimmi asks, trying to get clarification for something that shouldn't need clarifying. I'm not saying it's alright to go around killing people, but in these circumstances, we might not have any other choice. Once Bested by Crows knows, really *knows*, that Tray Walker is dead, then we're screwed. They'll be seeking vengeance and they won't stop until they've got it. Whether that means killing some or all of us, or taking Mireya hostage, I ain't got no clue. As of right now, it's a little hard to concentrate on all that, important as it is. Sawyer's got my dick locked in a death grip, squeezing it so hard I swear to God, the poor fucker's about to break. But it feels so damn good. Right now, I've got the two things in the world that mean most to me: the road and my woman. Doesn't get much better than that. Well, I won't lie, if I could at least get this girl to tell me she loves me, or at the very least accept that I love her, that sure would be fucking nice. I dream of sliding a ring on her finger, claiming her for all the world to see, but that ain't never gonna friggin' happen.

“Make things safe, Kimmi,” Austin says, and I can imagine that he's thinking of Amy, dropping his hand to touch hers where they're clasped around his belly. Me, it's all I can do to keep hold of my bike and not crash us into the dirt on the side of the road. The wind is whistling all around me, stinging the bare skin of my cock as Mireya slides her hand up and down, moving the skin on my shaft and tensing my muscles with pleasure. I don't know why she's doin' what she's doin', but I like it. “Let's see if we can ride this out. Like my mama always said, I don't start shit, but I sure as hell will finish it.”

There's a buzz on the com, and then on comes a song I can actually relate to, even though I kinda wish I didn't. 'Casual Sex' by My Darkest Days bursts out through the speakers as Austin lifts up his bike and hightails it the fuck out of there, flying ahead of the group like he needs some space to think. Me, I couldn't think my way out of a cardboard box. Mireya is coaxing pre-cum from the head of my dick, slicking me up nice and good, letting the wild wind sting it hard. She works me fast and furious, drawing the breath from my lungs, choking the life out of me while I fight against an orgasm. Not often that that happens. No man wants to hold back his load, but shit, if I'm not on the back of a damn bike.

I drop one hand to hers, hoping I can keep us on the road with the other. My fingers tangle around hers, but she doesn't slow, just squeezes tighter and pumps faster, bringing me to the edge and dropping me straight off the fucking cliff.

I come hard and only barely, just *barely* manage to keep us on the pavement. When Mireya's satisfied that she's fucked me up enough, she withdraws her hand and leaves me with my dick hanging out of my damn pants.

It's not easy to get myself put together, so when we pause in the next town to refuel, I look like a damn fool. I am fucked up six ways to Sunday, breathing heavy and leaning over with my helmet in my lap. Mireya slides off behind me and pauses next to my left side, glaring down at me with narrowed eyes.

"And what in the hell was that for?" I ask her, glancing up with hair in my eyes. I brush it away, but I'm sweaty and sticky from the heat. The hair refuses to budge, sliding across my slick skin as I stare at the love of my life and the grudging respect in her eyes. She's mad at me, yeah. I was right about that. But she's not livid.

"Next time you pick me up like that, you're done," she growls and then glances around like she's suspicious that someone might be listening in. "But thank you. For stopping me." She puts her hands on her rounded hips, and drops her chin to her chest. "When I kill those sons of bitches, I want it to be with my mind in the right place and my intentions on my lips. If I'm going to hell, I might as well make it worth it." Mireya lifts her head up suddenly and starts to turn away. Without a second thought, my hand shoots out and wraps her arm, halting her where she stands with one boot in a slick of oil.

"If there's any real justice in the world, you'll be marked a saint for removing those fuckers from the face of this earth." She smiles tight-lipped at me and tries to move away, but I'm not done yet. Instead, I pull her back hard and fast, slamming her body against mine and smashing my lips to hers. My fingers tangle in her hair and my heart beats a rough, aching rhythm of want. With half of Triple M looking on, Mireya grabs me right back and kisses me fierce, nipping my lips and drawing blood. I fight her back, begging and commanding both with my mouth, asking her to indulge the burning desperation she's fired up in my blood. But no. Guess I'm being punished.

With a chuckle, Mireya shoves back, using a rough hand on my tender crotch as leverage.

"Barb," she says, drawing the old woman's attention. She stands behind Mireya with a cigarette dangling from her mouth, either ignoring the myriad *no smoking* signs or just not giving a shit about them. Her white dreadlocks drape over her shoulders as she narrows her eyes on me. "Gaine told me the other night that he thinks about you a lot when he whacks it. Apparently, I'm not his dream girl. You are." And then Mireya spins away in a cloud of crow-black hair and curves that could kill. I watch her go and only just manage to pull my gaze away when Old Barb snorts at me. She gives me a once-over that says she isn't very impressed with what she sees.

"Boy," she asks, leaning close and squinting her eyes at me, wrinkles falling down her forehead like a damn avalanche. "I think you got splooge on your fuckin' shirt."

Gaine

CHAPTER 9

"You are such a fucking asshole," Beck crows, laughing his ass off as he follows me down the hallway to our rooms. Mireya's back with Austin and Amy, trying to figure out what to do with Christy. Me, I'm here suffering a constant barrage of insults about the damn jizz on my shirt. *Thank you, Mireya Sawyer.*

"Leave me alone, Beck," I growl at him, but he's not too good at taking hints. Instead, he follows me to the last door on the left and kicks his way inside, guffawing while I yank off my shirt and toss it to the floor. "I'm sure you're no stranger to walking around wearing badges of honor." I kick the dirty tee against the dresser and retreat into the bathroom with a fresh one. It's got a saying on the front that embodies my current mood to perfection: *Up Fuck Creek Without a Paddle.* Yes, sirree, that's me in a nut shell. "Don't you have women to harass? Go find the local bar and pick yourself up a chick."

"Now why would I be out doin' that when I've got a perfectly good asshole to fuck right here?" He chortles some more and I kick the bathroom door closed in his face, leaning over the counter with my fingers wrapped around the laminate. I let my head hang for awhile, trying to catch my breath. I'm not embarrassed. Okay, not *really*. I'm a little pissed that Old Barb turned me down for a tumble, but hey, that's the way the world works. You win some, you lose some. I smile. Frown. Mireya. I just don't know know what I'm going to do with that woman. I think briefly about joining Beck on his nightly prowl. I'm sure I could find a girl that would make the hurt go away. Thing is, I know that in the morning, it'd be back with a vengeance, screaming around me, telling me that I've betrayed my heart with my dick. I don't like that feeling, and it's a damn hard one to live with.

I sigh and lift my head up to look into the mirror, straightening myself and examining the tattoos on my chest and belly. I could use a new one. Ink always makes me feel better. I touch the broken heart tattoo on my left shoulder first, dipping my hand down to the viking on my chest, sliding my fingers down to the skull and the Triple M tat beneath it. And then I keep going, diving down and taking a naughty dip into my pants.

The whorls on my fingers feel like blades, slicing across my aching flesh and drawing more blood into my cock, making it solid and painful. I feel like I could fucking scream right now. At first, I didn't get Mireya's angle. I mean, who would turn down a hand job? But now I get it. That bitch knew exactly what it is that she was doing.

I use my other hand to rip open my pants, snapping the button off and sending it skidding across the white tiled floor. Beck slams his fist on the door and I ignore him, turning on the sink, so I can have some fucking privacy.

My right hand grips my shaft while my mind wanders, sliding right back to those fresh memories of Mireya's cruel fingers. I stroke myself, letting my eyes flicker closed for a moment while I savor the rush of pleasure that's coursing through my veins, poisoning me, spoiling me to anything or anyone else. Never thought I'd be this way. The day I turned thirteen, I lost my virginity to an older girl next door, just a few days before she left for college. And from that moment until the day I joined Triple M, I was a little nightmare on wheels. I had more sex in that brief time period than I have in the past seven years. But it wasn't great, wasn't even good. I'm in love. Never wanted to be, don't even really know how much I like it now, but I can't stop it. Love is an unstoppable force, a gale of emotions, pain and pleasure, joy and melancholy, ache and fulfillment. It doesn't discriminate and it never stops. It never goes away. I got bit in the balls and I can't pry off the jaws of fate.

I am so fucking screwed.

I reach forward and grab the complimentary lotion bottle that was left on the counter, sending up a silent apology to whoever put it there. Doubt they suspected that some guy would be slathering up his penis with it, wishing he was being swallowed up by a smart mouthed Spaniard turned Yankee with a tiny waist and heaving breasts, skin like bronze and eyes the color of melted fucking chocolate.

"Mireya," I whisper, opening my eyes and staring at myself in the mirror. I'm a shirtless mess with my pants hangin' loose around my hips, my cock out and rigid, standing tall and quivering with need. I try to start slow at first, work my way up into a more satisfying orgasm, but I can't keep it in. Soon, I'm pumping so furiously that I find I can't stop, not even when I hear the bedroom door open and the harsh murmur of Mireya's voice as she tells Beck to fuck off. If anything, it makes it worse. I grit my teeth and pump myself into a wild fury, imagining Mireya beneath me, writhing in pleasure, calling out my name, begging me for more. In my mind, she gives herself fully to me, opens up and lets me in. I call her mine and she doesn't protest, she lets me have her the way I want her to have me. Fully and completely.

I'm so into my shit that I forget that the door didn't get locked behind me. Just as I'm reaching that pinnacle, watching myself in the mirror, staring my demons head on, the door opens. The muscles in my belly contract and I let loose, spilling myself all over the bathroom sink at the same moment somebody screams.

"Shit." I stuff myself back into my pants and grimace as I turn to find Mireya and Christy standing just outside the door. Mireya has her arms folded across her chest and a bemused smirk on her face. Christy, well … shit, the girl just looks freakin' terrified.

"Don't you know how to knock?" I ask her as my worst nightmares are confirmed and Beck slides into view. Soon as he sees what's going on, he starts to laugh again. *Can't a guy get a freaking break around here*? Mireya rolls her eyes and gestures at my mess.

"Clean it up, cowboy. The girl here has to piss." She starts to move away, leaving me in a bit of an awkward position. "Amy will be along in just a minute. Austin and Kimmi have some shit to work out, so we're babysitting." She walks away with a sigh and a roll of her eyes. I think I hear her mumble *Madre Mia* under breath, but who knows.

"Sorry there, babe," I tell the frightened girl who just shakes her blonde head and steps away, floral dress drifting like smoke behind her. I can't imagine I'm helping the poor thing any. Being a part of an MC is a far cry from being a sheltered Southern belle. And then to have to deal with Bested and being tossed on the back of Beck's bike afterwards? She's got to be in shock. "Dude, lay off," I growl at my friend as he proceeds to switch on the charm and hit on the poor girl. I saw her flirting with him at the bar that first night in Wilkes, but I have a feeling she's not really into him.

"Dude?" Beck asks me, giving me a single raised eyebrow. I keep my glare locked on his face while I clean up and drop one of the white towels into the trash can. Don't know where else to put it. He rolls his eyes at me and ends up mumbling curse words as he pushes open the door and tips an imaginary hat at Amy Cross. Austin's standing behind her with Kimmi at his side, watching carefully. I imagine him to be sort of like a lion or something, watching over his pride. Anyway, that's how I feel when he looks at Amy.

"Everything alright in here?" he asks when he sees Christy's face. Tears are building behind her eyes, but she smiles anyway, nodding her head and holding out her hand for Amy who takes it and gives her friend a gentle hug.

"Everything's just fine there, Pres," Mireya says, a cigarette dangling from her lips. She watches the two girls embrace and something flickers behind her eyes. I wonder if she misses that kind of intimacy, if she wishes she had more friends. Mireya and women have never particularly gone hand in hand. I don't know the last time I saw her have a pleasant conversation with someone of the same sex. "And it'd be even better if you told us what the hell was going on." Austin nods his head and swipes his hand through his blonde hair. He's overwhelmed, that's alright. I get it. I watch him carefully for a moment and decide to speak up. Didn't get my chance on the intercom, thank you very much, Mireya Sawyer.

"Sparks, I think you should talk to Diamond." I get three sets of glares leveled on me from Austin, Kimmi, and Mireya. I hold up my hands to keep the peace, letting them know I'm not trying to start shit. "Listen to me first and then shoot me after if you don't like what I have to say." I drop my hands and move out of the bathroom to sit on the edge of the bed. Austin and Kimmi exchange a look and move inside, closing the door behind them. "Melissa knows most - if not all - of the shit that Kent was up to. She knows how he kept things running so smoothly. Now, I know you and Kimmi have been our breadwinners for fuck knows how long, but it's going to take more than that to sail this ship, especially with all of the crap that's going down. People are okay now, but what happens if they think you can't control the group? That you can't keep things the way Kent did. They'll get antsy and things will get weird. Think about it. Melissa Diamond is a train wreck, but she's probably our best hope of managing this without a hitch."

Austin stares at me for a moment with a blank expression and then breaks out into a grin.

"Now, tell me this," he says, lifting his head up a bit to glance at Amy. She smiles back at him, and Mireya rolls her eyes again. "Why did it take a damn infant to bring that shit up? Don't know why I didn't think of it." He slaps me on the back and it's my turn to roll my eyes.

"Fucking geezer," I mumble at him as he watches Kimmi check out our newcomer. She looks pleased with what she sees. Now, I don't know if Christy swings that way or not, but Kimmi Reynolds has been known to turn a few heads that wouldn't otherwise look her way, if you catch my drift. "Now go rob a bank or some shit. That's your specialty, ain't it?" Austin laughs, and Kimmi flicks me in the nose with her long nails.

"Glad you guys are so chill with this," she says, dangly earring swinging as she turns her head from me and focuses back on Christy. A double take. This doesn't bode well for Kimmi's current girlfriend, Margot. Poor thing. Looks like our female casanova is ready to move on. Wonder if she knows the girl's a virgin? I can practically smell her innocence from here. Christy is not like Amy, a facade of politeness wrapped around an animal. Nope. If their positions had been switched, Mireya might still be holding Austin in her grip.

I shiver and try not to think about Mireya's grip. God. My cock starts to stiffen anyway, and I drop my hands to my lap to try and cover it.

"Ain't gonna be any bank robbing going on tonight, but if we're doing Fort Walton, our plans have got to be solid. You don't mind if we step out together for awhile?" I start to shake my head, and then pause to look over at Mireya.

"You don't want any help?" she asks, and I notice that her voice softens just a bit. God, what I would give to have her look at me like that. Austin shakes his head.

"Much as I appreciate the offer, sugar, Kimmi and I have been a two-horse team for as long as I can remember. When Kent tried to get Melissa involved, it didn't exactly go over well. I'm going to say that we'll stick to what works." He pauses and the two of them share a strange stare over my head, communicating without words. Old friends can do that, you know. It's pretty fucking special. "You'll stay here and watch the group for me though?" Mireya smiles, but it's tight-lipped, nodding her head reluctantly.

"Yeah, sure, Pres. Whatever the fuck you want."

Austin takes a step forward like he wants to go to Amy and then pauses. Out of respect for Mireya, I watch him pull himself in, drop us a salute and leave the room with Kimmi practically drooling behind him. Thing is, I think I see Christy returning the stare. Hmm.

"I want to take a moment to thank you both," Amy says, turning to look at us with a gentle smile. "The way you handled yourselves in that bar was admirable." She pauses and her blue eyes lock onto Mireya's brown ones. "Especially you. I know we haven't had the best of of beginnings, but my mother always used to say that the best things are worth working for. I think we could work at being friends, don't you?" Mireya stares at her for a moment and then lights up her cigarette, shrugging like she doesn't give a shit. But I think she does. I really, really do.

"I'm going to take this outside," she says, raising her smoke up with two fingers and moving past the girls and out onto the patio. I follow after, wanting to give the two friends a chance to catch up. And well, maybe because I'm still a little bit off after having Christy catch me whackin' it.

"Go away, Gaine," she says before I can even close the sliding glass door behind me. I watch as she leans over the railing and sticks her leather clad ass out like she has no clue how friggin' hot she is. I know she does though. I've seen Mireya Sawyer flaunt it like a fucking peacock. She knows the body she has and the power she's got over men. I stare at her ass for a moment and step up beside her.

"Are you pissed at me?" I ask her, and she groans, dropping her head down and letting her cigarette dangle, ashes trailing off into the warm wind. The town below us stretches out, sleepy and quiet, fading into the sultry evening like a fairytale. I swear, sometimes I think these little Southern towns are in a universe of their own making, one where the hustle and bustle and bullshit doesn't reach. It feels so peaceful here.

"What for, Gaine?" she asks, and I don't really know what to say. I guess it just feels like she's angry with me all the time. I wish she'd let go a little bit. I wonder if Amy Cross could help her out with that? I think that girl just learned how to lose herself. It's a valuable skill, one that I think Mireya would benefit from. As stupid as I feel taking Beck's advice, I keep his words in mind and try not to pester her. Whining and bitching and moping around isn't going to endear any woman to me, especially not one that's tough as nails like Mireya.

"I dunno. Just thought that bike trick of yours was a little cruel. Sweet Jesus. And you wonder why I was jacking off in the bathroom?" She laughs this time, just a cruel, little chuckle, but at least it's something.

"I didn't wonder why, Gaine. I knew." She takes a drag and passes her cig to me. I look at it for a minute and accept it, sliding the stick between my lips with a smile. "But I had to teach you a lesson. And thank you. It was complicated." She sighs and spins around, leaning back over the railing so that her hair catches in the breeze and sways, a silken cloud of darkness that makes me wet my lips and shift uncomfortably. Mireya lets her eyes close and takes in a deep breath.

My gaze falls to her chest, to the rise and fall of her breasts, the line of dark cleavage. I shiver and feel myself responding to the sight. *Christ, Gaine, you shootin' for a marathon run today*? I keep myself angled forward, so Mireya can't see. I don't want her to think that all I'm thinking about is fucking. Far from it. If anything, I'd like to be the one to help redeem Mireya's soul. I hold my hand out and focus on my fingers, curling them in towards my palm. If I get the chance, I'm going to spare her anymore blood on her hands, even if she hates me for it.

I lick my dry lips and lean my elbows on the railing, letting the cigarette dangle from my mouth. Now that I've banned myself from bitching and nagging Mireya, I don't exactly know what to say.

"You got any ideas on how to deal with these girls for the evening?" I ask, trying to smile. The smoke falls from my mouth and tumbles end over end to the sizzling pavement below. I watch it go with a sigh. "I mean, Amy's had it pretty easy since she got here. Maybe a little hazing would be in order?" I look over at Mireya who's cracked an eye to look at me. Even half-lidded, her gaze is powerful, cutting through my chest and stabbing me straight into the heart.

"Can I break Amy's face in half?" she asks, but then she smiles and my heart flip-flops. I feel like a fucking tool when I'm around her, getting all these lame ass fluttery feelings and shit. I'm into the fairytale crap, but I'd rather not be the princess. Still, for Mireya, I might be able to make an exception. My smile turns into a grin.

"I think you already tried that, babe, and it didn't exactly go over all that well." For a second, Mireya's still and silent, and I'm pretty damn sure I've fucked up this quiet moment of in-between, but then she grins and stretches with a groan.

"Fucking bitch fights hard." She stands up and slips her leather jacket off her shoulders, revealing the sleeveless whatever-it-is that she's got on underneath. Looks like lingerie, but that's alright with me. I don't mind a good look-see. "For a little pussy cat that is." She puckers her red lips at me and tosses a wink, sliding open the door and then using her hip to push it the rest of the way. I don't miss the way her leather pants hug her curves and kiss her ass, rolling my eyes to the sky and praying for somebody or something to help my dick out a little. Poor fucker's had enough trauma today.

"Get your bitch asses dressed," she barks at them, sizing up the two skinny pale girls. Christy jumps, but Amy doesn't flinch. Actually, she smiles. "We're going out to buy a bike."

Mireya
CHAPTER 10

Evening is peeking its sultry head out of the sky and getting ready to swallow the day. There's less than an hour before the dealership closes, but I say fuck it. If you give off the right attitude, people will bend over backwards for you.

When we walk into the glass doors and move across the linoleum floor, we get some looks. This isn't exactly our sort of place. I doubt any of these fuckin' people have actually ever seen a real biker before. This fine establishment is probably here to service the local balding male population, middle aged men looking for a way out of their midlife crisis without buying a convertible.

My nose wrinkles right away. This isn't exactly my scene. These are pre-built bikes from the manufacturer, name brands that'll never live up to the road the way I want them to. I already miss my Bonneville.

Gaine walks beside me, watching my face, smirking just a

bit. He knows how this outing is going to go.

"Don't say a word," I growl at him, thinking about riding on the back of his bike, knowing that I will do anything to get off of it. And it's not because of Gaine, it's out of principle. Being up against men who think women shouldn't ride makes me want to ride that much more. I want to grind that pavement and destroy the road. I want them to see me coming from across the state, gunning for it. I want to destroy perceptions and prejudices and grind them into dust. I'm going to have a hard time doing it with a make-a-million Tinkertoy, but there it is. I'm going to have to let my riding speak for itself.

"You gonna be alright with a piece of plastic there, honey pie?"

"Call me honey pie again and I'll cut your nuts off while you're sleeping." I pause next to the counter and watch as one of the salesmen walks quickly towards our little group. Amy is looking around with a glint in her eye that tells me she's not going to be gracing the back of Austin's bike forever. I guess I have to cut the kid some slack. I might hate her guts, but at least she has some to spare. Christy looks like a damn deer in the headlights. She's taking in the motorcycles like they're monsters, ready to spring out and assault her at any moment. I haven't asked yet, but I hope nothing happened with Bested by Crows and her in that back room. I suppose at some point I'll find out, but I can't deal with that at the moment. Right now, this is all about seeing the best this shit hole has to offer.

"Don't try to sell me something," I tell the man in the suit, the one that doesn't even look like he's ever climbed onto a damn bike. *Madre mia*, this is not going to be easy. "I'm walking out of here with something that's ready to ride. I want the keys, today, right now." The man opens his mouth to speak and I cut him off with a raised hand, rings glittering in the late afternoon light. He pauses and nods his head, ever the salesman, trying his best to smile at me.

"Certainly. Just let me know if you'd like to take something for a test drive." He backs away slowly, like we might be dangerous, might be there just to whoop his ass and carve our names into his backside, and turns away to busy himself at the counter, eyes flicking up every now and then to take us in.

"Back country piece of shit," Gaine mumbles, tucking his hands into his front pockets and glancing around with a slight quirk of disdain playing about his lips. "Bet he doesn't know a Kawasaki from a Harley." I try not to smile, but I do anyway and spin on my heel, so Gaine can't see. No point in getting his hopes up. He's fun to be around, sure, but that's because he's young and stupid, and there are no strings attached. I imagine that if I fell onto his lure, I'd drown in that love. A pretty death, sure, but a death nonetheless, a sacrifice of the *self* for the *us*. I'm not ready for that yet. Maybe not ever. Yeah, probably not fucking ever.

"Jesus friggin' Christ," I murmur as I wind through the gleaming rows of metal and paint, the decorative toys to be parked in garages and cooed over, the ones people like to drive to the supermarket and then right back home for a bubble bath. These babies never get to stretch their wings, never get to wear a badge of pride, covered in slight scratches and dings, gifts from the open road. It's a damn shame. "This isn't going to be easy."

"Can't imagine that it will be," Gaine says, glancing over his shoulder and pulling my gaze along with him. Amy's straddling a Suzuki Inazuma and feelin' it up like they're an item. Her blue eyes glitter with the thrill of freedom, sparkling with the knowledge that she is her own boss out here, that the rules of the road are guidelines and that she's welcome to leave whenever she pleases. I stare at her for a moment, take her in, and wrap my hatred around me. *She stole Austin away.* I scowl and turn away, letting myself revel in an emotion that's become much more comfortable to me than simple amusement. I'm not saying that's a good thing; that's just the way it is.

"She's going to fit in a lot better than even I thought," Gaine says, and I wonder if sometimes he thinks about what's coming out of his damn mouth. I flick hair over my shoulder and stomp down the aisles, the heels of my boots clicking across the over waxed linoleum floor. The thing sparkles so damn much, my eyes are starting to flicker with sun spots. And don't get me wrong, I'm a fan of air conditioning but Lord in Heaven, it must be sixty fucking degrees in here.

I ignore my friend, the one who's desperate to be so much more and keep moving, fingers sliding across gleaming chrome and unblemished leather, wondering if I'm going to be able to find anything here that'll let me salvage some of my dignity.

Gaine follows close behind me, a heated presence in all of this sterile frigidity. It's like a freaking museum in here. I just want to buy a damn bike, not come in my panties at the looks of some pretty statues. I want something that's functional. Is that too much to ask? I keep moving and Gaine stays on my heels. I swear, I can feel the heat of his breath on my neck, his fingers hovering over my hips. When I pause to glare back at him, he's not quite as close as I think. *My imagination then. I haven't been getting laid enough lately.* I turn back around and keep walking, through another doorway and into the next room. I can't see Amy and her friend anymore, but I can hear their soft voices drifting through the quiet building, bouncing off the glass and teasing my ears with girlish whispers. So naïve. So fucking naïve. I almost envy them. Almost. Naivety is great and all, a soft place to lie your head, but that's not the issue. The issue is when reality comes crashing down, tearing you apart and ripping your innocence away, leaving you with nothing but violently shattered pieces. I pause next to a Kawasaki and rest my hand on the seat.

My mind is spinning away, dragging me back to my memories, blinding me with pain and humiliation, tainting me with betrayal. I shut it down before it even gets a chance to start and jump when Gaine lays his fingers on my upper arm, brushing the whorls of his fingertips across my skin.

"You alright?" he whispers, voice soft, understanding. I've told him my story before, my whole story. Don't know why I did it. I must've been *muy loca*, but I spilled my shit, just drenched him with it, and now I'm paying for it with gentle looks and tender caresses. Might seem like a good thing to some people, but to me, it's dangerous as hell. I pull away and roll my shoulders into a shrug.

"Just help me find a Goddamn motorcycle," I snap at him, taking out my frustration on the one person who really doesn't deserve any of my shit, but who takes it anyway. Willingly even. He follows close behind me and doesn't let up as I push past a curtain and into the smallest of all three showrooms. The floor in here isn't linoleum, just cement, and it's splattered with oil and droplets of discarded paint. In here rests the skeletons of the unfortunate, bikes that didn't make the cut. Most are just here for parts, sitting around in neat rows, missing vital organs and grinning in grimy darkness. I stare them all down, letting my gaze scan along the waste until I come across another row in the back, against the wall. Maybe I'm not supposed to be in here, but I'll be damned if I leave this place without seeing *everything* there is to see. Besides, if they didn't want customers wandering into the service area, they should've locked the damn door.

"You can talk about whatever with me, Mireya. You know that, right?" I roll my eyes and keep moving until I'm stopped in front of … something. I don't know what make or model it used to be. It's just a big jumble of parts now, but the engine looks good and it certainly doesn't look like anything you'd wipe your damn ass with. This isn't a Barbie bike, built for show, and made of plastic. This is solid, metal, old, probably American, definitely custom. I smile. I wonder if it rides?

"Stop being a damn pussy, Gaine. I don't want to have any fucking heart to hearts with you, alright? Go be a fucking faggot somewhere else." His fingers grasp my bicep firmly, but gently. He's holding tight, but he isn't being rough. He knows better. I can handle men that are rough, but I don't like it. It doesn't feel right. I mean, holding your own is one thing, but you don't have to like it. Gaine knows that.

"If lovin' so hard I can't breathe, can't think straight, can't even fuck another woman, makes me a damn pussy then so be it. Mireya, you're hurting. Old memories are getting stirred up. I can tell. It isn't hard to see that. Don't hold it all back. That's what you've been doing for years, and it isn't helping. You have to talk about it, babe." I turn to look at him, the smile melting off my mouth and pooling on the dirty floor under my leather boots like oil.

"You don't know shit about shit, Gaine Kelley. Fuck off and leave me alone. I don't want to gossip about past fuck-ups. And I definitely don't want to ride in reverse. I'm going to move forward and railroad Bested by Crows. That'll be my vengeance; that'll be my finality. Words are just words, and I have no use for them." I jerk my arm back, but Gaine doesn't let go. Instead, he follows, moving against me, pressing me back into the row of metal, so that my jeans brush against tailpipes and tires. The heat of his body overwhelms me, crashing down around my skin like fire, burning away the icy brush of the air conditioning.

"I know you don't like to hear it, and I know you're tough as nails, and I *know* beyond any shadow of a doubt that you can take care of yourself, but Goddamn it, Sawyer, if you're not stubborn as all get out. Sometimes, you have to talk about something to get it off your chest. I can see it sitting there, the biggest damn elephant in the room. You're hurt, lover. I can see it plain as day." He slides his hand up my arm and touches his fingers to the base of my neck, sending thrills of pleasure down my spine. Velvety heat envelops me again, whispers false promises in my ear. Never before have I wanted to throw myself into somebody's arms. And I don't like it. My mouth twists into a scowl, but before I can get any words out, Gaine's kissing me like he's afraid he's going to lose me. I don't know how that's possible since the fucker doesn't even have me yet, but he does it, somehow, someway ... I reach out and grab his leather jacket by the lapels, yanking him against me. I mean to push him back and then sock him in the face, but I don't quite get there. Instead, that heat and desire and desperation to be wanted as much as I want, fills me, consumes me and then spits me back out into the world, cold and wanting. I let go of his jacket and slide my arms beneath the leather, holding Gaine tight while he teases me with his lips, pressing barely there kisses against my mouth, avoiding the tangle of my tongue with his. He keeps it strictly mouth to mouth, less vulgar, more intimate somehow. I don't quite know what to think.

"Mireya?" It's Amy's voice, flitting through the curtain into this quiet darkness. It smells like oil and gasoline, rusted metal and cracked leather. Maybe that's why I'm so intoxicated? I stare past Gaine's shuttered lips and watch as she moves into the room, pausing when she sees us. Her small mouth turns into a perfect, little 'O' and she reaches back to stop her friend from following after her. "They're not here," she says instead, and then in a swirl of floral skirts, turns away and disappears again. Somehow, it seems she knows what I need even more than I do. Uppity, little bitch.

Gaine's fingers tighten slowly but surely, weaving into my hair and holding me still while he savors me, opening up a bit, letting me in, so that I can brush my tongue against his. We kiss slow and sensual, sizzling. I want to take the next step, but I don't, waiting for him to move first. He doesn't. He just keeps kissing, holding me like he's never going to let go, trapping me between old metal and uncertainty.

When I hear movement outside the curtain, I try to pull away, but he keeps us still, trapped between one heartbeat and the next.

"Mireya." The word is whispered against my mouth, spreading the wetness between my thighs. When Gaine drops his hand down and slides it under my shirt, I groan against his lips. "No matter what you say or do, or hell, no matter you *don't* say or *don't* do, I'm here for you. Got it? And it ain't because I'm a pussy. It's because I love the hell out of you, and I'm not willing to watch you fall by the wayside, bitter and broken. What happened then doesn't mean shit now. Yeah, I think you should talk about it, and I sure as shit think they should pay for it. But ... " He trails off and lets go of my hair to unbutton my jeans. His hand moves lower, into my panties, cupping my heat tight and then slipping a single finger into the moistness. "It." He thrusts hard, slamming his knuckles against my pussy. "Doesn't." Gaine slides his finger out slowly. "Define." A second finger joins the first, filling me up and making me gasp. *Jesús santo.* "You." Gaine curls his hand just right, hitting my G-spot and knocking my feet out from under me. The only thing that keeps me standing is his arm around my waist, burning a line alone the bare skin where my shirt rides up. He kisses my open mouth again and holds me there while he plays along my insides, brushing and sliding and thrusting, sending flutters through my belly.

Words filter in through the curtain, and I'm fairly certain I hear Amy's voice asking about gas mileage or something else as equally unimportant. I get that she's trying to help me, I do. She's leaving me alone here, with Gaine, in a garage in the middle of nowhere. Maybe she's hoping I'll find myself? That I'll have some revelation or something the way she did, something so powerful that I'll drop everything and start fresh, leave my old life behind and find something new. Who the hell cares. Right now, I can't even think. All

I'm worrying about is how long this pleasure is going to last before there's pain again, how far I'll go before the cycle of hurt starts anew.

I want to tell Gaine to step off and fuck off, but I can't speak anymore. My orgasm is sneaking up on me, coming from places low, settling deep and getting ready to explode from within. I gasp, breaking away from Gaine's lips, letting my noises sift through the quiet air. From outside the room, the voices get louder and then quiet away again.

"Do you want me?" Gaine asks. The question is simple *and* complex. I don't like it. It scares the shit out of me.

"How so?" I manage to grind out, narrowing my eyes on him, listening to the slick slide of his fingers inside of me as he teases the life from my body and leaves me limp in his arms. The only comfort here is knowing that if I grabbed his dick in my hands, that he'd drop to his fucking knees. "If you're asking if I want to fuck then sure. Otherwise, you know the answer to that question." Gaine frowns and pulls his hand away, pausing to spread his fingers apart and examine the shining wetness on his skin. I'm not ashamed. I fall back when he drops his arm, just a little and end up sitting on the ride I was admiring earlier, the one I'm going to buy, the *only* one in the store worth buying.

"You're stubborn as hell, you know that?" he asks and his voice wavers just enough that I catch a whole lot of Yank in his accent. Not that I'm complaining. I might've been born in Spain, but I've spent the majority of my life in the North, East and West, so it doesn't bother me. All of these

Southern trimmings are nice, but I don't need them. He drops his hand and looks down at me, dark eyes sparkling. The stubble on his face fills with shadows and gives him a darker, more masculine look. He seems older then, with the light absent from his youthful face. I'm not sure if I like it or not. I look down at the ground and then back up at him, rising to my feet, so that the toes of my boots brush his. My fingers grasp the waistband of my pants and push them down around my feet, crumpling them around my ankles like chains. But here's the thing: I don't mind. I'm not afraid of Gaine. I don't have to be worried that he's going to strip my womanhood away from me and leave me barren. Not that I couldn't take him, but it's nice to know that he wouldn't even try.

I turn around and bend over, letting my fingers touch the cold, white wall with its dirt stains and oil spots, letting my ass stick out, brushing it against the stiff bulge in his jeans.

"You started this, now finish it," I tell him, letting my belly rest against the motorcycle. It props me up, holds me still and sturdy, like it's always done in one form or another. Riding is my life. I don't have to have anyone or anything else. "Fuck me."

No arguments from behind. I hear Gaine slide his zipper down and arch my back when his hands touch my bare hips. A condom wrapper falls to the floor by my feet as I wait fully exposed and wanting, the touch of the air conditioner on my bare parts making me shiver.

"Do it in the ass," I tell him, gritting my teeth, wishing

for that slight edge of pleasure and pain. It's not like I'm new to it, but it'll still hurt, just a little. Gaine though, he knows how I like it. That's why I prefer the same lovers over and over again. Casual sex is fun, but this is better. I don't even think about missing Austin.

"You like to live hard and ride dirty, don't you, babe?" he asks before sliding his fingers into his mouth and then slicking them across my opening, warming me up. I don't need it or want it. I just want to fuck fast and frenzied.

"Do it. Now."

Gaine doesn't hesitate.

Wrapping his fingers around my hips, he presses his cock against me and slides in hard, shaking the motorcycle in a clink of metal. I grit my teeth and relish the feeling of being whole, of wrapping him so tight that there could no doubt in anyone's mind that in this moment, he belongs to me. *Like I care about that*? That's the last, negative thought I manage to get out before I'm overwhelmed with pleasure, riding a sting of sharpness, opening up and accepting him fully. My nails curl against the wall and the muscles in my stomach contract as I hold back a joyous scream, swallow it into my throat and pray to whatever fucking god will listen that nobody walks in on us.

Gaine rides behind me, holding me so tight I'm almost positive that there'll be marks tomorrow, and fucking me so furious that I know I'm going to be sore. But it's worth it. Oh so fucking worth it.

"Faster," I growl at him, listening to the rattle of metal

below us, imagining the road stretched out before me as Gaine's cock penetrates me deep and teases that sensitive line of flesh that separates him from my pussy. He grinds against it so hard, it's like he's trying to break through and pleasure both parts of me at once, slamming his hips against my ass with the sweet sound of pounding sweat soaked skin and a low, growling moan vibrating in his throat.

I toss my hair back and close my eyes, wishing we were in a bed or something, somewhere that we could let loose and scream and wrestle and grind and writhe for hours on end. Unfortunately though, it can't last. All good things must come to an end, and bad things last forever. While Gaine's body feels good now, while his feelings might be strong, they'll fade. One day, he'll realize I'm not the one and move on, and I'll be left feeling even more alone than I was before. But my nightmares, those remain. They stay behind and they torture me, year after year after year.

My orgasm builds again, climbing to a crescendo of wild ferocity that finally pulls that unwilling screech from my throat. I scrape my nails along the cement wall and listen to Gaine as he comes, shuddering inside of me and grabbing tight enough that his fingertips gouge my skin and draw just the slightest hint of blood. A few more slams of his hips and I'm going, too, falling off the deep end and drowning in wave after wave of mind numbing pleasure that I can't escape from.

When he steps back, when he finally pulls away, I'm a wreck, in tears that I can't explain, stumbling away and fixing my pants before I'm caught with … well, with my pants down.

When the salesman finally stumbles into the room with a wincing Amy at his heels, I'm smiling again, and it isn't pretty, more a grimace than anything else.

"I'll take this, please," I say, pointing at the bike, and for all the world determined that I am *not* going to be looking at Gaine fucking Kelley.

Mireya
CHAPTER 11

I ride my new bike back to the hotel while Gaine and the girls walk. I don't go too far though, just in case. You never know what kind of shit can go down at dusk. Everyone always worries about what's going to happen after dark, but not me. The real badasses, the bad guys you want to stay away from, they come out when the sky is still light enough to see, but just dark enough that it casts shadows. People expect bad in the dark; I expect worse at twilight.

My new ride's a piece of shit, for sure, but I'm confident I can fix it up on the road. I've done it before. It isn't easy, but I can make it happen. It's all about knowing people, about understanding how to get your way when you need a favor. I get guys to let me in their shops all the time, and I never have to suck a single dick. Not that I would, of course. But some might.

"How's it ride?" Gaine asks when I pull into the garage

and park. I'm sure he can tell from the frown on my face that it wasn't great. At least half the expression's for him, but he probably doesn't know that yet. I swipe some hair over my shoulder and sigh.

"It's not my Bonneville, but it works." I pause and look over at Amy and Christy. They're holding hands which I think is a little weird, a little juvenile, but whatever. I try not to pay them too much attention. "It's going to need some work, but nothing I can't handle." He tries to smile at me, turning up those ridiculously perfect lips into a grin. I ignore him. "Let's go back to the room. I need a shower." Amy giggles, and I toss her a searing glance.

"I'll bet," she says, but that's it. She tries to smile at me, too, but I'm not into making friends with girls who steal my exes, so there. I move away before anyone else can talk to me and Gaine follows, trying to throw me soft smiles and knowing looks.

"It was just a fuck, Gaine," I tell him before he starts to think otherwise. I mean, it's not like anal sex has been or ever will be considered the height of romance for God's sake. His smile falters a little, but it doesn't stop him from following me, dragging Amy and Christy along in our wake.

"When are you going to stop kidding yourself, Mireya. You and me, we're meant for each other." I wrinkle my nose and nearly have a friggin' heart attack when Beck's laughter bursts out from behind the lobby door. He pushes off the wall and stalks towards us with a rictus grin spread across his ugly face. "What the fuck do you want?" I snap at him, continuing on my way to the elevator. I don't care if I'm babysitting or not, I'm going to do what I want to do, everyone else be damned. If Amy and Christy don't like it, they can go to hell.

"Just wanted to let you know I'm on watch right now, and we ain't seen nothing to worry about yet." My shoulders get tight and my mouth purses. I saw the Triple M'ers hanging outside the parking garage. That was all the reminder I needed. *We're being hunted.* My skin goes cold and my heart starts to beat an irregular rhythm. This isn't how it should be. We should be chasing *them*, not the other way around. They're the ones who should be suffering right now, looking over their shoulders, not knowing *when* it's going to come, but knowing that it will. Eventually.

I hit the button on the elevators with a jab of my thumb and cross my arms over my chest.

"Yet is the word of the day, isn't it?" I growl, fingers clenching tight, dragging my nails across my skin. "But don't you worry your pretty little red head about that. They'll be here. Those idiots would follow Tray to the moon and back." *And that's why it hurt so much, his betrayal. I trusted him. He had full control, complete and full control.* I squeeze my eyes closed and flick them over, making sure that I'm wearing a mask over my emotions. The last thing I need is Gaine to look me in the eyes and know what I'm thinking about. I don't want his sympathy. I don't want anyone's sympathy. "So stop flirting with the desk clerk and keep your fucking eyes out." I slide into the elevator and let the doors slam shut before anyone can follow me.

I hear Gaine call out just before the metal cuts us off from one another, but I don't care. I need a moment to myself.

Bested by Crows is going to come, and they're going to get theirs, even if I have to take out everybody in the MC. From the assholes that betrayed me to the women that watched, I'll drag them all to the depths of hell and leave them to rot. If, *if*, there's anyone worth saving, then so be it, but she better be willing to step up her game.

I sigh and slam my forehead against the wall, resting there with my fingers lighting brushing the mirror. The soft sound of a piano drifts to me from the speakers above, painting a melancholy backdrop to my misery. When did life become such a chore to live? I don't even know what it is I really want. Love? Not anymore. Freedom? I guess I have that. Nobody's keeping me here expect myself. Vengeance? Definitely. But then, I have a feeling it's not going to leave me as full as I want it to. It'll be like a bandage to my damaged soul, not a cure.

I push away from the wall and step between the doors as they slide open, gliding down the hallway to my room. As soon as I step inside, my clothes start to come off and I end up sitting on the floor of a hot shower, my mind drifting to places best left undisturbed. The rapes play over and over again in my mind, faces of betrayal and feelings of humiliation that I try to wash away with soap and scalding water. Nothing works. I live it over and over again, the horror stirred up like dust in a stampede. I'm in there so long that Gaine lets himself in and flings back the curtain like he thinks I might be dead.

"Just because we've had sex, that doesn't give you the right to walk in on me when I'm showering." I don't look up at Gaine, just stay where I am with my arms wrapped around my legs. I can feel his eyes on me, can see his cock responding out of the corner of my eye. He pushes the curtain back into place and I listen as he takes a step back.

"I'm just checkin' in on you is all," he says with a sigh. I aggravate him. I can tell. But too damn bad. I never asked to mean that much to him. That's his problem. The room stays silent for awhile with nothing but the sound of running water to keep me company, but I know he's still there. Strange as it sounds, I can *feel* him. My nightmares run down the drain with the soapy water, pushed back by Gaine's presence. I might not realize it in that moment, but it's true.

The steam surrounds me, touching my skin with wandering caresses. I lean my head back and let water cascade around my face.

"I thought you might want to get out tonight, do something interesting."

If I listen hard, I can hear his breathing, rough and pained outside the curtain. He's aroused. Doesn't take a fucking genius to tell me that. Even though we just had sex, my body calls out for him, swearing up and down that my pussy is jealous, that it *needs* his touch. I tell it to fuck off, but somehow, I find my hand wandering between my thighs, brushing my clit ever so slightly, just enough to send a thrill through my body. “Like what?” I ask, and I manage to keep my voice even. I fall back, laying my head next to the faucet and resting against the wall. My fingernails brush across my opening and pause there, hovering, half desperate.

On the other side of the curtain, I catch just the slightest hint of a groan.

Gaine
CHAPTER 12

Mireya is driving me bat shit fucking crazy today. I can't get enough of her, and I want desperately to get away from her. The two emotions are threatening to strip my sanity and make me nuttier than a jar of fucking peanut butter.

My hand drops down to my jeans and brushes across the fabric there. I've been whacking it more than usual, like I'm still a damn kid or something. Mireya does that to me. She makes me so hot I can't think straight. I don't intend to touch myself then and there, but as soon as I make contact, I'm bitin' back a groan and trying to resist tearing that friggin' curtain off the wall, so I can get to her.

"I don't know, Mireya. Go out to dinner? See a movie? Something normal. We don't get a lot of that around here." I unbutton my pants, careful to keep the sound to a minimum. I imagine that the water will cover most of it up, but if she catches me, I'm a dead man.

"You want to go on a date, Gaine?" she asks, and her voice sounds a little faraway, not as bitter as usual. If I've learned anything by being around Mireya Sawyer, it's that half the things that come out of her mouth are curse words and insults, and the other half are reserved for caustic slurs and put-downs. It's not that she's a bad person, not at all. That woman has a heart of fucking gold. She doesn't know it, but I do. And one day, I'm going to figure out a way to show it to her.

I slip my hand under the waistband of my boxer briefs and grab my cock in a firm hold. It feels so damn good that I almost let a sound slip.

"What makes you think that's a good idea? We're babysitting, remember?" I wait for a moment, but I don't hear any signs that she's gettin' out of the shower, so I start to stroke myself, slowly at first but quickly building into a frenzy. Sure, we just screwed. But I'm not done. I'll never be done with her. Something about those saucy lips, those full breasts, her round ass. I can't get her out of my mind. I've tried a few times, but it never works. I'm hooked and there ain't nothin' I can do about it. Best I go along for the ride instead of digging my heels in. It can only hurt less this way.

"Amy and Christy can come. Don't see why they couldn't sit at a different table or nothin'." I squeeze harder and move faster, letting my eyes fall closed for just a moment, so I can pull up the image of Mireya with her pants down around her ankles and her body bent over that bike. I bite my lip to hold back a groan.

"I'm not going out to dinner with those bitches, so you can just forget about it." The words are classic Mireya, but the tone is not. *Did I just hear her moan*? Outside the door, I can hear Christy and Amy chattin' about something, probably our little rendezvous at the dealership. I don't know how they know, but they know. Amy's friend won't even look me in the face now. Doubt I'm making a very good first impression. I check the door, just in case. Thank the fucking stars I locked it this time.

"Then let's do something else, anything else." I don't want her to sit around and stew because if I let her, she will. She'll sit on the bed and watch weird ass soap operas and squinch her eyes, tighten her lips and disappear inside of herself. We might travel a lot, but we don't *get out* all that much. I want to do something I'd do if I lived in one place year round and met a girl I liked. I want to take her on a fucking date.

I pump my cock hard, wondering what kind of fool I am to jack it with her sitting only a few feet away. What would she think? Doubt she'd be all that thrilled about it. But then … I'm pretty fucking sure I heard another moan.

"You suggest something that interests me, and maybe I'll reconsider." I let my head fall back as her voice drifts around me, teasing my bare skin, strengthening the illusion that my hand is her body wrapped tight as steel, hot and pulsing and dripping wet.

"Shit, I don't know, Mireya. Why don't you tell me what

you want to do, and I'll do it. I'd do anything for you." I stop suddenly and pause in the awkward silence that follows. For any other girl, that might've been a romantic statement, but for her, it's just another fucking annoyance. If I can't figure out a way to stop pushing myself on her, I'm screwed six ways to Sunday and back again. I don't stop stroking myself. It's like I'm possessed or something, like I can't hold back even if I wanted to. "We could go for a joyride. It's been awhile since we rode just to ride." I bite my lip hard and massage the head of my cock, teasing the skin with rough fingers. "Shit, we could go for a damn walk. I can't even remember the last time I went for one of those."

"Fine."

Just that one word, harsh and clipped but with a wild undertone that sends me spinning around and snatching the curtain in one hand while I keep hold of my pulsing cock with the other.

Mireya
CHAPTER 13

Gaine rips the shower curtain back with a violent ferocity that spikes my blood and sends my tongue sliding across my lips, beckoning to him even though I shouldn't. The pervert's holding his damn dick like they're best friends and looking at me with his pupils so dilated that they make his eyes look black.

He's panting and staring down at me with an expression that's half delight and half *what the fuck*. I narrow my glare on him and slide my fingers in deep, filling myself with my own flesh, opening up and letting him see all of that delicateness on display.

"You fucking pervert," I snarl, moving my hand faster, in and out, wishing that he were in here with me, pressing me down with his body, ravaging my neck with hot lips and fucking me until I can't stand straight anymore. With Austin, the sex was fun, but with Gaine … it's almost miserable. I can't get a release, even when I come. I just want more, no matter how we do it.

"Speak for yourself there, babe," he tells me and then he's climbing into the bathtub fully clothed, kneeling between my legs and sliding his hand along the slick length of his shaft, biting his lip and looking down at me with dark eyes obscured by his dripping hair.

I fuck myself harder.

Water sprays across the floor, but neither of us care. I've let myself get wrapped up in this tornado effect that Gaine seems to have on me where he pushes everything else away and sucks me in. I can't stand it. I feel like I'm drowning, that I can't breathe, that my lungs are being filled with something other than air, a force that has no name, that I don't recognize. Gaine Kelley is dangerous for me, especially now in this state of in-between where anything can happen.

You think I'd stop then, but I don't. I'm fucking stubborn as shit, desperate to show myself that he doesn't mean anything to me, that he's a fuck buddy and that's it. I slide my fingers from my pussy and rub them across his cheek, grabbing his hair and pulling him down, soggy clothes and all. Our mouths crash into one another, biting and scraping and grasping. His hands find my breasts and caress my nipples, teasing them with rough fingers and holding them so tight that the flesh bulges around his hand.

I try to pull him into me, but he won't let me, drawing a snarl of frustration from my throat that's quickly drenched with another kiss, one that cuts me so deep I almost scream from the pain in my heart. I can't explain the emotions he brings out in me. I feel like I'm suffering, but like I'd do anything to suffer more, to writhe in his arms forever. *Debo estar perdiendo mi maldita mente.*

Gaine kisses his way to my throat and grazes the flesh with his teeth, dragging his mouth down to my breasts and biting my nipples so hard that I gasp and arch my back, pressing myself fully into him, feeling his erection but being denied it. *I'm going to kick his ass after this.*

He tugs on my nipples and flicks his tongue over them, bringing me to the edge of an orgasm with just his mouth while his hand roves down between my legs and takes over, plunging inside of both my openings, teasing that tender flesh between his thumb and forefinger. Gaine pinches the sensitive nerve endings and leaves me shaking with desperation and need, biting back a wave of insults and a scream. I imagine that if I let loose, Amy's little friend would piss her damn pants. I doubt she's ever heard a woman in the throes of passion.

"You're teasing me on purpose," I growl against his wet hair, wrapping my fist it in and pulling his face back to mine, so I can lick along his stubbled jaw and nip at his ear. My cheek smoothes along the roughness of his as I whisper in his ear. "If you piss me off, you'll regret it." He ignores my half-assed threats and continues to fuck me with his hand, kissing the tiny star tattoo at the edge of my eye and then moving down to the sensitive skin between my breasts, running his tongue over a tiny dusting of freckles.

"You're a real piece of work, Mireya Sawyer," he says, flicking his thumb up against my G-spot. I gasp and a flood of pleasure washes over me, pulling an orgasm from my lower belly, and sucking the breath from my lungs. For a split second, I can't think abut anything but Gaine and the weird feelings he draws from the empty well of my heart. And then I'm coming hard, biting my own tongue to keep from screaming. The muscles in my body clench tight as I shudder around him, wishing all the while that it was his cock, that he was being rendered motionless in my arms, taken down a notch from the simple act of fornication. As my lungs fill again with a much needed breath of steamy air, a cascade of liquid warms places low, dripping down his hand and joining the spray from the shower head. It feels like I'm takin' a piss, but there is no way in fuck I would pee myself. The orgasm draws it from me without asking, drenching the bottom of the tub with my own juices. I try to play it off as nothing, but Gaine notices, slowing the rhythm of his hand and sitting up to look down at me.

Gaine

CHAPTER 14

"Baby, did you just ejaculate on me?" I ask, the corner of my lip twitching in amusement. Mireya puts her hand on my chest and shoves hard, but I'm not going anywhere, not this time. I slide my hand from her hot cunt and run my tongue down the warm liquid that's running down my wrist. It's not just water, that much I know for sure, and this ain't just the usual. Mireya Sawyer is a squirter. I try not to laugh. I'm not making fun of her, not in the least. This right here, this is pure ecstasy on my part.

"What the fuck are you talking about?" she asks, scooting back and holding her arm across her breasts, covering next to nothin' except her nipples. Mireya's breasts are full and luscious, two beautiful bronze orbs glittering with moisture. Drops of water run between them and draw my eye down, down, down. "You can either wipe that smile off your face or piss off," she says and then mutters something dirty in

Spanish. Kinda glad I don't speak the language at the moment.

"It's nothing to be ashamed of," I tell her, bending down and putting my hands on either side of her slick, moist body. I want to strip down and rub myself all over her, feel every inch of that soft, smooth flesh pressing against me. The differences between our bodies excites me, makes my cock so hard it hurts. I want to grab her hips and fill her, so that she's tight with me, joined with me in that moment in a way she's not with anybody else, and I never want to let her go. I want to hold and kiss and fuck this woman until the end of time and then some. It'll never be enough. There will never come a time when I can just walk away from her without lookin' back. She thinks that, maybe, but it isn't true. "But I don't recall this ever happening before." Mireya narrows her eyes at me and gives me a look that could kill.

"I don't know what the hell you're talking about," she growls, and for a second there, I think she's pullin' my damn leg. But then I look closer and see that the red flush across her bronzed skin isn't just from the heat or the excitement. She's *embarrassed.* Mireya fucking Sawyer is flat out flamin', cheeks rosy and red. "Get your ass back down here and fuck me, you piece of shit. Or get out."

"Mireya, listen to me," I say as I press my body against hers, bringing my hand back to that molten spot between her thighs. "You've got a special talent there, that's all." She tries to knee me in the groin, but I manage to grab her knees and push her legs apart. Well, I'm sure it's not all brute strength. She's letting me or I wouldn't be doing it. Mireya might've gotten a good ass kicking from Amy Cross, but she's tough. She can hold her own. "Not all women can come like that, you know?"

"Go to hell, Gaine," she says and turns over, grabbing the edge of the bathtub and trying to haul herself to her feet. I grab her hips and pull her back against me, slamming her ass against my body, letting my cock shimmy between her cheeks. I manage to pull a breathy gasp from her lips before I angle myself to slide in, using her natural juices as lube. We don't need anything extra, just our bodies and a quiet moment in time.

"Mireya, you came. Some women can do it, and you're one of them. It's nothing to be ashamed of. To tell you the truth, it's kinda turning me on." The muscles in my belly contract, begging to slam into her and watch the flesh on her plump ass shake with each thrust, but I hold back, teasing and caressing with the head of my cock. I move in just an inch and hold myself there, letting her stretch to accommodate me. She's so damn tight, I can barely take it. "Come all over my dick, and I'll give you a special treat."

I grab her hips and hold on tight.

Mireya
CHAPTER 15

My logical mind wants to kick Gaine's ass, but pure, animalistic need is hard to fight. Like a horny pussycat, I arch my back and try not to purr. That would be really fucking hard to live down. Instead, I brace my hands against the shower wall and let out a growl as I push back and spear myself on Gaine's massive cock. He's not as long as Austin, but he doesn't disappoint. In fact, I think I like him better. He's the widest guy I've ever been width, almost thick enough to hurt, straddling that edge that I enjoy so much. I almost wish he'd spank my ass. Almost. Certain things are too much for my dignity to handle.

"I'll tell you what," I whisper, feeling the rush of water against my spine like a massage. At this point, I know that Amy and Christy must guess that something is up, but I don't give a rat's ass. This is about me, proving to myself what I already know isn't true. Gaine is not just a friend with benefits. I wish he was, but he isn't. I try to imagine a girl like Amy sweeping in and taking him from me forever, drawing pet names from his lips and putting a goofy grin on his stupid ass face.

It puts me into a violent rage. Yeah, sure, I didn't let Austin go without a fight, but I didn't feel like this ... I never ... *came* on him, that's for sure.

"You do the work and I'll forget to kick your ass later. How does *that* sound?" Gaine shoves into me with a grunt, slapping his body against mine with a splatter of hot water, soaking the tiled floor even more. I let him move inside of me the same way he did before. Same motion, different hole. I smile and then end up biting my lip so hard it bleeds when he increases his pace, going at me with the monstrous frenzy he held back before. Anal sex feels fucking delicious, but you can't pummel an ass the way you can pummel a pussy, just wasn't built for it. This, this was *designed* to take a good beating. "Harder, you stupid, snatch sucking son of a slut." Gaine slams into me and my elbows go weak, loosing my grip on the wall and dropping my face to the edge of the tub. My cheek hits the plastic surround with a grunt, but he doesn't slow. He moves faster and deeper, filling me up and making my insides tingle like they never have before.

If I was out to prove myself a point, I've just learnt the opposite.

Fuck.

"Stop!" I scream suddenly, and he does, just like that. Gaine knows my past, so he knows when to push and when to let go. This time, he backs off, sliding out of me and falling back on his ass in the tub.

I push myself to my feet and try not to let my past screw with my head, with my emotions. I need to know what this is and why it's there. It's just a little niggle at this point, but I feel like it could be more. That scares the crap out of me.

"*Estoy perdiendo mi maldita mente. Me estoy volviendo loca. Esto no puede suceder. Me niego a dejar que esto suceda.*" I stumble out of the shower, catching myself on the curtain and grab the towel that's hanging over a metal bar next to the door.

"What does that mean? Mireya?" Gaine stands up and fixes his pants, shoving his erect cock inside like it doesn't even matter. He comes after me, but it doesn't do him any good. Mireya Sawyer is an expert at running away.

When I open the door, I come face to face with Amy. She looks a little confused, but unconcerned.

"Are you alright?" she asks as I push past her, wishing with a tiny part of myself that I had that much innocence, that I could be that pure and simple. I feel like a twisted mass, a tainted piece of trouble that's better left alone. I open the door to the hallway before Gaine can even make it out of the bathroom and go running, sprinting down the hallway with dripping hair and no clothes, my pussy swollen and aching with desperation. It wants to be filled, caressed, teased. I *need* that release, and there's only one person I want it from. *Gaine*. The problem is, the more I'm with him, the more I want to be. The ache never seems to subside; it's always there, deep down, mocking me with something I can't have.

Love.

That's the worst four letter word in my book, and unfortunately, that fucker is out of print.

I keep running and don't stop until I'm sliding down the wall in the stairwell with tears running down my cheeks again. No matter what I do lately, I can't seem to stop crying.

Gaine
CHAPTER 16

I know I can't leave Amy and Christy alone in the room, so I'm tickled fucking pink when I find Beck in the hallway and grab him by the shoulder.

"Watch the girls for me?" I ask without an explanation. He looks at me with one red brow climbing towards his hairline, but he doesn't ask questions. He knows better than that. I've been doing this dance with Mireya for a long time now, and when it finally looks like it might pay off, that we might actually be able to come together for a waltz, she takes off running.

I follow the water spots on the carpet until I get to the door to the stairwell, pausing just outside to listen in. Sobs. I don't need to hear anything else.

I fling the door open so hard that it slams into the wall behind me and leaves a massive dent in the drywall. Fuck it though. They can bill me for all I care. I bend down next to

Mireya's crumpled form and take her into my arms, feeling her stiffen as I fall back against the wall with her in my lap.

"Let go of me," she commands, but it only lasts a moment and then she's falling apart the way I always thought she should. Sometimes, we have to break ourselves into pieces before we can be whole again. Otherwise, we're just a jumble of dented parts.

I kiss her hair and squeeze her so tight that my muscles strain against the sleeves of my shirt, threatening to rend them at the seams. She shouldn't be like this. She's strong, confident, powerful. This pain, this ache, this should've never been inflicted on a woman this perfect. I have never felt a stronger urge to kill than I do now. I want to find Bested by Crows and tear them apart, one by one.

I hold my woman in my arms and promise that I'll never let her go, even if I can't say it aloud. In my head, I run through it over and over again. *I love you, and I'll protect you, whether you want me to or not.* And it's not because she's a woman, it's simply because I love her. That's it, all there is to it.

"Leave me alone, Gaine. I have things figured out. I function a certain way. I can't do that with you harping and nagging all the damn time." Mireya swipes her hand across her eyes angrily and glares at me, all of that fire and passion burning in her blood. I can feel her body like it's a brand, burning me and drawing welts along my skin. I want more, and my dick rises, poking against her ass like the fucker he is. I don't push it though. I understand where she's been and what she can handle, and I never, ever want to overstep those boundaries.

Still, I can see the way she swallows. I notice the way she adjusts herself, so that she's straddling my lap. We both do.

"I don't want anything from you," she tells me, and I listen because, no matter what I say, she's mine and I'm hers. That's it. It's woven into the tapestry of the universe. It's fuckin' fate. I touch her high cheekbone, run my fingers down that sculpted jaw to the point of her chin. When I kiss her, it's just a brush of flesh on flesh. I don't press it, don't force it. I beckon and she comes, willingly. That's all I want.

Her tongue crashes into mine and her fingers scramble at my back, digging into the fabric of my shirt and yanking it up and over, past our hungry mouths until she tosses it onto the floor in a soggy heap. Her hands run down my chest and caress my muscles, feeling them contract as she moves. I let her see the pleasure and the desire in my face, but I don't do a damn thing. I just wait, letting her set the pace because I know that's what she needs.

When she reaches down for my pants, I let out a groan of relief. She doesn't waste another second, sliding down along me until I'm pressed so firmly against her that it's hard to tell where one of us begins and one ends. Just as it should be.

Her arms come around my neck and our eyes lock. As she slides up and down my shaft, soaking me with her juices, squeezing me tight, I just watch her. I watch and I look and I listen. And when she comes, soaking me, drenching the floor with her essence, I wait. Only until after I'm sure she's at the edge again do I let myself go. And when I come, when I spill my seed inside of her, I know for damn fucking sure that somebody's going to pay for what they've done.

Gaine
CHAPTER 17

"I ain't going to apologize for it," I say when we roll into the next town. Austin keeps throwing me nasty looks, and Beck is laughing his ass off. Wait till he actually finds out why Austin is looking at me like that. The teasing will *never* fucking stop. "What makes you think you're any better?" Austin just shakes his head at me, blonde hair dripping with sweat. It is hot as shit out here, that's for sure. I've never been to Fort Walton, but already my impression isn't the best. The whole place looks dirty and dusty, like none of the buildings have ever seen a drop of rain or the sidewalks a broom. Kind of freaks me out.

"I never said I was better, just that I don't get caught." He tosses me a wink and kisses Amy full on the lips before helping her off the bike. If the asshole hasn't told her he loves her yet, I'm going to kick his ass. He has no idea how good he's got it. The girl he loves doesn't mind loving him, fell into it pretty easy if you ask me. Mine's … a bit more complicated.

Our plans are all helter-skelter, that's for sure. From what I gathered at this morning's meeting, the majority of the group is staying at the hotel while the rest of us meet up with Broken Dallas. They don't know we're here, so we're taking a pretty big risk with this. If they decide they don't want us here, things could get bad. Austin and Kimmi seem pretty confident. They've worked with them before, so I guess they know what they're doing, but I never trust other MCs. More often than not, if they can fuck you, they will.

"You want to stay at the hotel?" I ask Mireya, but she won't even look at me. She's ashamed, I think, and maybe a little embarrassed, too. Opening up to someone like that isn't easy, I know. I try not to smile at her since I know it'll only make things worse and shrug my shoulders, slipping a cigarette between my lips. "I hope we're bringing firepower," I say around my smoke as I light up. "I'd rather not spend the rest of the weekend dead."

"Thanks for the boost of confidence, Gaine," Austin says, tucking Amy against his side before grabbing their bags and swinging them onto his opposite shoulder. "Now tell me, why isn't your ass staying behind?" I laugh as I watch him move away, all the while perfectly aware that Mireya's watching me, eyes boring into my back. If I didn't know better, I might just say she was interested.

"Because without me, there'd be nobody to make all the logical decisions." I give Austin a grin and blow smoke his way before stepping away from my bike and trying to forget Mireya Sawyer for a moment. On the one hand, I feel kind of elated. I mean, it seems like she might be getting to a point where she's ready to accept me, but on the other, I feel like I'm smothering her, drowning her in my affections. It's a fucking nightmare.

"You want to tell me why Austin's raggin' on you so damn much?" Beck whispers as he comes up beside me. His green eyes are sparkling mischievously, so I'm guessing he has some idea. Best way to deal with Beck is to stay confident and not show a lick of shame. Second he senses any weakness, he's like a cougar on a doe's back.

"Some old as fuck couple with a bundle of sticks shoved up their asses filed a complaint on Mireya and me for fuckin' in the stairwell." I shrug like it's no big deal and pull my cigarette from my mouth. Beck starts to laugh, rubbing at the red stubble on his jaw and shaking his head like he's never heard anything so funny.

"Hey, step off and fuck off," Mireya growls, storming past him in a wave of sweet perfume and raven hair. She doesn't even look like the girl I made love to last night, the one who stared me straight in the face and let it all hang out. They could be sisters maybe, but there ain't nobody on this earth that would believe this woman sobbed in my arms last night. I take a drag, but I don't say anything. One wrong move now could ruin everything.

"You are such a stupid fuck," Beck cackles as he catches sight of a young girl seated alone at one of the tables in the hotel restaurant. He licks his lips, but doesn't leave my side. Beck might be a slut, but at least he knows it's work first and screw later. "How the hell did you manage to get caught?" He chuckles again and keeps pace with me until he spots Melissa. I don't know what's going on between them, but when Beck's eyes catch on her, he changes. Now, I've been told that Beck Evans only has three emotions: horny, happy, and pissed the fuck off. But the way his green eyes dull and his hands clench at his sides, I'd have to bet that there's something else in there. Could be sadness maybe, or disappointment, I'm not sure. I let it go. I can only handle one problem at a time. After I figure out what's going on between Mireya and me, I'll see what I can do for Beck.

I wait in the lobby while everybody gets checked in, making sure I've got enough weapons to take down an army. No chances. I won't risk anything at this point in my life. I am *this* friggin' close to having the woman of my dreams and nobody is going to take that shit from me.

I sigh and lean against the wall, putting my cigarette out when I see I'm starting to gather glares, and watch as Christy follows Mireya like a lost puppy. She rode in on the back of her bike, clinging to her like her life damn near depended on it. And maybe it did. Mireya's new ride is a little worse for wear or at least it looks it. I don't have half the knowledge that woman does, so I guess I should hold my tongue, but when she starts the fucking thing, it's like a cannon going off. It's loud as shit and rattles like a bag of marbles. I get that she didn't want to be seen riding around in something better fit for a dollhouse than a highway, but why the clunker? Girl is a mystery to me.

"It'll be alright, you know?" Kimmi says, coming up from behind me and wrapping her fingers around my bicep with a sigh. She rests her head on my arm and I watch as her silver and green earrings sparkle in the afternoon sunshine.

"You broke up with Margot, didn't you?" I ask. Don't know why I even bother. It's blindingly obvious that she's not interested in the girl anymore. Kimmi goes through girlfriends the way some people go through toothbrushes. All's fine and dandy in the beginning, but after awhile, it just don't work the same anymore. Can't say I get it, but that's Kimmi Reynolds for you. I imagine that she's just never met anyone that makes her feel the way I do about Mireya.

She groans and turns her head, so that her forehead is resting against my sweaty skin. Kimmi and I are close; she's just one of the guys now. Better even because I get a woman's perspective on being with women. Pretty fucking handy.

"I just can't seem to get Basil out of my mind."

"Mint," I correct, thinking of that wisp of a girl that seemed to have stolen Kimmi's heart. Or at least she pretends she did. It was probably the closest she'd ever gotten to real love, but it wasn't quite there. If it was, she'd remember the woman's name. "But I don't think that's it. You've been checking out the new girl, everybody sees it." Kimmi rolls her eyes and stands up, taking a quick glance around the room before reaching into her shirt and adjusting her tits, making sure they bulge up out the top of her shirt like muffins.

"Chrissy?" she asks, and I shake my head with a sigh, brushing back some dark hair that's fallen in my face. It's getting a little long in the front, probably time to get it cut again.

"It's Christy," I correct, but Kimmi's already got her eye wandering, scoping out Triple M members first and then when they move away, focusing on some of the other guests. Nobody here seems that interested in our leather jackets or her skintight pants, our tats or our piercings. Doubt she's going to find anyone here to take back to her room.

"Whatever," she says, reaching up to adjust her ruby red waves, sliding her fingers through the strands and fluffing out her helmet hair. "She's cute, but I don't know. Kind of young."

"And virginal," I add. She smiles with lips covered in pearl pink lipstick.

"And a little of that, too." She watches Amy and Austin as they disappear into the elevator and grins. "I wouldn't be willing to take on such a massive task. I don't know about you, but it sounds like a lot of work to me. The sex later might be good, but the first couple dozen times are going to be shit." Kimmi pulls a cigarette out from between her damn tits and lights up, tossing me a wink along with her words.

"I don't know," I tell her honestly, glancing around the lobby and finding no trace of Mireya. Not that I'm looking for her specifically. *Yeah, fucking right, Gaine. You stalker piece of shit. Get your head back on your shoulders and knock it the hell off.* "I guess if you love somebody, you'll do anything for 'em, no matter how distasteful it might seem to you at first. When you've got them in your arms, you know you'll do whatever it takes to keep them there." I shrug. "So I guess being a virgin doesn't seem like that big of a deal to me." My friend laughs, her voice loud and raucous and echoing, bouncing around the quiet whisper of the room like thunder.

"You are a dying breed, my friend," she says as she fingers the massive necklace hanging around her throat. It looks like a miniature chandelier to me, but then, what do I know about jewelry? Unconsciously, my hand travels to my back pocket, to the tiny sliver of metal wrapped in tissue. *Fuck.* I don't make any move to grab it. I'm the only one that knows about it at this point. If Kimmi were to find out, I'd never hear the end of it. And Beck? Not even an option.

What would my friends say if they found out I've been carrying a wedding ring around in my pocket for three friggin' years? Yep. That's right. I *don't* want to know.

"I don't envy you the pain it will cause." Kimmi rises to her toes and presses a kiss to my cheek before sauntering back out the front doors and into the heat. I stay where I am, frozen, trapped in thoughts. I can't even *imagine* a scenario where Mireya says yes to a ring. It would never happen. When I told Austin a few weeks ago that I couldn't imagine her ever getting hitched, I was serious about it.

When I told her I loved her before, I had this romantic chain of events all planned out in my head. Things didn't work out, and so now I'm stuck with this ring. I've thought about getting rid of it, sure, but it never feels right. How can I take my feelings and just flush 'em down the Goddamn toilet?

I sigh and push off the wall, wandering to the bank of windows in the lobby. The hotel is situated up a long driveway, perched on a hill overlooking the small, dusty city.

It's the perfect vantage point to see Broken Dallas coming.

Long before I hear them, I spot them down the road, moving across the pavement like they own the place. And they do, I suppose. They really fucking do.

"Shit." I don't want to see where they're going. I know. That part's pretty damn obvious. What I don't know is what they're going to do when they get here.

I race across the lobby and hit the stairs, pausing at each floor with the hopes of finding Austin. Fortunately for me, this is a small town and an even smaller building. I find him quick, exiting the room he's going to share with Amy, a silly smile plastered across his lips. I don't blame him. He's head over heels, so I get it. And he's not a bad Pres, just an inexperienced one. He's used to robbing banks, and based on his track record, he's fucking good at it. But this is a whole different ballpark with a new set of rules and unforgiving consequences. Planning on coming here was fine, but we should've prepared more first. The fifteen minutes we've spent here might've cost us everything.

"Broken Dallas is en route," I tell him before he can even ask. I watch as his blue eyes widen and his mouth twists into a slight scowl. "I'd say we have about five minutes, maybe less." Austin nods and doesn't waste time with small talk, moving down the hallway and tapping on doors with his knuckles.

"Christ on a fucking cracker, this shit doesn't ever get easy, does it?" he asks me as we move into the stairwell and down, boots pounding against the linoleum floor. The chains on my pants ding against the railing as we spin down and around, hitting the lobby running with a small entourage in tow. People stare, but we don't pay them any attention. We don't have time to focus on them. Right now, all that's important is showing a strong presence and staying polite. It's true. Manners will get you everywhere with bikers. Trust me, I am one.

I check my pockets again, making sure my handgun is safely tucked inside the waistband of my jeans. I didn't used to carry it around. It was strictly for emergencies, always there in the back of my bike for when I needed it. Feels like everyday is an emergency now. If it's not Bested by Crows, it's something else, right?

Mireya meets up with me outside the doors, face paler than usual, red lips pursed tight. I imagine if I were to kiss them now, that I'd get my tongue bit off. She looks fierce as fuck today.

"How's it goin', lover?" I ask her as we move through the parking lot and pause near the entrance. We have to let them in here, there's no other choice, not if we want to stay on their good side. I take a deep breath and pray to God that Austin knows how to handle this. Beck looks ready to strangle someone with his bare hands and Kimmi's already loading a fresh magazine into her semi. *Fantastic.*

"Not so good. What the hell is going on here? I'm tired of dealing with this harassment bullshit. Can't we get a single freaking moment to ourselves?" She sounds like herself, but she still won't look at me. Good thing or bad? I don't get time to contemplate it.

"*They'll be comin' around the mountain when they come,*" Kimmi singsongs, but she doesn't look even the slightest bit frightened. A bit sweaty maybe and a whole lot of ticked off, but that's it. I'm glad she believes in Austin as much as she does or she'd have taken his place already. In all reality, she'd probably make better decisions than him, but she's not very diplomatic. All her good work would be undone the second she had a free moment to shoot off her mouth.

I pause next to my bike and wait. What else is there to do in this situation?

The rumble of engines starts low and grows louder quickly, winding up the road to the rusted gate that cuts across the front of the property. It's open, doesn't look like it's ever been closed actually, and it's only seconds before the group has pulled in front of us, all frowns and angry faces. There are no women here, only men. I wonder how much worse this shit is going to get before it gets better. My guess would be a whole hell of a lot.

"Good afternoon to you, gentlemen," Austin says, tilting his blonde head to the side. He's all smiles and good ol' boy charm. His voice is laced with Southern hospitality and underwritten with brute strength. Perfect.

"Who the fuck are you?" asks one of the men. He's got on a pair of sunglasses and a leather jacket with full colors, including the 1% in the center, to the left of their emblem, that says he considers himself a gen-u-ine badass extraordinaire. The only bikers that put that insignia on their shit think that they're outside the norm, that they're the special ones. Well fuck him *and* his sister. I keep my face neutral.

"Name's Austin Sparks. You remember me, don't you? We stopped through here five, maybe six, years ago to take care of some business. Kent was running the show then, but surely you remember Triple M?" He takes a step forward, but the man in the sunglasses doesn't smile. His silver beard looks like a tangle of spider webs in the wind, all wispy and shit. I hate him right off the bat. When his gaze moves straight past Austin and onto Kimmi, I get ready to fight. When he looks at Mireya next, I'm ready to kill.

I don't mind men being men or whatnot, but I don't like asshat motherfucker cock sucking pieces of misogynistic shit. The only man that hates a woman is a man who isn't even really a man at all. Only a nutless sack of crap would have a problem with a lady invading his space. If you know who you are and what you can do, you own it and you prove it. You don't put others down to make yourself feel better.

Only the weakest of the weak need to go about proving themselves that way.

This guy, their President I guess, looks old, wise. He doesn't seem so bad at first glance, but I sense that things here are not exactly what they seem. Did they see us roll into town? Don't think so. Did somebody relay information back to them? Probably.

They knew we were coming; this was planned.

I just hope Austin knows it.

"You goin' to answer me or not?" my friend asks, letting his voice drop an octave. None of these sons of bitches have gotten off their bikes yet. Bad sign. Violence is a sure thing now. This is going to escalate in a split second. I'm not going to have time to react later. It's now or never.

My hand slips into my jacket while Mireya watches, tire iron clutched between her fingers. I don't know where she got it or how long she's been holding it for, but I don't care. I have to do what I have to do. I have to stop this before she really sees why they're here. Teaming up with Bested by Crows is fine, but when it's for the reasons that are simmering beneath the surface here, it's a fat load of smelly ass bullshit. I can't respect that decision.

I pull the hammer back with my thumb and don't wait to hear whatever response they've got planned. My hand comes out and the trigger goes down, hitting the front tire of their Pres's bike and shredding the rubber to pieces.

Chaos explodes.

People are shouting and weapons are being drawn. One

or more of us might die here today, but I had to do it. *For her.* These men came here because they don't want women to ride motorcycles? To participate in the politics and the inner workings of the groups they give their hearts and souls to? Well, fuck 'em. Fuck 'em all.

I duck down behind my bike, making sure Mireya is safe behind hers, and I wait. Silence descends, cutting the frenzied activity like a knife. Nobody moves.

"Who the fuck fired the first round?" somebody from Broken Dallas is asking, but no one responds. They're not going to because nobody knows. Except Mireya.

Her brown eyes look orange in the harsh glare of the hot sun through the dust, turning the look she's giving me from fierce to deadly. She narrows her gaze on me and I know, just know that I'm going to get it later. I keep her in my sights and lean my back against the metal of my motorcycle.

"I don't want to start anything," Austin says, staying right where he is, standing up in the middle of this instant battlefield, chin up, shoulders strong. I don't think I've ever been prouder of him than I am in that moment. Despite the circumstances, I smile. I think he'll make an alright Pres if we give him some time. He's got the balls for it at least. "But I will if I have to. You got a problem with us being here, fine. You let us know and we're gone." Austin pauses and a gust of wind whips around his face, slapping his sandy hair against his furrowed brow. "But if you fuck with us, we'll destroy you."

Cheers go up from our side, loud whoops of excitement

and a thrill of danger. We don't do this sort of thing very often, but I have to admit, the rush of adrenaline is nice. I could get used to this. Maybe. Mireya isn't cheering, but she isn't unhappy either. Her face is perfectly neutral, schooled into this blank expression that's just begging to be read. I want to know what sorts of thoughts are going through her head. Does she suspect the same things I do? And if she does, does she know why I did what I did? I hope to hell she doesn't. Ignorance is bliss and all that, right?

I watch my friend standing tall amongst a sea of crouching bodies and get ready for folks to pop up like daisies, for gunfire to rain down from the sky like hail, and for blood to be shed in a needless ritual of crap. That's the way of the road sometimes, you know.

My muscles tighten and my body gets straight as an arrow, rigid and pulsing with pent up violence and barely restrained threat. I feel like a real man right here, getting ready to protect the woman I love. This primal bullshit would see me dead with a smile on my face, just so long as I knew she was going to be okay, that she could walk away from this without anymore scars, that one day, even if it's far off in the future, that she could smile and mean it.

I scoot forward and inch across the dirty pavement towards her. Her brows wrinkle up and she tilts her head to the side like she thinks I'm fucking nuts. As soon as I've crossed the small bit of space between us and hide myself safely behind her tire, she opens her mouth to growl at me.

My hands come up and grab her face, my lips meet hers,

just a slight slide of dry mouths, burnt and cracked from the sun over our heads. The crackling energy inside of me transfers over into her body, sending chills along her exposed skin, snapping her spine taut and bowing her back. It's like I'm feeding my spirit into hers, infusing her with the wicked wild energy I'm feeling right now. I pull back and spin, rising to my feet in a fluid motion of muscle and purpose. I'm going to back my Pres, and I'm going to make sure we get a chance to do what we came here to do. Robbin' banks might be illegal, but on my list of immoral sins, it doesn't rank near as high as lookin' the devil in the eye.

Okay, so I have no clue what that means, but I've heard Beck say it before and it fits. Anybody that think it's okay to tear the spirit out of these women deserves whatever he's got comin'. My thumb

cocks the hammer back and a smile lights my face. I don't know where it comes from, but I hope it looks as good as it feels. Austin doesn't even turn to look at me, just stays facing forward, blue eyes solid and serious. Nobody from Broken Dallas moves, and for a split second there, things look like they might turn out alright.

Guess I shoulda known better.

Mireya

CHAPTER 18

I know Bested by Crows is coming before they even show up. I know because it's the worst fucking thing that could possibly happen right now. I've learned that if I expect the worst out of folks, they deliver.

Gaine's an anomaly I don't even want to touch right now. What he's doing and why he's doing it, I have no clue. He wants to protect me like some ancient caveman? Fuck him. He thinks that because I lost it last night that he was some rights over me? I shake in anger just *thinking* about it. But then there was that kiss. I don't even know what to make of that. It felt good, electric, like I was sticking my nail into an outlet, letting the flavors of the world pass through me in electrons and white hot blinding energy. It was good, I'll admit that at least, but it doesn't change a thing. Gaine Kelley is not good for me, and I'm even worse for him. I've got to stop this before it goes too far. I thought I could handle it before, but I was wrong. Whatever pull it is that he possesses, I'm having a hard time resisting.

I watch Gaine spin up and away, pulling his gun on our rival MC, putting forth a foot I never thought I'd see. Gaine is logical, the one that makes all the good decisions, that keeps a clear head. And here he is throwing caution to the wind? For me. It's all for me.

I stand up, too, and reach forward, digging my hand into the back of Austin's jeans. Amy might not like it, but I figure I've been there before so fuck her. His gun comes out and rests heavy in my hand. I might not know shit about shooting, but really, there's not much to it, right? You pull the damn trigger and shit happens.

In a lot of places, this kind of crap would never have the chance to go down. The cops would get called, do-gooders would do what they do best and things would happen. As of right now, here in this small town, Broken Dallas is law and we're on their turf. Some of the other Triple M'ers might not know how these sorts of things work, but I do. I've lived in a 'real' gang, suffered at the hands of a 'real' MC. I don't know what might've happened with Broken Dallas and Triple M before, but Kent must've worked some of his magic on them because I could tell you from experience that things like this normally don't work out.

I aim the barrel at Will Walker's chest and hold it steady. Knowing I could blow his ass to kingdom come makes me feel better, but I manage, just barely, to hold back. Gaine was right. If I kill them in a fit of rage, I'll never be able to make peace with myself or my past. I have to make a conscious decision, and I have to do it right.

I keep my arm very, very still.

"I thought with Kent dead, the trap was set, the rat was caught. But that was no done deal. Our rodent is still very much alive, don't you think?" Kimmi asks, sliding out from behind her ride in a spray of wild hair and glimmering earrings. See, I really do like her. Any woman that can kick ass and look good doing it holds a special place in my heart. I'll just never tell her that.

"You have to imagine that he had allies, am I right? We're going to have to do a lot more weeding to take care of this garden," Gaine says, eyes focused on the rumbling herd of assholes rolling into the gate.

"Amen to that," Austin says with a slight quirk of a smile on his crooked mouth. The scar at the edge of his lip tugs at his face as he struggles to control his amusement at the current situation. "That's why I've got back up."

"Back up?" Gaine asks and then Austin's lifting his hand and beckoning with crooked fingers, drawing a group of Triple M'ers out from behind the rusted fencing, bringing the crouching bodies through holes in the chain link and out of bushes. There are definitely some bonuses to having a large group. Oh yeah, and to not shafting our women. Girls with guns, baby, all the way. I try not to smile.

"Afternoon, folks," Will says, climbing off his bike like he doesn't have a care in the world. He should. His impending death is near; he just doesn't believe it yet. But he will, most likely when it's too late. He walks to the edge of the perimeter Broken Dallas has made with their bikes and stands with his hands in his back pockets. Something about his demeanor is different today. His skin seems paler, more taut, stretched across his chubby as fuck face.

He knows.

This time, I do smile.

"You Goddamn bitch!" he screams, spittle flecking the dry air and evaporating as if it had never been. It's so friggin' arid in this damn town. I'm already counting down the hours until we leave. "You really did it, didn't you?" Will laughs, and the sound is horrid, like nails across a chalkboard, bitter and tinged with sorrow. Huh. Didn't realize he had the emotion in him. Doesn't make me feel sorry for him. There is nothing he could do at this point to redeem himself in my eyes. His soul is black as tar and twice as sticky. He's out and that's that. I won't rest until my demons lie dead and bleeding, but on my terms. Right here, today, Will lives. Tomorrow, he might not be so lucky.

I keep him centered in my gaze, but out of the corner of my eye, I spot Mack. He's wearing a helmet with a dark visor, and he hasn't bothered to take it off. I hope that under that mask, he's got tears streaming down his face. I hope he hurts half as much as he hurt me. I watch him and wonder, doing my best to imagine how losing a family member would feel. At least Walker didn't betray them; he was killed. There's something different about that, more melancholy maybe but not as damaging. Betrayal is an emotion that's hard to come back on. All the positives in this world are built on trust, and once that's gone, it leaves you nothing to live by. So here I am, twenty-eight fucking years old with a heart that can't feel, a brain that won't think, and a soul that's empty and barren.

I flex my finger on the trigger, tasting the surge of violence, the rush of power. Gaine did something to me when he kissed me. I don't know what it was, but I can feel my legs shaking and my stomach churning. I want to charge down this slope and out those gates, race across the dry landscape until I find the sea.

It's fucking weird. I don't get feelings like this. Bitterness, sarcasm, pain, I understand these things. This ... longing I've got growing in my gut is new, and I don't like it. I don't like any of the things Gaine's been doing to me lately. All these years I've managed to resist him and now, suddenly, he's cutting through me like a warm knife through butter. Why? When I killed Tray, I felt a wound being carved into my spirit, and all of this newness is rushing to fill it. I don't know what to make of it.

"Tray Walker was a good man, Mireya. Despite what you may think, he did a lot of good in this world."

"I don't give two fucks if he fed needy children or volunteered at a homeless shelter, that fucker deserved to die. He's lucky it happened so quick." When Will starts to interrupt me, I lift my gun in the air and shoot. Bodies stiffen, muscles harden, weapons are raised. I continue. "But let me tell you this, and I'm sure it'll make you feel better. There's no need for you to mourn your brother because you'll soon join him."

"You uppity little cunt."

That's it, all I need to hear.

I lower my weapon and fire at the nearest member of Broken Dallas. I don't know them, but they're here and that's enough for me. I don't shoot to kill, but I do hit the man in his calf, send him rolling back behind his bike as explosions erupt around me.

I stay standing during all of it, finishing off the rounds in Austin's revolver before slipping it into the back of my jeans. The chains on the sides of my pants come unclipped in an instant, and then I'm just out there, swinging them around and smashing the links of metal into faces, groins, bikes, whatever gets in my way. This isn't about killing anybody, at least not right now. This is about showing strength, seeing whose dick is the biggest.

I intend to show off a fierce as fuck lady boner.

Mack appears out of the dusty melee with his eyes red rimmed and the devil's dance in his step. He comes at me with intentions that are nothing short of malicious and finds himself with a line of metal around his neck. When I was younger, right after I married Tray, I used to dance with chains. I'd put on some heavy metal and an outfit that would make a hooker blush, and I'd get up in front of the MC and shake my fucking ass like there was no tomorrow, like that moment was all that mattered. It was fun, and I'll admit, I spent half of that period of my life in a drugged or drunk daze, but it didn't last. The honeymoon period ended and things went sour. Tray stopped asking me to dance and started making me. He stopped holding me in his arms and started pushing me into others'. He started treating me like I was less than his bike, less even than the dirt beneath his boots.

So I did what I'd always done, what he said made him fall in love with me. I showed him my spirit, I rode my girls through town and came back flushed and panting, but he wasn't the same. I don't know what happened to him or why, but it didn't matter, the moment I told him no and he laid his hands on me was the moment I died inside. Gaine thinks it was only Mireya Walker that passed away that day, that maybe he can get Mireya Sawyer back, but he's wrong. I don't want to come alive again because then I'll have to feel it all a hundred times worse than I do now. A necrotic soul doesn't bleed half as bad as a living, breathing, aching, loving mess. *Es cruel, pero es la verdad.*

"Have you missed me terribly, Mack?" I ask as I pull the chains tight around his neck and lift my boot up to his stomach for leverage. Dancing with those chains made me good at handling them. After all, it's not all that sexy if the dancer smacks herself in the back of the knee and goes down wailing, and it certainly isn't impressive if she can't flip and spin and twirl like a deranged baton girl in a beauty pageant. So here I am, dancer turned ass kicker and I am *destroying.* I make the chains as taught as I can, holding Mack's windpipes hostage as people spin and scream and kick around me.

I look at his reddened face, gasping for breath, hands outstretched and wonder how he felt when he was looming above me, taking things I never gave, hurting me in ways I never imagined. I thought of him as a brother, and he raped me. He raped me. He raped me.

With a scream of rage, I squeeze harder and bring Mack down to his knees, dropping him to the pavement like a sack of weevil ridden flour. Useless. My blood runs hot as the sun and my eyes start to blur, white hot memories of anger and rage crashing into me, taking over, destroying my sanity. I'm losing it again, and I have nowhere to fall.

And then I feel arms around my waist and my body spasms, loosing the chains just enough that Mack slips out, falling to the cement with a choking gasp. Sweat starts to pour down my face and my knees go weak as I slip a bit on the gravel and the dirt. Gaine holds me up with one arm and borrows one of the chains with his other hand, using it like a whip to snap a man in the knee caps. It's pretty fucking impressive, I'll admit.

"Let fucking go of me!" I scream, but I don't fight. I can't move. My body doesn't belong to me in that moment, it belongs to the howling demons inside my skin, the ones that fight for supremacy everyday, the ones that I always just manage to hold back. Lately though, lately they've been kicking my ass hard, beating down the door of my sanity. *I never should've killed Tray.* There. There it is. I've said it. It hurts to admit it, feels like a betrayal of self, but that's it.

That's the magic answer. I keep striving for vengeance when all I really want is peace.

I scream and flail, stumbling from Gaine's arms in a pulsating frenzy, a collection of confusion and barely suppressed rage. I can't believe this. I cannot even freaking believe this. How could I *not* want to kill these stupid fuckers? And how, how, how could I regret taking out the worst one of them all? Obviously, something is seriously wrong with me.

I squeeze my fists at my side and turn to look at Gaine.

Or someone. Yeah, maybe someone is wrong *for* me.

"You stay away from me!" I tell him in the middle of our mid-afternoon brawl. He looks at me like I've completely lost it, brushing his dark brown hair from his forehead as his eyes flick this way and that, absorbing the mess around us. Seems kind of counterproductive for me to start a shit storm in the middle of a tornado of crap, but that's kind of what I'm good at. I'm not proud of it, but there it is. "You don't touch me, you don't pander to me." I point my finger at him and pause just long enough for him to shove a guy in the chest and send him stumbling back into the whirlwind that is Beck Evans. The redhead grins the entire time. "You treat me like an old friend and that's it, Gaine. This cat and mouse game is over."

I turn away and smash the instep of a man in a Bested by Crows jacket. I have no clue who he is, and I don't care. If he's a part of Tray's gang then he's trouble. Fuck him and the horse he rode in on.

"Mireya!" Gaine's calling after me, but I'm not listening. I'm letting my fury boil up and spill out, letting it cascade down around me and crash into the rioting crowd like a tsunami. I take my frustration out on anyone that gets in my way, swinging my single remaining chain around like I'm still dancing for my first husband and his friends, for the people I called family and who called me cunt, saw me as nothing more than a place to hang their hat. "Mireya!"

I move away from Gaine, purposely trying to lose him in the melee. It isn't difficult. There's a lot going on here and none of it is simple or easy. It's just a big, fucking mess. There are a lot of people that are going to be hurting come tomorrow morning. I get terrible déjà vu then, remembering the first time I'd seen Bested by Crows in years, at the bike show in Amy's town. We went to trash their bikes, and they came to trash us. None of my attackers were there then, so it was easier to distance myself. Here, they're all the fuck over.

I fight my way to Kimmi's side because I know that when it comes down to it, even if she hates me half as much as I pretend to hate her, that she won't tell anyone about the tears that shine wet on the dusty planes of my face.

Mireya
CHAPTER 19

It's two in the morning, and I'm still awake. I'd rather not be, but the moon won't let me sleep. She was beckoning to me through the curtains and drawing me out here to sit on the edge of the pool with my thoughts. The water might have chlorine in it and be swimming with water bugs, but at least it looks pretty. I dip a finger and try to grab some control over myself. I don't feel like me anymore. I blame Gaine for it because he's the closest person to me, a victim of friendly fire, but maybe it's true. He's been desperately trying to see inside the cracks of my psyche all these years, so I guess he's finally done it. He's in and I am screwed. *¿Qué voy a hacer*?

Tray Walker.

I twirl my finger through the water and watch the trail of ripples, comparing my clumsy motion with the weightless dance of the insects on the surface nearby. They're probably laughing at me, at this ridiculous woman with the horrible past who can't make up her mind for shit.

Right now, sitting here in this quiet loneliness, I know that I was right. I know why I feel so conflicted. I want Bested by Crows to suffer for what they did, but I don't want to be the one to act on it. I figure it's because I've already been through enough shit. I have plenty of nightmares to keep me awake at night. I'm not a saint myself, so I have more than enough to atone for. You add that on top of all the horrible things that have ever happened to me and there you have it. I'm tired. I'm done with all of this.

I drop my palm to the water and hold it there, feeling just the slightest kiss of liquid against my flesh. It feels like Tray's blood. Well, in my mind it does. In reality, it's nothing like it. It was sticky and hot; my mouth filled with the taste and scent of copper, like I was sucking on a jar full of old pennies. He convulsed like a fish out of water and bled out right then and there in front of me, life fading from him like color draining from a photograph. One minute, he was in color, the next he was black and white.

I want to like it that I did it, to cackle with glee at the memory like a wicked witch in a fairytale with some hope of a happy ending. But I don't. Don't get me wrong though. In no way do I feel guilty for what I've done. Did Tray deserve to die? You make your own decision on that, but he did deserve to pay and I extracted my remittance. Was it right? I don't fucking know. But I won't do it again. If I do, I'll just be splitting myself up into even smaller pieces. Right now, there's a chance I can recover. Later, maybe not so much.

I glance up at the roundness of the moon and wish I could join her in the sky, join *las estrellas* and sparkle for eternity in blissful peace. I laugh and the sound echoes around the empty pavement, stirring up the day's dust to dance a solo just for me. I'm not usually so poetic, so I know something must be wrong. *Fuck you, Gaine Kelley. I don't know who you think you are, but if I keep having these Shakespearean thoughts, you are done for.*

"Mireya?" I almost pull a knife when the voice sounds from behind me, soft and unassuming but also unafraid. I turn to find Amy Cross standing with her arms crossed over her chest. She's dressed in a pair of pink silk pajamas with a hotel robe thrown around her shoulders. Her blue eyes catch the moonlight and throw it back at me, like she knows all its secrets. I squeeze my fists and try not to scowl. I don't want to deal with her or Austin right now. I can't even get into that. Ten years of chasing that fool man around and I have nothing to show for it. What a waste of time. It just goes to show that no matter how strong I think I am, inside, there's a pathetic, quivering cunt just waiting to get out. I don't know if Tray and his cronies put her there, or if she was there all along, but I'm tired of looking at her ugly face. I've cried, what, three times in as many days? I don't cry. That's not me. That's her, all her.

"What the fuck do you want?" I ask Amy. It's not enough that I'm nursing sore knuckles and a bruised face, that I got the shit beat out of me even as I kicked some ass today. Things went well for us, but I'm still hurting, and now I have to deal with this. I throw her a poisonous glare and a once-over that says she'd do best to back the hell off.

"May I?" she asks, gesturing at the edge of the pool nearest me. I give her a look that says no, but apparently she misinterprets my silence for a yes. I glare at her heart-shaped face and her pale skin, already warming up with color from the sun. The worst part about her isn't just how pretty she is, how her chestnut hair falls straight and silky around her shoulders or how her lips always look like they're just about to smile. The worst part is that she's fitting in here, that she slipped right into this life like she was a piece missing from the puzzle. Austin looks at her like she's a god and her face mirrors his. They belong together, whether I want them to or not.

I look away.

"Austin hovering around the door somewhere?" I ask, gesturing my hand at the dimly light entry to the lobby. I hear Amy's clothes rustle as she shakes her head and slips her robe off her shoulders, rolling up her pant legs and dipping her feet into the cool water. When I glance back at her, I see a small shiver work its way up her legs. It was hot as fuck out here today, but the water is freezing ass cold. Don't know how they manage to pull that one off.

"He's not back yet," she says, and I can see in her eyes that she's worried. I am, too, but I refuse to show it. Kimmi and Austin have done this midnight rendezvous shit for years. It's just now that I'm hearing what it's all about, but it makes sense. I almost feel betrayed that they didn't tell us sooner. Robbing banks. Who gives a shit about that? There are people in this world who have too much and some who can't have anything, who don't fit into a particular mold. That's us, Triple M. We're not just bikers, we're people with pasts that would light up the sky if you set them on fire. We need this group and this life to keep our spirits alive. It might come at the cost of others, but then, nothing in this world is free. We work for our livelihood in different ways.

"Gaine?" I ask instead because if Austin isn't back, then that means Christy and Amy were still in our room. I doubt he'd let her out to wander by herself. The initial fight might be over, but we're still here and neither of the other gangs wants us to be. If they come at us again, it's going to be with an even worse intent. They're going to come for us, and it's not going to be in broad daylight in the middle of a hotel parking lot. No, next time, they'll grab us when we least expect it, in a place that makes it easy to take things a step further. And I'm no optimist, so I know what's coming. Rape and then death, that's it. Or for poor Amy, they'd probably just rape her and then take her with them for a fate worse than death. I feel irritated with her myself.

"He sent Beck with me," she says, and I throw a narrowed glance over my shoulder. I don't see the asshole, but then, when Beck doesn't want to be seen, you won't see him. I don't know what his story is because he refuses to tell it, and I don't mind. I don't exactly walk around blabbing about how my mother was a Castilian artist who painted vampires and fairies and cats with demon wings. I get the weirdest urge to tell Amy about her, but catch my tongue just in time. I don't want to have girly gossip with this bitch; I just want her to go away.

"Then we're safe as long as the military doesn't descend with nukes." I reach for a cigarette I started earlier and left in the ashtray nearby. I put it between my lips and inhale. Amy laughs at my joke which I don't think is funny at all and then throws me a sweet smile.

"You're absolutely gorgeous, you know that?" she says, and I raise a dark brow, taking in her petite perfection and her soft curves. So this is the kind of woman that Austin was after all along. Nice. The polar opposite of me. Where I'm dark, she's pale and light, where I'm gruff, she's polite. *Fantástico.*

"I'd thank you for the compliment, but then I'd remember you stole my boyfriend and I'd have to get pissed off. I don't really want to deal with that right now if you don't mind. Why don't you go back inside and watch Lifetime or something?" Amy laughs again and the sound doesn't echo like mine. It's light, like bells, and simply peals away into the silent evening. *Bitch.*

"I didn't come out here to talk about Austin," she says and my lip curls as I pull out the cigarette and toss it into the pool. Amy looks at it aghast, but clears her throat and says nothing.

"Gaine then," I say, figuring that must be it. She saw us

fucking, and I'm sure she figured out what we were doing in the bathroom. Plus, I know she sees the way he looks at me. "The last thing I need right now is for you to throw your two cents in. He still loves me. Fine. I get it. But I don't want to love him. That's all there is to it." Amy's smile grows a little wider and then she's glancing over her shoulder and checking to see if she can spot her bodyguard. Beck is visible now inside the glass doors, flirting with one of the night staff. I roll my eyes.

"That's not it either," she says as she reaches down and unbuttons her top. Underneath, she's got on a swimsuit. It's the color of honey and half as sweet. This thing looks like it was designed in the early fifties or something. It covers *everything*. Amy takes off her pajama top and lays it aside, standing up and dropping her pants to the cement. "I just wanted to come down here and make sure you were alright."

"Yeah, so that's why you wore your grandmother's swimsuit under your pajamas, right? To check in on me?" Amy laughs again and sweeps her hair up on top of her head, twisting it into a bun and snapping a hair tie from around her wrist onto it to keep it still.

"This," she says, pausing to gesture at the beige jumpsuit she's got on. "Is most certainly not my gram's swimsuit. It's far too scandalous, don't you know?" Amy points to the curve of the suit on her upper thigh. "Gram's was much more conservative. Went straight down to her knees." With a wink and a nod, Amy launches herself into the cold water and disappears in a perfect swan dive. I watch her move beneath the water for a moment, and don't even bother to look up when boots appear beside me. Beck is an idiot, but he's good at what he does.

"Are you two skinny dippin'?" he asks, squinting into the darkness and trying to catch a glimpse of Amy. I put my cigarette out on the toe of his boot, and he doesn't even notice. He's too focused on trying to catch some free tail. Wish I was that single-minded. Must be nice being Beck Evans.

"Only in your wildest fucking dreams," I tell him as Amy surfaces with a gasp and treads the water with a smile on her face.

"Everything alright?" she asks him as he tucks his hands into the front pockets of his jeans and grins.

"Be even better if you two lovely ladies were to put on a show for me." Amy laughs, but I don't. Beck might seem funny at first, but after a couple of years, he just gets annoying.

"That desk clerk is leaning over the counter," I tell him and he moves back, so Amy can swim forward and lean her arms on the cement edge near my feet. "Her ass is in a prime viewing location. Go away and do what you do best." Beck pats me on the head and laughs again. He's always fucking laughing. Must be nice.

"She's more colorful than a leprechaun's ass burstin' with rainbows," he says and Amy snorts.

"What?"

"He thinks she's gay because she's not interested in him.

Beck always thinks that." I start to stand up, irritated that my quiet slice of space has been ruined and pause when Amy's hand touches my foot.

"I mean, who wouldn't want a little cut of this beefcake?" he asks, and then laughs at his own joke. See what I mean? Sometimes, I think it's a front for something darker, but I guess I'll never know. I don't have the time or leisure to delve into Beck Evans and his many intricacies. "Only reasonable explanation is that she prefers titties. Can't say that I blame her." Beck shrugs and, satisfied that he's not missing any nudity, moves away again. As soon as he's out of earshot, Amy grabs my attention.

"You know, I brought a book with me, one of my favorites. I think you might like it. I'd be happy to let you borrow it if you want to read it." Before I can object, she forges on, leaning out of the water, eyes sparkling. Reading is obviously her thing, but it isn't mine. I don't want to get lost in somebody else's story. I'm already having enough trouble trying to navigate my own. "There's a character that kind of reminds me of you. Sali Bend, I think you could relate."

"Bonding with fictional characters isn't my thing, but thanks for thinking of me."

"The only good lie is one that sticks. Otherwise, it's just all bullshit." I give her a narrow eyed look, and she smiles. "A Sali Bend quote that I happen to think fits." Amy reaches up and hauls herself out of the water, plopping down next to me with a splat. "We all need an escape every now and again, an opportunity to lose ourselves, if only for the moment. I look at you sometimes and I can't help but think of my mother." Her face falls, but the expression doesn't last. It hits rock bottom and bounces right back, leaving her with a bittersweet smile.

"A preacher's wife?" I ask her as I straighten my legs out and let my feet hit the water with a splash. The coolness washes over me, bringing a sigh to my lips. I bite it back, refusing to show Amy anything but my harshest side. I think about that damn video again, and I wonder how much it played a part in my fate. What would've happened if I hadn't sent it? I glance over at her and can't help the feeling that somehow, things would've ended up the same. I don't necessarily believe in fate, but sometimes shit is just meant to be. I roll my eyes at my own inner thoughts and Amy smiles wider.

"A person who thinks she should be one way, but might be happier if she let herself be another."

"And what makes you the ultimate, fucking authority?" I growl at her, scooting back, feeling my chest tighten with anger. This bitch is going to come down here, disturb the one freaking peaceful moment I've had in a long while, and then psychoanalyze me? Nuh uh. Not happening. "Listen here, *sweetheart*. You don't know me, so don't act like you're a freaking expert all of a sudden. I don't need your advice, and I sure as hell didn't ask for it." I lean in close, but Amy doesn't flinch. She sits stone still and listens to my rant without the slightest hint of fear or anger in her blue eyes.

"You don't know where I've been or where I come from or what's going on in my head." Amy nods which surprises me into a brief second of silence.

"No, I don't. You're right. I'm sorry. I know I shouldn't make judgments like that." She pauses and reaches out a hand, placing her fingers on the back of mine. "But if you want to tell me, I'm here. You can say whatever you want, about anything you want, and I'll listen. I'm actually quite good at that." She pauses again and this time, swallows nervously. "Even if it's about Austin, you can talk about it." Amy stares at me with such a warm expression in her eyes that I don't know what to do or how to handle it. I don't have female friends. I just don't. And I definitely don't have heart to hearts either.

I stand up suddenly, my lace nightie billowing in the wind around my ankles, and open my mouth to speak.

I find that in reality, there's absolutely nothing that I can say.

I leave Amy at the pool with Beck and march up to my room, rapping my knuckles gently against the door and waiting for the sound of movement inside.

"It's me," I say before Gaine gets the chance to ask. I let my fingers rest against the wood and try not to think too hard about the erratic thumping in my chest. Obviously, he's having an effect on me, maybe he always has and I just never noticed. I guess I might've taken him for granted all this time. I try to think back on my weakest moments, the moments where I needed someone the most. Did I run to Austin? Only for the little things. When it came down to it, when it really counted, it was Gaine I was spilling my soul to.

I step back and swallow my resolve, letting it slide down my throat like a dry lump. I'm cutting him off. Period. If I keep playing this game with him, things will change, and I'm not sure I'm ready for that.

"You have a nice swim?" he asks me, and there's no hint of anything in his voice but mild interest. I look up and find that he's not smiling, not gazing at me with affection. Guess he listened when I told him to back off. It's what I wanted, so I try to be happy about it, try to pretend that I don't feel anything in the air when I slip past him and move into the room.

Christy's asleep on top of the bed, curled up into a ball. This journey is going to tax every last ounce of strength from her. I hope she's willing to pay for it with all she's got.

I check the clock on the nightstand and decide that I don't have time to shower. Austin and Kimmi should be back soon and then we'll be moving out again, hopefully to someplace free of conflict. I run my hands down my face and breathe in the sharp scent of chlorine. I know I'm wishing for something that'll never happen. I might have made peace with my needs, but that doesn't mean Bested by Crows will go away or that this … war on women will stop. I can only hope it doesn't get bigger than this. I mean, I get that there's an antiquated consensus among some gangs about women being pledged members, and I've dealt with my fair share of half-assed insults and bullying, but I've never seen it get so serious. Bested is going to turn this into an all out war if we're not careful.

I move over to my suitcase and let my mind wander.

"Is it alright if I step out for a bit?" Gaine asks, surprising me. I turn my head and glance at him over my shoulder.

He's staring at me with a carefully blank expression now, like there's a lot he could or would say if he had the chance. I don't give him one.

"Yeah, fine with me." I pause, mouth open, and think about saying something else. But there is nothing to say. The best thing for me to do right now is to keep my distance from him. "But be careful, alright? The air might be settled, but it'll only take a gust of wind to stir it all up again." Gaine nods and moves away, reaching for the door handle without another word. It doesn't feel right to let him go, but I don't have much of a choice. I have no control over him or what he does.

The door closes and cuts us off from one another, leaving me alone with whirling thoughts and curiosity that I can't satisfy. Where Gaine is going and what he does right now is none of my damn business.

I get dressed quickly and close up my bag, tossing it next to the door in anticipation of leaving early in the morning. There is no way in hell I could sleep right now.

When Amy gets back, slipping inside with her key card, I'm sitting on the bed contemplating my next move. Obviously, I'm the start to all this, so I have to be the one to finish it, too. Murdering those fucks would obviously be the easiest route, but I won't let myself go there. If I'm going to keep any part of myself, I have to make sure that I stick to what's going to work for me. Meaning I don't get to keep Gaine, meaning Will and Mack aren't going to die by my hands. I sigh and close my eyes, leaning back on the bed and listening to the swish of fabric as Amy changes her clothes.

When something lands softly near my head, I open my eyes and see that Amy's tossed me her book. It's wrinkled and smells like coffee where it's been stained over the years.

"What the fuck is this?" I ask her as I lean up on my elbows and throw her my worst possible death glare. Christy startles awake then and stares stupidly at the two of us, moving her gaze slowly around the room like she isn't sure where she is.

"Give it a try and see. You never know what you might discover when you walk around with eyes wide open."

"Is this another book quote?" I growl at her, snatching the novel and flipping open to a random page. I can't even tell you how long it's been since I read a book. I don't even *want* to know. My guess would be in the *years*. I have vague memories of holing up in my grandmother's closet and sneaking peeks at her murder mystery novels, but those have been virtually railroaded by all the other shit I've done in my life. I wonder what would happen if I took it up again, what sorts of things from my distant past would come alive.

"It might be," Amy says coyly, moving over to her friend and sitting down on the bed next to her. She takes her hand in hers and smiles. "Did you sleep alright?" she asks and Christy nods.

"Better," she says, voice throaty and scratchy from sleep. "Gaine told me a story about a badger that got into his high school gym." She smiles, and I have to hold back my lips before they follow suite. *That asshole.* "It actually helped put me to sleep."

"Oh, trust me, the longer you know him, the more times you'll hear it and eventually, you'll start dozing off in simple anticipation of listening to that crap." Both the girls laugh as I scan my eyes down the dark print, pausing when I catch sight of a particularly vulgar phrase.

His balls slap my chin as I struggle for breath, relishing the thick heaviness of his flesh between my lips.

Huh.

I keep reading.

Glance lifts my face to his, using my hair like reigns, and smiles down at me while his friend goes to town, fucking my pussy so hard and fast I feel like I might come already. God, I asked for a threesome, but I never expected this. Sali Bend is a connoisseur of dick, and this is most certainly a feast.

I slam the covers closed and flip the book around, so that I'm pressing the spine against my lips. The muscles in my stomach clench as my eyes shift across the small gap between the beds and find Amy's. She's grinning at me, garnering a confused look from her friend as she glances back and forth between us. Inside of me, something strange happens, some rusted gear comes unstuck and starts to spin.

"Try not to stay up too late," she warns as I let loose and spill a chuckle from between my lips. Oddly enough, it sounds much more like my mother's this time.

"To read this trashy, ridiculous smut? Fat chance."

By the time Gaine shows up, face white and eyes faraway,

I've finished the whole damn thing.

Gaine
CHAPTER 21

I don't know where I plan on going when I leave, but I'm not sure what else to do. I can't sit in that room with Mireya and watch her fight against me. I *know* she's starting to feel things for me, but I can't get her to admit it. I don't want to hound her ass, but I also hate sitting back and waiting. I've spent far too much time doing that already.

I don't know what happened to her during that fight, but something changed. She's both more receptive and less. I don't get it at all.

I run my hand through my hair as I pace down the hallway, moving towards the stairs and taking them two at a time. There are Triple M'ers everywhere, watching, waiting for something to happen. And it will. We all know it. After seeing Broken Dallas, I'm admittedly a little terrified. I don't want this disease to spread, to be fearful of my surroundings wherever I go. If this scuffle turns into a war, life will never be the same.

I hit a side door out to the parking lot and nod at my friends, making sure they know I'm alright. I probably shouldn't be leaving by myself, but there's nobody I want to take with me. I just need a moment alone to think.

I start my bike and zip out of the parking lot, moving slowly, cautiously. Just because those dumb fucks walked away after our fight, that doesn't mean anything. They could be waiting for me right around the corner.

It's only after I *don't* see them for awhile that I start to get worried. I start thinking all sorts of horrible things for Austin and Kimmi, find myself absolutely positive that something bad is happenin' to them. I'm sure they're fine, of course, but the dark brings out the demons and when they howl, it's hard to hear much of anything else. I start thinking of Mireya then, wondering if I made a mistake by leaving. What if something were to happen while I was gone? I would never forgive myself.

I ride through the blackness for awhile, past all the darkened storefronts and restaurants. If Amy thought her town was bad, this one is even worse. There's not a single place open at this hour, not even the bar which looks more like a diner on the outside than anything else.

With a sigh, I turn around at the end of the street and work my way back again, searching for the bank. I have to pass the road to the hotel and continue on in the opposite direction for awhile before I find it.

I don't stop, just continue past it and circle around again.

There's no activity that I can see, and I start to wonder if maybe Austin and Kimmi are finished in there already, if they were successful. That dream we've been nursing of heading to the beach and relaxing for awhile sounds damn near orgasmic at this point. Mireya could use some space, I think, and it'd be nice not to have to worry if I'm stepping on her toes every five minutes. Absence makes the heart grow fonder, right? So maybe if I were to play hard to get or somethin'? I wonder how she'd react if I brought a woman up to my room?

I head back towards the road to the hotel, determined not to stick my head any further up my ass. Just as I'm dipping low for a sharp turn, I catch sight of feet in the grass near the sign. They're bare, glaringly out of place in this dry darkness. This isn't the sort of place where folks hang out after sunset. There's a moment there where I lick my lips and try to decide if this concerns me at all, if I should pause or just keep going. Against my better judgement, I stop. Hey, I try to be a nice guy, that's how I live my life. If that were my friend in the bushes there, my sister, my brother, whoever, I sure as shit would like someone to stop and at least give 'em a poke, make sure they're alright.

When I get close by, I start to feel something weird inside, a twisting and churning, like an internal alarm. My movements slow and my ears strain to take in the scenery around me. I don't hear anything, but I smell a trap. Just when I'm about to turn away, go find Beck or somethin', I hear a groan from the direction of the feet, like a quiet sob.

I crouch down and crawl forward, slinking across the grass, taking in the two, dirtied soles before me with a growing pit in the center of my belly. *I know this person*, I think long before I reach out to touch them, before I dive into the foliage and discover the rest of the naked body. From the back, there are no obvious identifiers, but I've still got this horrible feeling in my gut. I should stop right now and drive up this hill like I've got wolves on my heels. But I don't. I can't just leave a naked girl lying in the bushes. If I did, I'd be no better than Bested by Crows.

"Hey there," I whisper as I bend down and touch the back of her head gently. I try to keep my voice calm, but I can feel my lip twitchin' a bit, doing its damnedest to curl up into a scowl. I can tell you without any shadow of a doubt who's responsible for this shit. I just hope the girl doesn't have to pay the ultimate price for it.

She doesn't respond, but I can see her back rising and falling as she struggles to take in shallow breaths. I can't see her face yet, but already, I'm sweatin' up a storm. *Who the fuck is this and why is she here*? *What the hell does this even mean*? I reach out a hand and grab her by the shoulder. I know I should leave her as she is, call 911 or some shit, but I'm so used to living off the grid that it doesn't feel right. If I have to, I will, but first, I'm going to find out who this is.

"Listen, honey," I say, leaning in close. I touch my hand to her shoulder and feel a sheen of sweat. No surprise, I guess, since it's hot as balls out here, but there's a clammy undertone that I don't much care for. Whoever this is, she's not in the best of shape. I move my fingers down her arm and grab hold of her bicep. "I'm going to turn you over, alright? So just stay calm and relax. I promise I won't hurt you, babe." I touch warm, sticky wetness and pull my fingers back. The liquid blackness coating my fingertips can only be one thing. "Shit." I turn the girl over and she whimpers. I make sure to catch her other shoulder and lower her softly into the grass. I catch flashes of purple bruises in a thin shaft of moonlight and have to bite my tongue to keep the bitterness out of my voice. "Hey there," I whisper as I brush some hair off her bloody face. "You awake there, sweetheart?"

I study the girl's features as best I can in the low light, but I still don't recognize her even though I feel like I should. Until I look down, past her bruised belly and catch a glimpse of her legs. Scooting closer, I see a black tattoo there.

"Aw, fuck." I know who this girl is now. It's the one Mireya picked up at the bar, the one I almost had sex with. I lean forward on my knees, checking her pulse, feeling her forehead. This isn't good. *I'm responsible for this.* At least partially, it's true. "Jesus Mother Mary," I whisper, rolling my eyes to the darkened sky. MC business should stay MC business, but this girl ... She has nothing to do with us. So what do I do now?

I grab my phone from my back pocket and pause when I hear the rumble of motorcycles coming my way. If it's Broken Dallas or Bested by Crows, I'm screwed. If they catch me, I can kiss my freedom goodbye. We had our standoffs and our brawls. Next time, it'll be more than just warning shots and chains. Now that I see this girl, I know that this shit is elevated.

I pull my phone out of my pocket and call 911, not for my sake but for hers. It's not what I want to do; pulling the authorities in here probably isn't the best idea, not for anyone, including them. Broken Dallas has been known to start shit with cops. The woman that answers the line asks what my emergency is.

I wet my lips and try to decide how best to deal with this. As soon as this call is over, we've got to get the hell out of here. Period. I don't know what to do about Austin and Kimmi, but if I don't call in an ambulance for this girl now, there's a good chance she won't make it out of here alive. I feel like I'm betraying my MC for my conscious, but I can't take it back now. I touch my hand to the woman's cheek. *Goddamn bleeding heart bullshit.* I close my eyes and take a breath.

The motorcycles roll to a stop near my bike and idle there while I speak to the operator. I don't give her my name, even though she asks, just the address of the hotel.

"I don't know what happened to her, but it doesn't look good. You'd best be on your way quick." I hang up the phone and slip my jacket off my shoulders, pausing before I lay it across her body. If I leave it here, I'm putting everybody at risk. Regretfully, I pull back and ready my gun. If it comes down to it, really comes down to it, I'd like to take a few of those assholes out before I go. I check the cylinder real quick and then sit back to wait.

"Gaine?" It's Austin's voice, just barely audible over the growling of his engine. "Where the fuck are you at?" I keep my revolver out, just in case. I mean, it doesn't take a Goddamn genius to figure out that this was a trap of some sort. *Or a warning.* We're running on borrowed time here.

I move out of the bushes to find Kimmi and Austin waiting for me. When they spot me, they both lower their weapons and breathe sighs of relief.

"What the hell are you doing in there?" Kimmi snarls, looking around like she expects to be ambushed at any moment. Scary thing is, I don't think she's overreacting. Sometime soon, somebody, whether biker or cop, is going to pull around that corner. "And who the fuck is that?"

I move forward and straddle my bike with a sigh and a regretful glance. I hate to leave the woman here, but I have no other choice. It's time to move on or get caught. I leave my helmet on the back of my bike and put my weapon away, keeping it in easy reach, just in case.

"That," I tell them as I close my fists over the handlebars. "Is a girl who ended up in the wrong place at the wrong time." I think about Mireya and how she'd feel if she knew. A girl who was, presumably, beaten and raped by the same men that attacked her. A girl who ended up on their radar because of us. I can't tell her. Hell, I can't tell Beck either. This is something that Austin, Kimmi, and I are going to have to keep to ourselves.

"Should I be worried?" Austin asks from behind me. It's hard to know how to respond to that question.

"If you mean, is this a trap of some sort? I don't know. Maybe more of a message than anything else, but I'll tell you this. We better get the hell out of here before it's too late. An ambulance is on its way." I turn and glance over my shoulder, catch a glimpse of Austin's face. Whether he and Kimmi were successful at the bank or not doesn't matter right now. If the cops come and find this girl while we're still at the hotel, we are up shit creek without a paddle. "And I'm sorry," I add before either of them get a chance to say anything. The apology's not just for them, but for the girl, too. Leaving her alone in the grass feels like a betrayal of my soul, but I've already put Triple M in enough danger as it is. It's time to go, before Mireya finds out and something else snaps inside of her.

"Alright then," Austin says with a sigh. He sounds tired already, and it's only his first week on the job. If we end up in an all out war, with our girls on one end and strangers on the other, all suffering over some dumb piece of shit like Tray Walker, the man's going to die from the stress. I hope this shit ends. Soon. I wonder briefly what might happen if I took matters into my own hands? "Let's rally the troops and light up the night." He tries to smile, but it doesn't reach his eyes. "That vacation we needed before is a necessity now. Let's cool our heels in the surf while we wait for this crap to die down. In a few weeks, we'll head to the West Coast where nobody's heard of Bested by Crows and this shit is buried in the dust behind us."

He revs up his bike and starts up the hill with Kimmi following close behind. She doesn't say anything, but I can see in her face as she passes that she's nervous. Not good.

I sigh and follow after them, doing my best to believe that it'll be as easy as Austin says to escape this without anyone else getting hurt. My mind goes right back to Mireya again. I know that on some level, she believes this is all her fault, that her past is chasing after her with a vengeance. I've got to get her out of this before she's pushed to the breaking point, twisted and broken beyond all recognition. Whatever's going on inside her head right now is leaving her vulnerable and open, in a place that won't be able to withstand another backlash of pain. Healing is great, but it leaves fresh patches in your soul where hurt can climb deeper if you let it. It's my job to make sure that doesn't happen. I think about her face today, when her chains were wrapped around Mack's neck, and I wonder, was that hesitation I saw boiling behind all of that rage?

Mireya
CHAPTER 22

"Okay, kitty cats, time to go," Austin says as he pushes into the room with a frown on his scarred lips. Amy lights up the moment he walks in the door, and me, I feel nothing. *Maybe I should be glad she came in and took him off the menu.* It's giving me a chance to focus, to move onto other things. *Like Gaine Kelley.* I frown and wait for him to walk in next. He doesn't. My heart starts to pound as I throw the book aside, forgetting the glee I felt when I pounded through the story in just a few quick hours. Either the book was short or I'm not as dumb as I thought. Anyway, it doesn't matter. When I finished reading it, I felt ... better. Now I just feel anxious and short of breath. *What the hell*?

Amy stands up, but Austin doesn't approach her, just starts grabbing bags and tossing them over his shoulder. The plan was to leave early in the morning, but I didn't expect we'd be going *this* early. Something's wrong. Amy notices, too, pausing awkwardly at the end of the bed like she expected some sort of *nice to see you* kiss or whatnot. I try not to roll my eyes. The fear in my gut won't let me anyway.

"Where's Kimmi?" I ask instead. Really, the only person I'm interested in is Gaine, but I don't want anyone to know that yet. Not even myself. *You're cutting him off, remember*? Austin pauses and tries to smile, running a hand through his blonde hair and coming away dripping with sweat.

"Gettin' the group together. Things went well, and we got some good money, but the alarm got tripped on our way out. We've gotta move before folks start askin' questions." He waits while Amy pulls Christy to her feet and grabs her book, tucking it into her purse as she moves forward, the muscles in her face tight, ready. Christy just looks terrified. I guess joining a biker gang is a lot harder when you're not fucking the new President. I force the bitter thoughts back, trying to remember how nice Amy was to me at the pool. Not that it really matters. I mean, nice is fine and dandy, but she did waltz in here with zero experience and pull the rug out from under me. I wonder if my hatred for the bitch is going to have to start being strictly on the outside, like it is with Kimmi. After all, after our fight in the lobby, I can't let anyone know that I'm actually starting to like her.

"And Gaine?" I ask, seconds before he walks in the door.

For a split second, I don't see his ashen face or his

darkened eyes, all I see is Gaine and my body reacts like it's been lit on fire, warming up and shining bright. Inside, I feel that panic start to cool, that anxiety lessen. *What the fuck*? It's definitely, *definitely*, time to pull back and give myself some space. I blame my reaction on the romance novel which, admittedly, has made me a little hot and bothered, and try to frown when I start so speak. No sense in letting him know I was worried. He doesn't need to be led on anymore. I know what that's like, and even if the person who's doing it doesn't realize it, it hurts like hell.

"What the fuck happened to you?" I ask as I rise to my feet and brush my hands down the front of my jeans. Unlike the two little princesses here, I'm already packed. "You see a ghost or something?" Gaine turns his gaze to meet mine and his eyes widen almost imperceptibly. If I wasn't looking straight into them, I probably wouldn't have noticed. He stands there silently for a moment before moving forward quickly, almost like he's falling towards me. When he's within touching distance, I hold up my hands and throw him my worst glare. "Gaine, what the hell is going on with you?" He reaches out for me, but I take a step back. "Don't you dare put your hands on me. I want an answer." I look from him to Austin, who's finally taken Amy into his arms and put his tongue down her throat. It doesn't bother me as much as I feel it should. I love Austin, but I don't think I'm in love with him. My mind goes back to Tray and Kent, and how I surprised myself by sending Amy into the bathroom. Why did I do it? Why try to protect her? For him. I wanted him to be happy. And Gaine ... is it the same for him? Of course it is. I want him to be happy, too. That's why I'm going to keep my distance. It works better for both of us.

"I got all mixed up and took a wrong turn, almost crashed my bike is all," he says, but I can tell that's a lie. My eyes narrow, but I don't get the chance to respond before he's leaning forward and pressing his lips hard against mine, touching me but not forcing anything. *And then he kissed me, and my heart exploded, just shattered into a million pieces and poisoned my body with love and lust. A virus and a disease, both catchable, only one curable. Love is the virus, of course, and while we can treat the symptoms, there's nothing we can do about the actual bug itself. Lust, well, that can be cured with a quick rut or a slow, steamboat of lovemaking extraordinaire, the kind where smoke curls out of your ears and your toes cramp up so bad you can't think. Huh. Glance Serone and Sali Bend, together forever. Who the fuck woulda thunk*?

I shove him back and wipe at my mouth like I really believe the smut in that stupid book, like I think I'm going to catch something from him.

"The hell, Gaine?" I ask as I try to avoid Amy and Austin's stares. Christy, I could give a shit less about, but the other two ... I don't want them to get any ideas. "I don't know what just happened to you, but if you're going to lie to me, don't even *think* about putting your lips anywhere near mine. I can't stand the fucking taste." I move around him and start towards the door.

"Mireya," he begins, but I cut him off with a middle finger and a grumbling of insults under my breath.

"*Hijo de puta*," I snarl. "Son of a bitch." I'm not an idiot. He needs to start realizing that by trying to protect me, he's only making me feel worse. I don't need to be protected. I can take care of myself. I just want him to realize that. Does he think I don't know why he shot out the tire on that bike? I know what those men were there for. I get it. They don't like bitches riding. Fine. I don't give a shit. I'm going to ride until the day they break my legs and leave me for dead on the side of the road. Even then they'd better be careful because if I can, I'll crawl my way to another bike and start all over again. I won't go down easy. I didn't then, and I won't now. If I can survive the hell Tray put me through before, I get through this. So what? A couple of gangs want to 'teach us a lesson', show other groups that they're not okay with the way we are? Screw them. They should know that the ultimate rule of the road is that there are no rules. I thought we were all out here to be free, to live the way we want to live. If codes and titles and patches are all that matter to them, then they're not really bikers anyway. The 'life' isn't about following a specific set of predetermined bullshit. If it was, it wouldn't be any different than the rest of society, than the place we're all looking to escape.

I wipe my arm across my lips again and move out to the parking lot next to my bike. The wind teases my hair as I pick up my helmet under my arm and gaze out across the quiet town. An alarm got set off? I call a lie. I can see the bank from here and nothing looks amiss. Whatever it is that the two of them are fibbing about, they'd better let me know because sooner or later, I'm going to find out and everything is going to go to shit. I squeeze my fists tight. Gaine wants to prove that he sees me as an equal, then why try to hide things from me? I have a right to know. Keeping stuff from me only further proves that he doesn't get it, that he thinks I can't handle the truth.

I put my bag away and slip my helmet on, climbing onto the cracked leather of my seat while I wait. Christy comes out first with Beck at her heels. He escorts her over to me and helps her get settled before moving away and pausing with his gaze focused out, towards the highway. Did they tell him what they didn't tell me? I can't decide. When Beck turns around, he's just smiling as usual.

"At least it's a good night for a ride," he says to nobody in particular. In the distance, the sound of sirens echoes across the emptiness of the terrain. I wet my lips against the dry air and flip up my visor to glare at the stupid redhead. He stands with his hands in his pockets and his muscles relaxed. The approaching red and blue lights don't bother him in the least. Guess they shouldn't bother me either. Even with a crew this big, we'll be out of here before the first squad car pulls into town. Still, it doesn't explain *why* they'e coming or what's going on. Guess I'll have to make it my mission to find out.

When Gaine comes out of the building, I don't look at him. He does pause near my bike for a second, but whatever words he thinks he should get out don't come and he ends up moving away. The gap between us grows wider than it's ever been. For years, we've been so close that I didn't even realize we were. When Austin pissed me off, I told Gaine. When I had an issue with Kent, he was the first person I would admit it to. And he's still the only person that knows my mother shipped me off to America, so she could pursue her dream of painting without the burden of a child. The only person that knows how much my grandmother meant to me, and how distraught I was when she died in a car accident. He's the only person on this planet that will ever hear the story of *why* I married Tray and took up this lifestyle. I was heartbroken and alone, that's all it really comes down to. If my grandmother hadn't passed away, I doubt I'd be here right now.

I sigh and drop my visor.

It's not that I don't like the open road, I do. Now that I've tasted it, I could never go back, but I can't help the wandering thoughts, especially when I'm in a situation like this. I could've lived a normal life and hell, if I'd met Gaine under different circumstances, maybe we'd be together. Maybe. But right now, this way, I can't do it.

I watch him climb on his bike, head low, shoulders tight under his jacket. Whatever he saw is eating him up, and that scares the shit out of me. That pain and guilt I see on him now, was that mine to take, to handle as best I could? I don't want him holding burdens for me. I know he thinks he should, but it isn't right. That's my responsibility. I think of Will and Mack and wonder what he'd do if I told him how I felt, how I'm tired of all the pain and the heartache, that I want them out of my life but don't know how to do it without getting my hands dirty. Would he try to take vigilante justice for me? I curl my fingers around my handlebars and promise myself that there is no way in hell I'm going to tell him how I really feel. As far as he's concerned, I'm thirsty for blood. Period.

I will not let Gaine risk himself for me. Not today, not tomorrow, not ever. My burdens are mine and mine alone. If anyone else got hurt because of them, I would never be able to forgive myself.

Gaine
CHAPTER 23

Our ride starts out ridiculously quiet. The intercom remains silent, no music, no mindless chatter. It's just engines and anxiety stirring the air tonight. I don't like the feeling in the group, not one bit. They're scared and they're nervous, and they're starting to get disgruntled. I'm sure they're wondering what happened tonight. I mean, it's not like they couldn't see the emergency vehicles in the distance. Kent was good at hiding his dirt. Us, not so much. If we're not careful, people are going to start wondering if Austin's strong enough to hold us together. I don't want to deal with that mess. Sooner, rather than later, we're going to have to take extreme action.

"I don't want to take the interstate," Kimmi says, and I hope to hell she's on a private channel. "There's a group out here that I don't trust. If Bested really wants to stir up shit and get everyone up in arms about us, this is the place to do it. *Seventy-seven Brothers*. You heard of them?"

"Nope." This from Beck.

"Well, the last time we passed down that interstate, we ran into them. It was a long time ago, before Gaine was even a part of Triple M, but they tried to start shit with us. They have a pretty strict code and anyone who falls outside of that is fair game. It would not surprise me if they were forming against us. They have a point to prove now. This has gone way past Mireya and Tray. This is about principle now, and if there's one thing I've learned in life, it's that principle means everything to some people." I wait for Mireya to launch into a furious attack on Kimmi, but there's nothing but silence. She's not on the channel. Shit. She's already pissed about my lying to her. If she finds out about this, there's going to be no coming back from it.

"Let's lie low and try to keep out of their hair then," Austin says as he drifts towards one of the upcoming exits. "If we can get everyone safely to St. Marlin's then I'll be tickled fuckin' pink. A few days to breathe would be nice, and I don't think a visit to the beach would hurt anyone neither." He tries to make light of the situation, and I hear him chuckle. "I sure would love to see Amy in a swimsuit, I might add."

"Saw it last night, boss, and it was mighty fine. Girl has got a body." Beck opens his damn mouth and inserts his foot. I smile, too, but I know it doesn't reach my eyes. I don't feel it deep down. This expression is strictly on my face. I think of the girl lying in the grass back there and I wonder what they did to her and how I'm ever going to be able to make that up in life. And then there's Mireya ... Do I tell her? I think about that for a second, but the answer is obvious: no. If she wants to hate me for lying to her, then so be it. I can't watch her be dealt another blow by these motherfuckers. I just need them to go the fuck away and leave us alone. Even if it takes another ten years, I'm sure I can get her to forgive me. I *know* I can.

I keep my eyes focused on the pavement in front of me, zoning into myself and letting my motorcycle warm me up from within. When all hell's broke loose and you got no one to turn to, your ride is there for you. Stupid as that sounds. It'll hold you up when you're down and take you places you never thought you'd go. If I could, I'd ride for days straight, stop only to refuel. Instead, I try to think of Mireya's lips on mine, her hands in my hair. It's going to be a long time before I ever get the pleasure of holding her in my arms again. One step forward, two steps back, right?

We ride straight on, the silence of the group heavy around us. It's like there's a climax building that we can all feel, a crescendo that's coming too fast. We don't have time to think, just to react. That's life, I suppose. It doesn't give you warnings, and it refuses to wait its turn. There ain't nothing I can do about that except go along for the ride.

We move together like a flock of birds, a perfect unit, burning up highways and tucking miles under our belt like they mean nothing. When the sun rises in the sky, we don't stop, we continue underneath its boiling gaze for as long as we can, moving as fast as I've ever seen. The longer I sit there, the more time I have to think. The more I keep going back to Mireya's face, to those chains, to her expression after I grabbed her.

She's done with this, I know she is. She's ready to move on. God, I can fucking feel it! It's driving me nuts. How can I expect her to accept me, to take the next step together when she's chained to the past? With Amy in the picture and Austin tied up in heartstrings, I thought I was good to go, that the last obstacle to her heart was gone. I was wrong. This is it. She can't rest until this crap is done and buried.

"Where we at, Pres?" Beck asks after awhile. The noise is so unexpected that I swerve a bit and catch sight of Mireya moving up beside me. She looks so perfect on the back of that ride, even if it is a bit rickety for my tastes. Her body is round and smooth, bent over like a race car driver. Even with Christy clinging to her for dear life, she looks graceful and strong, like a predator hunting prey. There's power there, and confidence. All of that paired with an ass I could stare at forever. It's almost too much. I force my eyes back to the road, but I know my cock is rock solid, waiting for her, always waiting.

"Just about there," he replies. "I'd say we've got less than an hour until we hit the coast."

"And just enough daylight to hit the beach," Kimmi adds with a smile in her voice.

"I want to talk to you all when we get there," Mireya says, and I'm glad to hear she's on the channel now. "I've got something to say if that's alright." She pauses. "If my opinion even matters."

"Of course it does," Austin responds automatically, but I doubt she's convinced. "If y'all have something to say, feel free. Hell, even if you don't got something to say, tell me, so I know you're in. This isn't going to work without your support. It's damn near impossible to go it alone." His voice trails off, and I know he's thinking of the massive burden he's just swallowed. It's going to be tough, but I know he can do it. "So, sugar, you tell us whatever you want and we'll listen."

"Good," Mireya says, and I can hear the frown in her voice. "Because you're not going to like it."

Mireya
CHAPTER 24

Eating the wind nourishes the soul, and it gives you plenty of time to think.

By the time I get to the hotel in St. Marlin's, I know exactly what it is that I'm going to do. I just hope everyone else is behind me. If they're not, then fuck 'em. I am tired of this crap, tired of running from my memories, already sick to death of the effect it's having on Triple M. I look down at the MMM tat that rests in the crook of my elbow and take a deep breath. Gaine's not going to like my plan, that's for fucking sure, but he's going to deal with it. I'm not going to give him a choice. Despite what he might think, I'm capable of making my own decisions.

I grab my bag and watch as Christy climbs off. If this all works out, and I make it through this shit okay, I'll be a better sponsor in the future. *Lo siento*, Christy, I think as I watch her eyes take in yet another new space, a different climate. I'm sure there are all sorts of things going through her head, enough to fill a novel twice the size of Amy's smut rag. *Which you loved, you dirty slut. Don't deny it.* I ignore my inner voice and toss my bag over my shoulder, letting it hang heavy against my spine. Considering it's all I own in this world, it doesn't seem so bad. When you travel this much, you learn to appreciate non-material things instead. I collect sights instead of items, sunsets and vistas, towering high-rises and quiet, suburban streets. Everything has its magic hidden somewhere. The only thing I give a shit about is my bike, and that's more like a friend or family member instead of an object. I throw up a silent prayer for my Triumph Bonneville and pretends that it's not lying trashed on the side of the road somewhere. It deserved better than that.

"What have you got with you?" I ask the girl, surprising her. She looks up at me, blue eyes wide and untainted. Whatever Bested by Crows did to her, they didn't rape her. If they had, I could tell. They barely roughed her up. Not enough time, maybe? Given the opportunity, I know they would've done much, much worse.

Christy picks up her bag, one of three that she had shoved in her trunk. Beck picked one at random and tossed it onto his bike. I never thought to ask if she had all the essentials.

"Nostalgic stuff mostly," she replies, voice soft and tentative, almost like she's afraid to speak to me. "My clothes got left behind. I've been borrowing Amy's." I look her up and down before sighing. She's wearing one of Beck's extra jackets with full patches. Kind of pisses me off, but what can I do about it? It's not like I have a bunch of extras lying around, and without the time to get her a new one, she'll have to make do. Can't make the bitch ride in floral print skirts, now can I?

"I've got some extra leather pants in my bag, and a pair of boots." I give her skinny, blonde ass a once-over. She's half the size I am, so they might be a little big, but they fit me like a second skin, so I guess it's alright.

Christy smiles at me as I turn away and start towards the entrance. Gaine's already waiting inside, leaning against the wall with his eyes closed. When I step in the door, he opens them and looks at me, doing his best to pull up a smile that I don't return.

"When I said I don't like lies, I meant it." I keep walking and ignore the sound of him sighing behind me. His footsteps move across the carpet and fall into step with mine, keeping Christy at my heels.

"I didn't mean to lie to you, Mireya. It's just … I don't want you to deal with more than you have to. It's nothin' against you, babe. I know you can take care of your own shit." I roll my eyes.

"Then why don't you let me prove it?"

Gaine grabs me by the shoulders and spins me to face him. His face is dead serious right now, dark brows crinkled, brown eyes shining. His hair falls into his face as he runs his tongue across his lower lip.

"Because you don't need to. Because I've already seen what you can do. When you're tired or stressed or weary or you need help, it's okay to ask, Mireya. I would. It's not weakness to rely on someone you trust."

"But I don't trust you," I tell him, and his face falls. "Why should I, when you have no issue lying to me?" I stare him down hard.

"Mireya, some things are better left in the dark, but if you really want to know ... " Gaine sighs and shakes his head, tightening his fingers ever so slightly on my shoulders. "I'll tell you. After you get your meeting, let's go to the room and we can talk about it." He releases me and moves away, towards the elevator.

I motion for Christy to follow after and make sure she's settled in with Amy before I move into the adjoining suite and close the door. Everyone's already waiting for me.

I look at them all, study their faces and try to memorize them. This is going to rip me to pieces, but I have to do it. This is the only way. I close my eyes and take a deep breath. When I open them, my resolve is solid. There's no going back.

"I know we have a lot of crap to deal with right now, a lot of changes to get used to, but none of that can be done until I deal with the mess I made. If I hadn't killed Tray, none of this would be happening." I forge on before anyone can jump in and feed me bullshit about how that's not true, about how all of this would've come to pass some way or another. That's not true at all, and I know it. I don't want to hear anymore lies. If I'd felt deep down and listened to myself, left Tray alive, unconscious on the floor of that room, we'd be sitting here talking about stupid shit like Vice Presidents and Road Captains. As of now, all the focus is on this, on me. "I wanted Tray to suffer, and frankly, I'm glad that he's dead. It's a relief knowing that he's not out in the world anymore, but … " I trail off and turn away, putting my hands on my hips and moving towards the windows. Outside, in the distance, I can see the blue glimmer of the ocean. It brings a smile to my lips that I quickly wipe away. I can't deal with that right now. At this moment in time, I have one thing on my mind and nothing else is going to happen until I can figure it out. "I wish I didn't have his blood on my hands." I wait for someone to say something in response to that, but this time, they're all quiet. "I thought I wanted to kill the others, but I just … don't. I don't want to be like them, to sink to their level. I've dealt with enough crap in my life. I just want to move on." I turn back to face the group, to look at Kimmi's wrinkled brow and pursed lips, Austin's deep frown, and Beck's sad smile. I do my best to avoid Gaine's eyes. "But I can't, not with them chasing us from one end of the country to the other. I don't want a hundred other gangs pulled into the mix, and I sure as shit don't want Triple M to be made an example of. So. I'm going to get rid of them for you."

"Okay," Kimmi begins, sounding confused. "So, what, you're going to hunt them down and shoot them? Is that what this is about? I hate to say it, sister, but that was my plan all along. As soon as we can, we take them out, and we don't look back. That's just the way it's going to have to be." I let her finish, smiling as I listen to her words.

"Not exactly. Actually, I'm going to leave for a little while."

Gaine stands up when he hears this, but I don't give him a chance to protest. I'm sure he'll try later, but it doesn't matter. I can make my own decisions, and I've made this one. This is the only way I can feel satisfied with the outcome.

"I'm going to go leave, and I'm going to make sure they know it. When I'm gone, they'll back off. I know they will. They might chase me, but I'm not worried about it."

"This is bullshit," Gaine says, moving forward. His black shirt is stretched taut across his body, highlighting his rapid breaths and his quivering muscles. He's pissed. And panicked.

"This is my choice, Gaine," I tell him and watch as it dawns on him that there is *nothing* he can do to stop me. If I want to leave, I have every right to do so. What I don't expect is the way my chest opens up inside, how I feel like I'm falling and I can't stop the descent.

"Why?" he asks and his voice is so quiet, it's hard to hear. Nobody else speaks. I think they can sense that there's something going on between Gaine and me that even I don't fully get yet. I look at his face, at the fear there, and I don't expect to have such a strong emotional reaction to it. I move a step back.

"This is the only way I can clear my conscious and protect Triple M." I stare Gaine down. "It's the only thing I've ever cared for in my life that's still around. I'm not letting this crap turn into some underground biker brawl bullshit. If I leave, they'll stop chasing us. They'll stop recruiting other MCs. They want to avenge their brother, and I'm their target. Kick me out," I tell Austin, looking into his brown eyes. "Or at least pretend you did. That's going to be your story. It'll make me an outlaw, and it'll protect you all from a whole load of bullshit. I don't want to kill anyone else, and I don't want anyone here to do it for me. You don't need blood on your hands, and I am not fucking letting any of you get yours on theirs. Got it?"

"Mireya," Austin begins, but Gaine is coming closer to me, moving forward like he's being drawn.

"Don't do this," he tells me, glancing back at Kimmi and Beck. "We're a family here. We've been one for years. You can't just walk out." I feel a sting behind my eyes, but I'm not taking it back. I won't. This makes sense to me. I want to sacrifice myself to make things better. I don't want to argue about women and motorcycles. We already have a tough enough time as it is. If I leave, this quiets down and fades into the background again, hopefully until the day it disappears forever. Prejudice garbage doesn't sit right with me, and it's not okay. I can stop it by simply climbing on my piece of shit bike and heading into the sunset.

"I figure I'll hit up a few shops and make some repairs to my ride. After that, I'm just going to drive until I figure out what to do next. Maybe, in time, they'll get over it, and I can come back. Until then, I'm going to do what I do best."

"Mireya," Gaine growls, and I call tell he's pissed, but that he's fighting the emotion back. "This is ridiculous. How could you do this to us?"

"You mean to you?" I ask him, feeling a burn in my eyes that I don't like, but that I've been getting awfully familiar with lately. "How can I do this to you? I'm sorry Gaine, but I'm never going to be the kind of woman that falls into your arms and swoons."

"That's not what I want from you," he tells me, voice breaking a bit, dropping that Southern sultry charm he's picked up over the years. "I just want you to be happy, and I know if you leave, you won't be. This self-sacrifice isn't worth it." I laugh, but the sound is just bitter, not at all pleasant.

"Sacrifice?" I ask him, feeling the other three stares in the room like they're lasers, driving into my spine. Gaine's look, though, is hot enough to melt. He looks like he wants to move across this room and grab me, hold me hostage and never let me go. But he wouldn't. He'd never do a thing like that, and that's what makes this so hard. "Hardly. I'll get to ride when I want and where I want." I look over at Austin. "And as fast as I want. No rules, no responsibilities. It'll be like a vacation."

"And if you get caught?" Gaine asks, and my stomach churns. I haven't said anything to them yet, but I'm taking somebody's gun with me. I don't know whose, but it doesn't matter. As long as it's got bullets in it, I'm good. If I have to, I'll kill them. If it comes down to a truly desperate situation, I'll kill myself. I'll never let my body be tampered with again. It's mine, and only *I* control what I do with it.

"Can I make a suggestion?" a voice asks from behind me. I turn to find Amy and Christy slinking into the room. They're both staring at me with different eyes, eyes from another world, orbs of blue that calculate risks and rewards in a completely different language than the one I use.

"I suppose," I say, turning to her and feeling Gaine's presence like a bullet behind me, hot and ready to pierce. I'm going to have to avoid him until I leave. I was hoping we could … hang out one last time. Amy's book gave me all sorts of ideas, and the only person I could bring up in my head that I wanted to try them with was him. But it's not going to happen. I didn't realize how much I would care. Making the decision in my head was one thing, seeing it hit him like a brick was quite another altogether. *Madre mia*, I hope I'm making the right choice.

Amy smiles at me, and I feel a little surge of disappointment. Maybe I could've made peace with her and her stupid friend, too. I feel like I could, like I'm at a point in my life where it would be okay. I glance back at Kimmi, too. It would've been nice to have some female friends in my life. I spend all this time defending women and trying to protect their rights, but I don't ever actually hang out with any. It's kind of pathetic.

"This is a big decision, and I see where you're coming

from." She moves forward and reaches out a hand to touch mine. I look at it, but I don't smile back. I can't. If I move my face at all, I'll cry, and I've done way too fucking much of that lately. I haven't sobbed in years, and I'm paying for it. All of the past pain is coming back, breaking through my dam and drowning me. "Some decisions we make; others are made for us. You might think this is a little of both, but it's not. This is all you. You have choices."

I stare at her for a moment before a scowl hits my face like a train, knocking me back with a surge of anger.

"Bullshit!" I scream at her, feeling my facade of calm slip away. It's always been pretend. I don't know how to act, how to behave, how to feel things. All I know how to do is get angry. That's it. I'm a fucked up eighteen year old girl inside, one with scars so deep they cut straight through to her heart. I can't pretend anymore. I'm *done* pretending. "I don't have any choice! I can't see the people I love get hurt, and I can't charge myself with anymore dirty deeds. I am fucking broke!" I hit my fist into the wall and spin before Gaine can come up behind me. "I made my decision and I'm sticking to it. I'll say my goodbyes tonight, and I'm leaving in the morning. If you don't like it, too damn bad. This is the way things have to be."

I turn and grab the handle to my room, moving through it as Amy calls out behind me.

"Sleep on it," she asks, and I pause. "Sleep on it and let's talk about it again tomorrow." Gaine moves forward and I step back, turning to throw him a wet glare, the muscles in my face taut from forcing the tears to stay back. He moves into the room but doesn't touch me, just goes into the bathroom and slams the door. “We can go to the beach and look at the ocean. That always changes things. Do that and then decide,” she whispers as I start to close the door. I don't want to hear it anymore. I'm not going to change my mind. They need to accept that. The sooner they do, the easier this will be. “And Mireya,” she says before I get a chance to block her out completely. I look at Amy's heart shaped face, at her moist eyes, and I see that she doesn't want me to go. I don't know why. I've been nothing but rude to her. “About Gaine, you said you didn't *want* to love him. Think about that. How can you not want to do something you've never done?” And then she winks at me and the door slams shut in her face.

Gaine
CHAPTER 25

I feel like a train's hit me, like I'm never going to be able to stand up again. I'm paralyzed, frozen in place, blinded with fear and frustration. I can't make Mireya stay, that's true. But there is no way in hell I can let her go. Do I follow after her? Do I ride my bike like a damn stalker and chase her around the country? If I did that, she'd never let me live it down. My chance at her heart would go from slim to impossible.

"Are you going to tell me or not?" she asks a few hours after her initial confession. I'm lying on the bed with my hands clasped behind my head, eyes closed. I've been here most of the day. Everyone else has come and gone, enjoying the new bounty of money that's been sprung onto the group. I don't know how much it is, but Austin's been pretty generous with it. Still, Mireya and I end up sharing a room when we don't have to. She could've walked out and gotten another at any moment, and she hasn't. I try to see that as positive.

"Tell you what?" I ask, and I don't like how angry my voice sounds. That's not what I want her to see. I can't control her with rage and a bad temper. She has to stay because she wants to. Anything else just won't work.

I open my eyes and look at her face. It's softer than usual. Her saucy lips are tilted down in the corners and her sharp eyes are open wide, looking at me like she's never seen me before. Or maybe more like she's never going to see me again. I absorb her into my system, staring at the fall of dark hair around her shoulders, the straight ebony blackness that ends in a gentle wave. Her body is just perfect, like a goddess descended from Mt. Olympus. It's round in all the right places, full, ripe. I doubt Mireya would ever be interested in having kids, but she's got the right body for it, solid hips and the softest fucking breasts.

I don't try to hide my erection from her.

"What you lied to me about." I laugh, but I don't mean to. It just comes out, nervous and shaky. As soon as I tell her about that girl, I'm sealing her ticket out of here. I may as well pack her bags now. I sigh and run my hands down my face as I sit up. I've got to come up with a solution, an atypical one, something that she'll never suspect because I'm pretty damn positive that she already has a retort ready for every protest in the book.

"Mireya, take my bike." I look up at her as she wrinkles her nose. The softness is getting erased already, and I've only just seen it. I lock the image in my mind and promise I won't forget it for the rest of my life. "It's better than that piece of shit you just bought. If you're going to go, I'd feel a lot better if you took my baby with you." I try to smile, but it doesn't come across right.

"You want to give me your Tiger?" she asks incredulously. "You've tweaked the shit out of that thing. It's got your fingerprints all over it." I stare straight at her, hoping that somehow she'll see in my eyes that I don't want her to go, that I can't bear to watch her drive away.

"Only because you helped me with it. You know I don't know shit about playing with machinery. I can ride it hard, but I don't know what the hell you're always going on about. Multi-plate clutches and steel trellis frames." Mireya's face stops wrinkling up and she almost smiles. Almost. I rise to my feet and move towards her, trying to keep that easiness we've had in our friendship for so long. I don't know why it's such a jump for her to accept that we're a couple. We've kind of been one, on and off, for awhile now. We've slept in each other's arms, shared secrets, fucked like friggin' rabbits. All I want is to be able to tell her I love her, to hear her say it back. That's it. Simple. I keep going, forcing the mood to stay light. "Single piston sliding caliber brakes?" I ask as a question, touching my fingers to her bare upper arm. She's got on a black tank and dirty jeans, no makeup. I don't often get to see her like this. She's gorgeous, jaw-dropping, flawless. I like her even better this way than I do when she's got her smoky eyes and red lips, though I wouldn't complain about that either. It's just, Mireya's perfect to me the way she is. "I don't know shit about shit. I just like to ride the damn things."

"Don't play dumb with me," she says, and I notice she sucks in a breath when our flesh makes contact. Her chest tightens and the rise and fall of her breasts increases as her breathing speeds up. "I know you know your shit, and I can't take your bike. It's a part of you." She looks up at me and shakes her head. Black hair brushes my arm and sends my body into a messy, sweating frenzy. "Stop saying such stupid fucking crap and tell me what you need to tell me.

"Mireya," I say, and I can't hold it back anymore. I wrap my arms around her, sliding my fingers beneath the fabric of her shirt. I don't miss the way she arches her back and pushes her chest into mine, squishing her breasts against me. "My bike is a part of me, but you're an even more important part. I'd hate to see it go, but I don't know if I can stand to watch you leave." I raise one hand to her hair, curl my fingers into it. She's looking at me with her slanted eyes opened wide, her lips frozen in a gentle part. I've only seen her like this once, the night I told her I loved her, the night she spilled all her secrets to me. I screwed things up then, but I'm not going to screw them up now.

In an instant, I know what I have to do.

Tonight, I'm going to leave, and I'm going to find Bested by Crows myself. That's it. That's all there is to it. There might be some scuffles after this, but that's going to be it. If I take out their Pres and his closest buddies, the group will either fall apart or be forced to back off. They don't have a big club. Just a few strategic hits should be enough. What's an army without its generals anyhow? And I figure if they back off, the other MCs might pull back a bit, too. As long as we stay away from them, we'll be alright, and this disease won't get spread all across the continent, taking innocent girls down with it. I try not to think of the woman with the tattoo. I have no way to check on her, so it's pointless to even entertain thoughts about her.

"Don't say stupid things like that, Gaine." Her words come out soft, barely audible. "You're trying to distract me with disgusting, fluffy shit. You know that's not my scene."

"I know, but I can't help myself. When you find the woman you love, you just start to spout fairytale crap in times like these." I lean forward and breathe against Mireya's mouth, pressing my lips against her lower one, savoring her in that moment, wishing I could hold her there forever.

"Times like what?" she asks as I kiss her, get her mouth wet with mine and enjoy the feel of her nipples hardening against me. She's not wearing a bra, but her breasts are still raised and full, held up by the strong muscles in her chest. I move one of my hands up slowly, caressing her tentatively, seeing how far she'll let me go. She told me to back off, but now she's leaving. Surely she has time for one last hurrah?

"Times where you find out that you're losing the one person that means the most to you, where you're powerless to stop it, where you know you'd do anything, give anything to keep them with you." Mireya's eyes flutter closed and her hands find the waistband of my jeans, sliding in and brushing against my skin.

"You can't change my mind, Gaine," she repeats, and I nod, kissing her full, breathing in her sweet scent and holding it in my lungs. I can't change her mind, but I can alter the circumstances. If I leave, she'll have to stay. That's it. I might never see her again, but at least I know she'll be safe here, happy. She's got Beck and Austin and Kimmi, and I think that eventually, she'll have Amy and Christy, too. Mireya could make friends with them if she wanted. I know she could. And one day, I hope she'll find a man that makes her feel the way I feel about her.

"I know."

I lift her up and set her on the edge of the dresser, slipping between her legs and pressing my hard on against the hot sweetness there. It's damp, moist from excitement, and it makes me crazy, makes me forget what I promised to do.

"Tell me first," she says as I move my mouth to her neck and start kissing my way down her shoulder. I pause and the image of Crystal's bruised body floods back into my mind. Shit. Well, at least I remember the girl's name. Somehow, that makes things a little better.

I sigh and move back, just a bit, keeping Mireya's hands on my stomach. This isn't going to be good.

"You have to promise that you'll spend the night with me," I tell her, swallowing back fear and trepidation. I didn't want things to go this way, but they have and I'm going to deal with it as best I can. I hope everything will work out, that I can pull off some miracle and make it back to her alive, but if I don't, it's okay. As long as I remove those fuckers from her life forever, I'll be happy.

"Are you fucking serious?" she asks, getting pissy and trying to push me back. "You'll only tell me the truth if I promise to *sleep with you*?" She shoves against me violently, and I grab her tight, pressing my forehead to hers.

"You don't have to touch me if you don't want to," I promise her as she reaches up and grabs me by the piercing in my eyebrow, using it to pull my face away from hers. "I just want you to stay here tonight. We can watch a movie, play a game, fuck, I don't care. We can dress up in drag and go to a bar if that'll make you happy." I manage to pull a small smile from her face. "But you can't leave when I tell you what I saw last night. And you can't blame yourself." The smile disappears as quick as it came.

"Blame myself?"

"For Crystal," I tell her and she blanches. I swallow and take a deep breath, keeping my hold on her firm, pressing her body to mine. "I found her last night."

"No." Mireya tries to pull away from me, but I won't let her.

"She was naked and pretty roughed up. I called an ambulance, but I don't know if she's going to make it. I don't know how bad it was. It was dark and hard to see."

"You called an ambulance?" she asks, putting together

the pieces. I put the entire MC at risk for that girl, and I don't know if Mireya's going to be pissed about it or not. God. I stay still, letting her absorb the information. Really, though, that should be the least of my worries. This isn't about me and what I did. It's about what *they* did. "Bested by Crows?" she asks, and I nod. There's nobody else with the motive or the ability.

When she pushes away this time, I let her, watching as she stomps over to her bag and rips the zipper back with shaking fingers. She digs through the clothes quickly, shoving shirts and pants aside like they've personally offended her. When she comes across a book, she pauses and lifts it up, thumbing through the pages like she might find some sort of answer in them.

"It's not your fault," I say, moving across the room and pausing behind her. "You didn't make them do what they did." Mireya laughs a caustic laugh and spins to face me, the book clenched so tightly in her hands it looks like she's about to start tearing pages from it.

"I picked that girl up, took her into the garage. I gave her a false sense of security, Gaine." She shakes her head and her hair goes flying, moving around her face like bats. "And I killed Tray. I got them started on this misogynistic bull, and now there are strangers paying for it?" She practically screeches this last part, like she can't possibly believe this is happening. "MC business is fucking MC business!" The book goes flying, and I have to duck out of the way. When I pick it up, a passage catches my attention.

He takes me up to the roof, where the sky is clearest and the birds sound loudest, and we fuck like animals, like two souls unbound from their earthly shells. We screw until the day turns night, and I don't regret a single second of it. If I only had one moment left to live, I'd want to spend it in Adam's arms. As things stand, he's leaving tomorrow, and I know without a single doubt that I'll never see him again. I have to savor the moment, to appreciate the beauty in this single second and cherish it in my heart forever.

I toss the novel onto the bed, and reach my hands out to grab hers, holding tight, letting that burn I feel in my blood transfer between us. She can feel it, too, I know. It's there whether either of us wants it to be. We're made for each other. I don't say that aloud of course, but in my heart, I know it's true. Ain't nobody going to tell me fucking otherwise. I'll die for her. That's what I have to do to end this. And maybe I'm not thinking clearly, maybe I'm blinded by my desperation, by years of longing, but it feels right. I touch one hand to my back pocket, to the ring I bought so long ago and will never get to see her wear.

"Mireya," I say as I pull her closer, slowly, tentatively, desperate to get her back in my arms again.

"That bitch, Amy, must've slipped it in my bag," she mumbles, but underneath her scowl, I see tears.

"It's not your fault," I repeat, reaching up to touch her chin, drawing her gaze to mine. As soon as we connect, as soon as we plug into one another, the tears start. They roll down her face, wet and glistening, a torrent of emotions that

I can't resist.

I want to cry, too, but I'll be damned if I show her a sliver of melancholy. Right here, right now, I'm going to show her a damn good time, leave her with a memory that burns hotter than fire, that scalds each and every time she thinks about it. I don't want a single other man to be able to top this moment. I'm going to do this shit right, going to destroy any leftover longing for Austin or anybody else. Before I go, even if it's just for a single second, I want Mireya Sawyer to be mine.

"Forgive me, lover," I tell her as I bend down and slide my hand behind her legs, scooping her up against my chest. At first, she looks startled, then pissed off, but the tears won't stop falling and she can't maintain the anger. "You didn't kill that girl, and you didn't do anything wrong. This isn't your fault. Walker deserved ten times what you gave him. If I'd gotten my hands on him, things would've been a hell of a lot worse."

"What the fuck are you doing?" she asks, pretending she didn't hear me. I know she did. I know my words are getting to her right now. A tiny sliver has opened up in her tired soul, and I've got to get in while I can, work my way inside and show her how I feel. This is it, my last chance to prove it.

"I'm taking you up to the roof."

"The roof?" I smile and kiss her lips hard, like a pair of newlyweds crossing the threshold on their honeymoon. I let her know everything I feel in that kiss, using my tongue to say things I don't dare speak aloud. When I pull back, I let my smile morph into a grin.

"That's right. Your book inspired me. I can't help myself now."

"This is fucking stupid," Mireya says, but she leans her head against me, years of pain and anger and frustration draining from her in waves, bleeding across the hideous hotel carpet and staining it with her past, a past I hope she can leave behind her after tonight.

You're making the right choice, Gaine, I tell myself as I carry her down the hall, past puzzled faces of fellow Triple M'ers. Mireya doesn't look at any of them, just keeps her forehead pressed against my shoulder and stays limp, letting me hold her up for what has got to be the first time ever. It feels good, like I can finally be helpful to her. From the day I joined Triple M, ran away from a perfectly good life that I'd thoroughly abused, I've been looking for a moment like this. A moment that was so bright, it burned my eyes and scraped my soul. This is it. I've found it.

When I hit the door to the roof, I'm happy to see that it's unlocked. I can't imagine what I woulda done if it had been bolted shut. Probably pushed Mireya up against the door and made the sweetest fucking love to her that I could. But this is better.

As soon as I step out, the breezy ocean wind teases our hair, tangles it together and kisses our faces with salt. I can hear the waves in the distance, calling out to us, soothing us with the soft cry of the earth. It's fucking perfect.

I set Mireya on the stone wall that surrounds the edge and hold her tight, knowing that this is dangerous as hell, but that I'd never let her go. With my hands wrapped around her, she could never fall. I won't let it happen. I'd hold her up with the last of me, prop her body up on my soul if I had to. There's no price that's too high to pay for Mireya Sawyer.

"I'm going to shoot their nuts off," she says, and I pause, hoping this means she's changed her mind. "Once they know I'm not with Triple M anymore, they'll come after me and they won't expect shit. I'll maim them and spit in their wounds, and then I'll leave again. I'll find a place they'll never look and I'll wait them out." Mireya looks into my eyes and touches the side of my face. "I want to want to kill them, but I don't Gaine. I think I've had enough darkness in my life for now. Anymore, and the flame will go out. I'll be nothing but shadows." My throat clenches tight and I have to squeeze her tighter to keep my emotions in check. I'm going to use sex to express myself. I'm a guy, that's what I do. I can't cry, not right now. I already promised I wouldn't end up as the fairytale fucking princess. "When I know you're safe, I'll come back. This isn't forever, Gaine. It's just for awhile."

I cut her off with another kiss, pressing my fingertips into her flesh, licking her lower lip, nipping at the edge of her jaw. Mireya moans and wraps her arms around my neck, leaning back so that her black hair billows in the wind, gets caught in the cool breeze and tickles my face. She leans back so far that she's nearly horizontal, exposing her chest to me, letting me kiss her breasts through her shirt and then down, past the spot where the fabric bunches up and her belly's exposed.

When I hit her jeans, I keep going, using my hands on her hips to hold her still as I kiss down the seam in her pants, biting and nipping at the wet spot on the fabric until her cries are loud enough that I can hear them above the wind and waves. Pulling back, I smile and tug her closer, reaching between us to unbutton her jeans. When she reaches for mine, I push her wrists back.

"All I need is you, lover, and I'm good. Just relax. You deserve a break."

I pull her off the wall, so that I can shimmy her pants down and toss them aside where they get caught on the stone and then tumble over.

"Goddamn it, Gaine," she says, but there's a ghost of a smile on her lips. "You dumb ass idiot. How am I supposed to get back to the room?" I grin and grab her shirt, ripping it off and throwing it purposely over the edge this time.

"Maybe I'll just leave you here until you change your mind about runnin' away." I grin, but she doesn't find the joke funny. Her face falls again, and I step forward to catch it with a kiss, running my thumbs down her cheeks and pressing her naked body against mine. The heat in my heart moves out and warms my body from head to toe. My cock stiffens and rubs painfully against my pants, begging to be let out, to show this woman how much she means to me with each thrust of my hips.

I lift her up and set her back on the wall, kneeling between her legs and dropping my face to her pussy, nipping at the dark hair and pressing rough kisses to her thighs that make her writhe above me. I don't hold back, keeping one hand on her back and using the other to enter her hot heat, feeling that fluttery pulse against my skin and holding back a growl in my throat. I want to grab her and grind her against the stone with my hips, bruise her ass as I slam her against the unyielding wall while I scream my frustration at the world.

But that's not what Mireya needs right now. She needs a man that understands her, that can touch her firmly but gently, who can take charge but leave her with the knowledge that she can change things, at any time, for any reason. I might be taking the lead right now, but she controls me, and I'm not ashamed of it. Beck can joke around and call me pussy whipped if he wants. If giving the love of my life what she wants makes me a prissy ass faggot, so be it. I'll don a dress and wear a crown. Mireya means more to me than any of that. And fuck, if anyone wants to question my manhood, I'll invite 'em to watch me slide my dick deep into the cunt of the hottest woman that's ever walked this damn earth.

I kiss Mireya between the legs, taking my time and making sure I get every fold, every crevice, before I work my way back up to her clit. I take the hardened flesh into my mouth and swirl my tongue around, moving her towards the edge with my lips. I listen to her moans, judging each movement of my mouth and timing it with her cries. When she finally hits her orgasm, she comes all over my face, drenching me with her hot juices and drowning me in lust.

I can't take it anymore.

I stand up and wrap my arm around her waist, yanking her against me hard, kissing her and forcing her to taste her own warmth. The salty sweetness of her sifts between us as we fight against one another, hands grasping, fingers clawing at naked flesh. I pull back just long enough to slip my shirt off and drop it over the edge, to let her unbutton my pants and free my aching cock.

It hurts so good that I can't wait. I move her forward and grind her into the stone. Her ass squishes against it, pressing tight to the lip of cement as I move the head of my cock to her opening.

"Mireya Sawyer," I tell her, and I wait until she opens her eyes and looks straight at me before I continue. "You're stubborn and frustrating and ornery as fuck, but I love you more than I love to ride."

"Gaine," she warns, but I can't hold back. It's now or never.

"I love you more than I love this group, more than I love myself. Mireya Sawyer, I just fucking love the Goddamn holy fucking hell out of you. That's it. That's all there is to it." She tries to protest, but I cut her off with my mouth, thrust forward with my hips and fill her completely. Her body swallows mine, clamps down hard around me, muscles fluttering as she milks my cock for all it's worth.

I grasp her by the back of the head, dig my fingertips into her hair and moan. I don't care if anyone can hear me. This isn't about them; this is about *us*.

"Gaine," she says, protesting between kisses, hissing my name out on the end of each breath as I push inside of her, finding her cervix and bumping it with the head of my cock. Her sweaty, naked body is wrapped in mine, filled with me. I want to hear her say those words, but I'll settle for this. Right now, right here, I know that Mireya Sawyer is mine.

"I love you," I tell her simply, wanting to say it again and again and again, as many times as I can before this is over. She keeps her eyes closed, groans as I bite at her neck, leaving red marks as I go, sucking gently on her soft, bronzed skin. Exotic, wild, beautiful. That's how I see her. A streak of angry perfection with her legs wrapped around my body and her hands touching my chest, feeling up my tattoos, tracing down my muscles.

I can still smell and taste her pussy on my face, and it's making me crazy, churning my lust into a frenzy. We grind against the wall, grunting and whimpering like animals, drawn halfway out of this world and into the next.

It doesn't last nearly long enough.

Mireya's moans to turn to screams, increasing in frequency until she explodes around me, hugging my dick with her body, coating me with molten hot juices that drip down my balls and land on the gravelly pavement at my feet. I don't want it to end, but I can't hold back. I kiss her with everything I've got, squeeze her tight and come inside of her.

For one, happy, blissful second, I am the happiest motherfuckin' man on earth.

That feeling doesn't last near as long as I wish it could.

Mireya
CHAPTER 26

Gaine slips his shirt over my shoulders and helps me sneak back to the room. I don't look at him, don't speak to him. I can't. My whole body is shaky, and it's gotten hard to breathe. My emotions are in a frothing frenzy, and suddenly, despite my previous conviction, I'm conflicted.

How can I leave this behind? I wonder as I stumble back to the room, warm and covered in sweat and saliva. My pussy is swollen, throbbing with pleasure with each step I take. Gaine's seed mixes with my own come and drips down my thighs, leaving me a fucking mess by the time we get to the room.

He loves me.

I knew that, of course, but to hear it again? It almost broke my heart and my decision. I can't let him know that. I do my best to avoid looking at him. If I do, I'm afraid I'll break down again. My mind keeps trying to swing back around to that girl, Crystal. Basically, I've got her blood on my hands, too. If I hadn't picked her up, convinced her to come down to the parking garage, she'd still be alive. Bested by Crows didn't go easy on her, I'm sure. I can't even think about what might've happened. I have to stay strong and stick with my decision.

"Can I get you anything, babe?" Gaine asks me, but I just shake my head and crawl into bed. When he slides in beside me, I stiffen, but I don't push him away. With his hard warmth wrapped around me, I'm asleep in minutes.

What wakes me up is the sound of footsteps in my room. And it's not just one person, it's several. My eyes burst open and my hand creeps towards the nightstand. I stuck my tire iron in there, just in case something like this happened.

"She asleep?" I hear a familiar voice ask. It's Austin.

"Musta had a real good time up on that roof," Beck says and then, of course, he laughs.

"Don't you motherfuckers know how to knock?" I snap as I sit up suddenly and cause Kimmi to jump. Her blue and silver earrings swing like pendulums.

"Jesus Christ, Mireya. What's your problem?"

"What's *your* problem?" I growl at them, wondering where Gaine's gone. I can still feel him wrapped around me, moving inside of me. Goose bumps break out across my skin as I glare at the three of them. "Why the fuck are you sneaking into my room in the middle of the damn night?" I grab the clock and spin it to face me. It's three in the Goddamn morning.

"We did knock. You must've been out like a light," Austin says, putting his hands on his hips.

"And?" I ask, stifling a yawn and surreptitiously stretching out a hand towards the spot where Gaine was sleeping. The sheets are cold. "What do you want? I have to say, breaking into my room this late at night is a little weird, even for you." The three of them exchange glances.

"Mireya," Austin begins and then pauses. "Is Gaine here? We've got something we want to say to you, but I'd sure like it if he were around." I squeeze my fingers against the sheets.

"You haven't seen him?" I ask, and Austin shakes his head. I glance over at the bathroom door, but it's wide open. There's nobody in there. A cold feeling begins in the base of my spine and starts to work its way up. "Maybe he's at the bar?" I ask then, thinking that it wouldn't be surprising if he'd gone for a drink. I know this isn't easy on him. I know … that he loves me. I get it. I did. I just can't reciprocate it right now. It isn't good for any of us. I think of Crystal and wonder if she's still alive. Either way, if my enemies are willing to take their anger out on a complete stranger, someone barely related to me, how will they be if they get their hands on someone else, someone like Kimmi? The fiery lesbian would not do well being ground to dust under their boots, forced under their bodies. I can't let that happen.

"Just came from there," Beck says with a grin. "Didn't see him."

I look around and spot Gaine's suitcase. It's still there, where he left it, but the boots he kicked off by the dresser are gone. My heart starts to race and my pulse quickens. *No, he wouldn't. Would he*? I start to get a suspicious niggling in my gut, one that makes me white hot with fear.

I throw the covers off and ignore the fact that my ass is hanging out. I move to the window and check the parking lot. Fucking Christ. My eyes dart around, trying to make sure I haven't missed it, but no, Gaine's Tiger is gone. He's gone.

"Holy shit," I growl, my knees going weak. I grab onto the windowsill for support and lower myself slowly to the floor. "This can't be happening." The pieces start to click into place.

"What's going on?" Austin asks, moving over to me and helping me up. His brown eyes bore into mine, completely serious now. "Talk to me." I shake my head and push away from him, stumbling back into the nightstand.

"I've got to go," I whisper, turning to my bag and digging out the first outfit I can find. I slip Gaine's shirt off and Beck whistles appreciatively. I ignore them all.

"Goddamn it, Mireya," Austin says, moving closer to me, not at all bothered by my nakedness. "You're a part of this fuckin' group whether you like it or not. You're not going anywhere. Doesn't matter if their grudge is with you or not. Fuck with one of us and you fuck with all of us."

I slip my shirt on and toss him the meanest glare I know. Okay, his words are sort of nice to hear. But it doesn't matter. I can't even think about that right now, can't think about anything except Gaine. Because I know where he is, and where he's gone.

"I'm talking about Gaine, you idiot," I snap at him, dragging my pants on and buttoning them quick as I can. "He's gone. He left."

"Left?" Kimmi asks, and then something clicks. Her eyes go wide and she moves to the window to look. "He left," she says, shaking her head and spinning around quickly. "He's going after them alone, isn't he?"

"What the fuck do you think?" I scream at her, sitting on the edge of the bed hard and slipping on my boots. *This is all my fault, the reason I wanted to leave.* Tears prick my eyes, but I push them back. I can't lose it now. If we hurry, there's still a chance we could catch up with him. If he gets there before we go, he's toast. I can kiss Gaine Kelley's strong arms and gentle smile goodbye. If that happens, if he dies, I don't know if I'll be able to take it. If I lose him … I stand up and grab my keys, sticking my tire iron into the back of my pants.

"Where do you think he went?" Kimmi asks, adjusting her red leather corset and biting at her lower lip. "We've been riding for hours. They might not be anywhere near us right now."

"Gimme just a sec," Beck says, pulling out his cell phone and playing with the screen for a moment. I have no fucking clue what he's doing, but I wait. When it comes to this sort of thing, Beck actually has his uses. Based on some of his tattoos, I've got a weird suspicion that maybe he's ex-military or something, but I've never been able to prove it, and I've never asked. "I installed one of them GPS things on his phone," he says, playing dumb when I know he knows exactly what he's talking about. After a moment, his stupid half smile turns into a frown, and my heart stops.

"What?" I yell at him, getting up close and staring him down. Beck looks at the screen and then up at me. "Is he far ahead of us?"

"Not too far," Beck says, tucking his phone into his back pocket.

"Then what's the problem?" My asshole friend, the one with the terrible sense of humor, who's dumb as a Goddamn doornail, looks at me with a grave expression.

"Well, from what I can tell," he says, glancing back at Austin and Kimmi. "He isn't moving, so … either he's stopped for gas or he doesn't have his phone on him anymore." There's an unspoken *or* in that sentence, something that tells me Beck doesn't believe either of those things. I finish his sentence for him.

"Or," I say, taking a deep breath and squeezing my fists at my sides. "They've already got him."

Gaine
CHAPTER 27

I expect to ride through the night before I come even close to encountering Bested by Crows, but it doesn't happen like that. I ignore Kimmi's instructions and end up on the interstate, going as fast as I can, pushing my Tiger to her limits while I apologize under my breath. I'm not just chasing demons here, I'm running from Mireya. If she catches up to me while I'm out here, I won't be able to go through with it. I have to hurry before she wakes up and comes after me because I know she will.

About an hour outside of town, I hear them coming.

Even though I don't expect to see them yet, I'm ready, pulling over to the side of the highway and hiding my bike in some bushes. I crouch down and wait, watching as they come around the corner, colors flying, bikes shining under the orange streetlights. My plan is to follow behind them and take them out when they least expect it. I don't think

I'm going to get them all, but if I can grab Will, Mack, and the other faces I recognize from the roadblock, I think it'll be okay. I'm hoping that they'll split up again, let their guard down and park their rides at some point.

What I don't expect, don't even friggin' consider, is that they already know I'm coming. Somebody saw me leave and they passed on the word, just like they've been doing all along. I don't know who it is at the moment, but as soon as I hear the crunch of boots behind me, I know it's true.

I turn but not quick enough, pulling my gun out and aiming it at the nearest body. I manage to fire off a single shot into one of the leather clad chests before I'm being grabbed and shoved to my knees. Boots slam down on my back, into my head, smash the bones in my legs. It happens so quick that I don't have time to shout, to struggle, to defend myself. Before I can even roll over and put up a fight, something hard smashes into my skull and renders me unconscious.

Mireya
CHAPTER 28

Austin pulls together a large group of people to take with us while I pace outside next to my bike and let my mind run wild. I can't even believe this is happening. I can't even fucking believe that Gaine would do something like this. *Really, Mireya? You're surprised that someone loves you enough to try to protect you, to risk his life to save yours?* Did I want to leave Triple M? Fuck no. I would've been miserable, I'll admit it, but I was willing to do it to keep them safe. And now, if we don't catch up to Gaine before it's too late, he might not make it at all. If Bested by Crows gets ahold of him, the only hope we'll have is that they'll hold him as a hostage in the hopes of getting me instead.

I throw up one of my grandmother's favorite prayers, hoping that in some way, she'll be here with me tonight. I could use a bit of her strength.

"*Dios te salve, Maria. Llena eres de gracia: El Señor es*

contigo." I swallow hard and fight back the pain in my heart. It's not too late yet. I could be grieving for no reason. Hell, Gaine might be stopped at a late night diner nursing a cup of coffee and regretting his stupid ass decision. I keep praying. "*Bendita tú eres entre todas las mujeres. Y bendito es el fruto de tu vientre: Jesús.*" I close my eyes and listen to the sound of the doors opening behind me, the hurried footsteps across the pavement. "*Santa María, Madre de Dios, ruega por nosotros pecadores, ahora y en la hora de nuestra muerte.*"

"A-fucking-men," Austin finishes for me, drawing my gaze around to his stoic face. He holds out his hand and gives me a pistol. I have no fucking clue what kind it is, but it's heavy and full of bullets, so it's good enough for me.

"*Amén,*" I whisper as I press it to my lips and then stuff it in the back of my pants. Hopefully I won't shoot myself in the ass before we get there. I look around at Beck, Kimmi, at the rest of the familiar faces, people I've known for years and said few, if any, nice things to. I wonder if they all hate me, if I'm the most unlikeable person in this group. *Not to Gaine you're not.* I ignore that annoying inner voice, the one that's decided to spring up at the worst possible moment, to try to remind me of all the wonderful things he's done, how amazing he's been. It's sort of the last thing I need right now. "Thanks," I say because that's all I can get out, the only positive thing I can think to say right now. If Gaine survives this, if I survive this, I promise that I'll *try* to be different, that I'll let people in. I have to. I've been saying I want to move on all this time, thinking that vengeance and blood would get me there. In reality, I had the ingredients I needed all along. I suck in a deep breath. "Now let's get the fuck out of here."

I turn around and straddle my bike, squeezing it between my thighs and letting the heat of the metal warm me up from within. Right now, deep down, my core has turned to ice, and I know that if I find out anything's happen to Gaine, it'll stay frozen solid.

These motherfuckers do not want to see this ice queen in action. If anything can make them retract their outdated thoughts on women, it would be getting their dicks shot off. Don't you think?

Gaine
CHAPTER 29

I have got to be the worst damn hero there ever was. What kind of man am I that I can't protect the woman I love? How pathetic must I be? These are the first thoughts that cross my mind when I wake up, lying on a cement floor in a darkened building. There's movement all around me, but I can't see shit. My eyes are blurry and my head is spinning, throbbing and sticky in the back. *Not a good sign.* Jesus Christ, I'm about as useless as a screen door on a submarine.

Did I take any of them down? And if so, did I grab one of my targets? I sure as shit hope so. My sacrifice better be worth it, or I'm going to go to the grave a fool and an idiot. I close my eyes and bring up the memory of Mireya's hot body in my arms, my cock in her sweet pussy. For a minute there, she was mine, and I know I can die happy if she gets away from all of this bullshit. Thing is, I know I haven't done enough damage to change anything.

Yet.

She's going to come after me now, I know it. I have to make this count before it's too late.

"Fuck," I growl as I open my eyes again, struggling to keep the room from spinning as I focus on boots and bikes and low voices. As soon as they know I'm awake, they'll probably break my hands. Maybe smash my kneecaps in. The next few hours of my life are going to be torture. There are no ifs, ands or buts about that.

I just need to see how much damage I can do beforehand.

I push against the bindings on my wrists and ankles, testing them for strength. Whoever tied me up did a damn good job of it, and whoever knocked me out should win a fuckin' award. I can barely see, and I'm nursing the worst headache I've ever had in my life. But I have to keep going. After all, what would Mireya think if she found out my rescue mission ended before it had ever gotten started? And the teasing I'd endure from Beck? Hah. He'd dance on my damn grave.

I move my gaze around the room, ignoring the ache in my skull, while I try to get a head count. At the same time, I touch my pockets and see if they've left anything in them. Unfortunately, the only item I feel is the rusted wedding ring. My heart skips a beat as boots approach my face. High-heeled boots. The fuck? I think about closing my eyes, pretending I'm still out, but I don't know how much good that'll do me. Best I get this show on the road and see what sort of *Indian Jones* type magic I can muster up. You know the kind I'm talking about, like taking out ten armed men with a single whip. That's what I need right now. That or some duct tape and a Swiss army knife, so I could MacGyver my way out of this shit.

"Gaine?" the voice above me sounds surprised, but not apologetic. And familiar. Way too fucking familiar. "I have to say, I'm a bit surprised to see you out here by yourself, but I can't say I'm going to be complaining much." My heart skips a few beats and my skin breaks out into a sweat. Ah, shit. Anybody but her. *Please Jesus.* When Melissa Diamond bends down and throws me a sultry smile, I almost piss my damn pants.

Mireya
CHAPTER 30

I gun my engine and haul ass down that highway, but it still feels like I'm crawling, skipping along the pavement at a merry pace.

"Fuck! Can't we go any friggin' faster?" I snarl into the intercom, desperate to reach the spot on the GPS where Gaine's phone is still sitting. An hour later, and it hasn't moved. I'm starting to flip shit.

"Goin' as fast we can, sugar. Hold tight, alright?" I want to speed ahead of the group, but I know I'm going to need them. To get Gaine out, if he's where I think he is, we're going to need every last body. And we're going to end up back at the hotel with a few less. This is what I was trying to avoid and now, here it is. There's nothing I can do about it. *Gaine, you fucking idiot*, I think. *How on earth did you ever think this was going to work out? Are you blinded by love? Is it making you as crazy as it's making me?*

I swerve violently and almost crash into the median.

"You alright there, lady cakes?" Beck asks as I regain control of my bike and move back into the group. I open my mouth to respond, but I can't speak. My tongue is twisted and I feel sick inside. *I don't want to love him.* But I do.

"Why is this just hitting me now?" I scream into the mic. I'm sure I'm scaring the shit out of the rest of the group, but I can't hold it back. Gaine. I'm in love with Gaine. I say it aloud. "I'm in love with Gaine."

Cheers ring out across the group, whoops and hollers that surprise the ever living crap out of me.

"Thank God," Beck whistles, popping a fucking wheelie on his motorcycle like the stupid asshole he is. "You finally figured it out. Amen and praise Jesus. I've been watching you two sons o' bitches for years. This has been a long time comin'. Congratulations, darling."

"Fuck you, Beck," I snarl back at him, but inside, that bit of cold warms. Let's just hope I'm not too late to see it unthaw completely.

Gaine
CHAPTER 31

Melissa Diamond looks me in the face with a wicked expression, reaching out to brush my hair across my forehead. I don't know why she's here or what the fuck is going on, but at least I know who the rat is. Like husband, like wife, I guess. It shouldn't surprise me, but it does. I saw her face when it all went down, saw her spirit spiraling down in the days after. This isn't something that was cooking up alongside Kent; this is something new. I don't know when or how this got started, but Melissa is most certainly the one feeding Bested information. Goddamn it.

Maybe if Austin and Kimmi had talked to her before, we might've seen this coming? I thought she could help the group out; I never expected her to hurt it.

Her sultry smile turns sad as she leans in and rolls me onto my back, running her fingers down my chest. Her blonde hair brushes my face as she moves forward to whisper in my ear.

"I always wanted to fuck you, Gaine. You know that." I don't have any friggin' clue what I should say to her, so I keep quiet. This is an unexpected twist, that's for damn fucking sure. *She goin' to rape me or something*? God, I hope not. "But you always turned me down. I respect you for that. You have a good heart." Melissa bends down and grabs my hair with one hand, pulling my head back and kissing me while shouts and catcalls ring out around us. None of them are worth the breath to repeat. I squeeze my lips tight against her tongue, work so damn hard at fighting her that it takes me a second to realize what she's doing with her hand. A metal blade slides underneath my back and nicks my wrist, drawing blood even as it cuts my ropes. *What the fuck*?

When she pulls back, she touches her other hand to my cheek.

"But you're too late. I've got this one taken care of, sweetheart. Live to fight another day, okay?" Melissa rises to her feet and stretches her arms above her head. From behind her, Will fucking piss ass Walker appears and slides his arm around her waist, pulling her close and smiling at me as he does it.

"Good evening, Mr. Kelley. So nice of you to drop in and pay us a little visit." I look up at the man and all I see is red. I don't see a face or eyes or lips, just a shadow of a person, a wisp so inconsequential it can be shattered with a simple beam of light. "I can't imagine you expected things to go this way, but then, you shouldn't be so neglectful of your old ladies. Give 'em an inch and they take a mile." Melissa smiles at me and puts a hand on her hip, sliding it back slowly, watching my face the entire time. When she dips her fingers into her pants, I'm clueless. All I'm thinking about is how I can use the knife she gave me to get Will Walker. It seems like my best hope for some sort of ending to this crap.

I lunge forward, using my stomach muscles to pull my body to my knees and reach out with the knife the same moment that Melissa pulls a gun, her twisted lips gleeful and her blue eyes shimmering with tears. When she fires off an entire chamber into the crowd, bodies fall and blood stains the walls behind them.

Mireya
CHAPTER 32

As we approach the spot on the map where Gaine's phone supposedly is, we're forced to take an obscure exit to keep on track, moving through industrial buildings, shipping centers, and large warehouses.

We're all on high alert, but I don't think any of us see it coming.

Shots explode around us, peppering the ground and bursting like fireworks in the air. Some bikes go down, mine included, and unfortunately for me, Gaine's not here to catch me this time. I hit a pothole as my bike spins out of control, and find myself flying through the air. It's actually a lucky outcome, considering the other options. A few of my friends go down in flames, crushed under their bikes and smashed by the ones behind them, steamrollered and broken in places I can't even imagine. Me, I hit the dirt with my shoulder and feel an agonizing pain rocketing through my bones, cutting me to the core and pulling every last breath out of me.

"Keep going if you can," I hear Austin shouting through the com. "Don't stop. Follow behind Beck." Ignoring his own orders, my new Pres, my former lover, slams on the brakes and comes to a screeching halt in front of me, sliding off his ride and falling back behind the metal. His visor comes up as he reaches out and helps me into a sitting position. I have to grit my teeth against the pain in my shoulder, but I manage it. I have to. This physical pain is nothing like the emotional pain I'll suffer if I lose someone important to me. "You alright, sugar?" he asks as he examines me for bullet holes.

"Fine," I growl, pulling away from him and peering around the front tire. There are bodies in the streets, but the the gunshots have stopped. As soon as we get the chance, we'll check them and see who's alive. For right now, we stay back here, partially protected by the gleaming metal and chrome. I pull out the pistol and get ready to shoot. "But what the fuck do we do now? I don't have time to sit here in a stalemate for six hours." Austin opens his mouth to respond when more shots ring out from inside one of the nearby warehouses, pinging off the metal walls with screeching cries that make my ears bleed.

Gaine.

"Mireya, don't!" Austin calls out, but it's too late. I stand up and start running in a low crouch, maneuvering behind obstacles and managing, somehow, to stay ahead of the gunfire that follows me. I keep going until I find Beck's bike, abandoned on its side in the dirt near an open door. If he's in there, I know there's at least a fighting chance that everything will be okay.

I move inside after him and nearly end up dead from a stray gunshot that grazes my shoulder and draws a cry from my lips. I roll to my side, behind a pile of scrap metal and end up next to Kimmi and her steady hands as she takes fire, aims, and shoots. A body drops and reveals a surprising sight across the room from me: Gaine and Melissa crouched behind a row of motorcycles.

What the fuck?

Gaine
CHAPTER 33

My knife manages to make contact with Will's thigh, and I leave it there, choosing instead to grab Melissa around the waist and drop her to the ground. Couldn't happen any sooner. In a split second, there's an explosion of heat and sound all around us, drowning us in the burst of gunfire as it echoes around the enclosed space.

Will is screaming and drawing a weapon from his belt, lifting a shaky hand up towards the two of us. Time slows for me, and I don't see straight. I don't think straight either. I can't. My anger is too intense, my rage too pure. I reach out and pull Melissa's gun from her fingers, aim it down and press the barrel into the elder Walker's head.

"I wish it could last longer, end sweeter, and destroy you from the inside out." I close my eyes and pull the trigger. Wetness splatters my face, but I don't waver. Being a part of an MC means thinking on your feet, keeping in control of the situation. My eyes open and avoid the carnage, choosing instead to focus on the knife as I yank it out and use it free myself at the ankles. Melissa's already taken charge and grabbed the extra gun, scooting close to the row of motorcycles nearby, so she can have a place to shoot. I follow after her, lifting my weapon up and aiming at the opposite end of the room, hoping I'm a good enough shot to hit some targets.

"I'm surprised to see you here," I say casually, and Melissa smiles. It's not a happy smile. In fact, she looks like she might've gone bat shit fucking crazy, but at least she's still on our side. Whether she's the rat or not, I don't know, but it's pretty obvious that she's not sticking around to do Bested by Crows any favors.

"I'm surprised to still be alive," she says, sweeping blonde hair from her forehead before steadying her gun again and taking aim. "Thank you."

"Don't mention it," I respond as the door explodes open and in walk Beck and Kimmi, trailing some other Triple M'ers behind them. They take stock of the situation in an instant and move for cover, trapping Bested by Crows in the middle of our two groups. *I might actually make it through this.* I hold my shots as I watch Beck work his magic, crawling around behind the scrap metal pile he's using for cover and bursting out into the open. It takes him three friggin' seconds to grab a man and snap his damn neck. Six more to knock another asshole out with his elbow and eleven more to kick Mack Walker in the nuts, bring him to his knees and steal his damn gun.

I'm so wrapped up in all of this crap that I almost miss a man in a red T-shirt taking aim at my best Goddamn friend. But Mireya doesn't. I don't see her until she's standing up and taking a shot at the back of his ugly fucking skull, flecking the air with red and pink for a moment before he drops to his knees and gives us a clear view across the room at each other.

When her eyes meet mine, she narrows them and pinches her lips. I can't tell if she's happy to see me or just pissed off. And then I see the wet sheen in her gaze, and I can't help myself. I rise to my feet and move across the space between us, listening to the strange absence of sound.

"There's more of 'em," Beck says, kicking Mack in the side and nodding his chin at a group of Triple M'ers sneaking in the back. "Just down the road with the Pres." His severe frown flips straight up into a grin. "Let's go kick some ass and then get the hell out of here before their little friends show up to pay us a visit. I think we're in *Seventy-seven Brothers* territory." He starts to move forward and then pauses when he sees Melissa rise from behind the motorcycles, gun in hand, blood staining her face and hair. They look at each other for a long, long moment, one that I can feel stretching out and warping the Goddamn space-time continuum. I smell another romance on the horizon.

Beck holds out his hand and she takes it, moving across the room like she isn't even really sure how she got here in the first place. That woman has issues, but if there's anyone that might be able to help her out with them, it's Beck and his sense of humor. That shit could cure anyone. Anyway, I know what it's like to be in love with someone that isn't ready to love you back. Yet.

"Mireya," I say as she moves forward, towards Mack, her eyes on me. When she gets close enough, she lets go of her gun and holds out her right hand. At first, I think she's going to touch me. I know I'm desperate to grab her, hold her, kiss her. I always will be. Instead she slaps me so hard that my jaw aches and the left side of my face goes numb.

"You dumb fuck," she growls as her eyes brim with tears and she glares daggers at me. "What were you thinking?"

"I wasn't," I whisper back, listening to the sounds of shouting outside the warehouse. "But Mireya, I – " She steps forward again and grabs me behind the neck, kissing me so hard that I stumble back and nearly trip over the legs of a body on the ground. One that's still moving. Despite the fire in my blood and the beauty pressed against my lips, I pull back and look. We both do.

"You Goddamn bitch," Mack screams as he rolls to his side and starts to get to his feet. I look at him and then over at Mireya. Her face is calm this time, but her hands are shaking. She stares at him as he stands fully and, instead of turning to face us, takes off running. Mireya watches him go and for a moment, I think she's going to let him live.

"I'm sorry, Crystal," she says, and then raises her arm, grabs hold of the gun with both hands and fires. Mack drops to the ground, still and silent, seconds before the first screech of sirens cuts through the air around us.

Mireya
CHAPTER 34

Blue and red lights tease the gray walls in front of me, kissing the dirty cement with frightening color. *La policía.* I'm not ready for cops. I still have blood on my hands and regret in my heart. I still see Tray's face in my mind and there's a freaking pistol clutched in my fingers. I turn to Gaine, to that pillar of strength, to the one person I know that has never let me down, that's always been willing to try, who refuses to judge me, even when I judge myself.

"Gaine," I whisper, and the word falls quiet, drifting down to the still bodies like a leaf in the wind. Outside the warehouse, I can hear Austin shouting orders, bikes revving up, a chorus of frightened whispers. Strong fingers slide down my wrist and hold tight, giving me the strength to turn and look at the face of the man that I know loves me, that I might just love back. I swallow the pain in my throat and wait for the help I've always needed, but refused to accept. It's okay to say I want somebody around to hold me up in the worst of times. I've already proven I can go it alone. Now, I think, it might be time to prove I can go it together. It's a whole different set of challenges, another host of rules. Some things might be better, others worse, but it'll be new. "I need a fresh start." I pause. "But I'm still pissed at you for running off like that. Fuck you."

Gaine's face is sober, but tender. Despite the seriousness of the situation, he manages to smile, to turn up his full lips and draw me into his love, away from this horror.

"It's over and done," he tells me, and his voice is almost as soft as the touch of his hands when he presses them against either side of my face. I move forward and touch my mouth to his, knowing that it's not over yet, not completely. I might go to jail. Or I might get into it with another MC. I don't know. All I know is that the men that betrayed me have left this world and fled to the next. Emptiness fills me then, and I know that I'm the only one that can decide what to fill it with. "Now, let's get the fuck out of here before we get arrested. I bet Austin's sweatin' like a whore in church." Gaine grins, pushing past the pain and the ugly, and giving me the strength I need to run from that warehouse and never look back.

Mireya
Epilogue

We ride for a long time in the quiet dark, my arms wrapped around Gaine, my injured friends bandaged up as best we can and draped on the backs of other riders. My own trashed ride is lying abandoned in a dumpster. The second one in as many weeks. If I keep going through motorcycles like this, I'm going to end up permanently glued to my ... I pause. *Ay, Dios mio.* I have no idea what to call Gaine. Boyfriend isn't right, never was. He's more than that now. I can finally admit it, even if it's grudgingly. I press myself close and revel in the warmth of him, of knowing I have someone I can count on. *Finally.* I sigh and let myself drift away, past the old nightmares, past the new ones, and into a place where I just am, where I'm resting in the moment, not caring what happened in the past or what will happen in the future.

I have myself, and I have Gaine.

For now, that's all I need. Well, that a new ride, but that'll come eventually. I'm not worried about it.

As we move across the earth like a stampede, carving our names into the wind and grinding the dust with our wheels, I feel Gaine's body start to tighten, like he's anticipating doing something dangerous. Again. Since I have no fucking clue what that could be, I wait, expecting the worse. After all, life hasn't exactly been good to me. It's in my nature to see the glass half empty. So you can imagine that when he pulls off on an exit without so much as a word to anyone, I'm a bit surprised.

"Where the fuck are you going?" Beck asks, voice crackling through the intercom. I know it's only a matter of time before Austin turns the caravan around and chases after us the way I used to wish he had before. But not anymore. I feel things for Gaine that I never felt for him. Besides, even if I did love him, I couldn't separate him and Amy, not anymore. If any two people were meant for each other, they were. *And you and Gaine*? Please, I'm not quite ready for that lovey-dovey crap yet. Love's complex. It's not easily dissected or understood. One day, I'll get it. For now, all I'm willing to do is accept it with pursed lips and an eye roll or two.

Gaine doesn't answer, not until we're pulling into a parking lot and he's lifting off his helmet like he's coming up for air, swinging his leg over the bike and turning to face me full on. The smell of salt tickles my nostrils and promises that the ocean isn't far off. I could use a vacation, we all could. I narrow my gaze on the man that's managed to touch my heart, to cut through the rusted chains and splay his fingers wide on that blackened bit inside of me. Slowly, very slowly, it starts to pump.

Sweat pours down Gaine's face and neck before soaking into the black fabric of his shirt. In the distance, the rumble of motorcycles sounds like the world's finest music. I wouldn't trade it for anything else in the world.

"Sawyer," he begins, swiping a hand across his forehead. A droplet of moisture pools invitingly on his lips as I yank off my helmet and hold it under my arm. His dark eyes reflect the stars and keep my gaze locked on his. I start to shake, and I don't know why. Before he even gets out another word, I'm in tears. Rough thumbs brush the liquid from my cheeks as he presses his forehead to mine, takes in a deep breath and says words I never thought I'd hear again, that I never wanted to hear. "Will you marry me?"

"Marry you?" The words catch in my throat and leave me speechless. I was trying to sound pissed off, but it came out more breathy than anything else. "Are you out of your fucking mind?" I can barely whisper past the lump in my throat, my eyes lifting up to the bright sign above our heads. A quickie marriage on the fly doesn't sound like the most romantic thing in the world, but in that moment, on the road, on the run, with Gaine by my side, it is. Somehow, it really is.

From his pocket, he pulls out a ring. It's wrapped in tissue paper and rusty as hell, but the red jewel in the center shimmers with secrets.

"I got it a long, long time ago," he tells me, voice soft, catching a ride to my ears on the gentle breeze that salts the air and stings the eyes. I wipe the liquid from my face and try to stay still. My hands shake, but I pretend not to notice and so does he. "When I first told you I loved you. I bought it then, and I've been cartin' it around ever since. It's a little worse for wear, but I couldn't think of anything else worthy enough to take its place." Gaine reaches out and takes my hand, and I let him. He uncurls my fingers with his and sets the ring down gently, like it's worth a million bucks.

I stare at it for a long while, listening as the group gets closer, moving in towards us in a drone of revving bikes and howling spirits. I think of Tray, but only briefly, just enough to know that this is different, that Gaine and I are meant to be in ways he and I never were.

I should think long and hard about this. Lord knows *mi abuela* is probably spinning in her grave now, clucking her tongue at me and telling me that no man is worth it. But this one is. This one is more than just a man. This is Gaine Kelley, and I'm in love with him.

"I love you." The words burst from my mouth before I can stop them, before I can overanalyze my feelings and come up with something different to say, something bitter, something that isn't half as truthful. I've fucking fallen for him, after all this time. Or maybe I've been in love all along and never knew it? Whatever the case, his hands find my hips and lift me up, knocking the helmet to the ground where it clatters in the silent, still air. His lips find mine and we kiss a kiss that can never be topped, that tastes like self-discovery and fresh beginnings. It isn't sour, doesn't reek of old, and best of all, it means something. No, not something, *everything*.

"I love you, too," he says before sealing the deal with a sizzling tangle of tongues and hands that rove too much for this wide open parking lot. I push back with a gasp and look him in eyes that sparkle. "I sure as shit hope that's a yes," he whispers against my lips, dark hair teased by the breeze, body hot as coals against mine. "Because if it's not, I'm going to look like the world's biggest fucking asshole when the rest of Triple M shows up."

I think for another second, just one more second to be sure, but I don't need even that. My heart is beating now, climbing faster and faster with each passing second. Warm blood flows through my veins and heats up my thighs, teases my nipples, warms my chest. I'm ready for the road, for the future, and I'm finally fucking ready for Gaine Goddamn Kelley.

"Yes." That's all I have to say, and that's enough. He knows. He smiles; I smile.

By the time our MC pulls into the parking lot, we've already said *I do*.

About the Author

C.M. Stunich was raised under a cover of fog in the area known simply as Eureka, CA. A mysterious place, this strange, arboreal land nursed Caitlin's (yes, that's her name!) desire to write strange fiction novels about wicked monsters, magical trains, and Nemean Lions (Google it!). She currently enjoys drag queens, having too many cats, and tribal bellydance.

She can be reached at author@cmstunich.com, and loves to hear from her readers. Ms. Stunich also wrote this biography and has no idea why she decided to refer to herself in the third person.

Happy reading and carpe diem!

www.cmstunich.com

Made in the USA
Lexington, KY
13 September 2013